Read a preview of the next book in the Devotion Heights book series after the acknowledgements.

Novi & NOLEN

DEVOTION HEIGHTS SERIES – BOOK 1

JIA JAMES

Published by JiaJames LLC. / JiaJames Books

JiaJames LLC.
732 S 6TH ST
Suite N
Las Vegas, NV 89101

Print: ISBN: 979-8-9932991-0-5
Audio: ISBN: 979-8-9932991-1-2
EBook: ISBN: 979-8-9932991-8-1

Cover design by Jia James
All Graphic Design work created by Jia James LLC.

For more information, visit:
http://www.jiajames.com

Dedication

To the man who inspired this story —
the one who taught me what love truly is.
You loved me completely.
Your love stirred deeply within me and
you filled it with passion, understanding, and truth.
Ours was a rare and extraordinary love,
and I am forever grateful to have known it.
Because of you, I came to know the depth of what it means
to be seen, cherished, and loved without restraint or hesitation.
And although, I don't know if I will ever experience that kind of love
again, or that feeling of deep connection with another man,
But...
I do count myself fortunate to have known it once.
Some people spend a lifetime searching and never find it.
I was blessed enough to have lived it.
Though time has moved on,
a part of me will always remain where we once were,
carrying the light within those sacred spaces of my soul,
and the ache I've learned to live with
in the quiet places you once filled.

"Zero — no higher."

Author's Note

This story contains mature themes and explicit sexual content intended for adult readers.

Prologue

Between the Cross and the Flesh

She used to think desire was a devil in disguise — a quiet ache sent to test the faithful. But that was before she met *him*.

Now, she stood in the mirror of a dim hotel bathroom, shirt clinging to her damp skin, breath shaky from what had just happened — and what might happen again.

This wasn't supposed to be her story.

She was the worship leader, the first to arrive at soundcheck on a Sunday morning, and the last to leave rehearsal on a Thursday night. She was a mother of two, a dutiful wife to a man called by God… or at least that's what the church thought. She was holy. Or at least she tried to be.

But holiness didn't stop her pulse from quickening when he looked at her. It didn't steady her breath when his fingers brushed against hers by chance. It didn't quiet the hunger for something that defied reason, something that *felt* more like truth than sin.

His name was Nolen Jahlil. He was a husband, a father, and a drummer with hands that knew both rhythm and ruin.

And somehow, when he touched her... just barely... she felt like something ancient had been reawakened inside of her.

Something sacred. Something unspeakably forbidden. She hadn't planned for this. She hadn't even asked for it.

But love, *real love* — the kind that knows your shadows and sings anyway wasn't a thing you'd choose.

It chose you.

Now the line between devotion and destruction blurred more with every stolen breath. And every prayer she whispered for deliverance was met with silence. Or worse — longing.

She touched her lips where he'd kissed her last. Soft, slow, like scripture written across her skin. There had been no guilt in it. Only clarity.

But clarity doesn't protect you from the fire. It just makes you walk into it with open eyes. She closed hers now, swallowing a sob that had nowhere else to go.

She was about to lose everything.

And still — she would do it all again.

CHAPTER 1
Sanctified Flame

They never meant to see each other that way — until they did.

The first Sunday of August always drew a larger crowd to Devotion Heights International Church. Heat rose from the pavement in soft waves as polished heels and patent leather shoes clicked across the parking lot. And in this great city of Baltimore, known for a city of rowhomes, steeples, jazz riffs and jagged edges - Sundays still belonged to the church, where ritual offered a rhythm older than the streets themselves. The building stood tall and modern, framed in sleek glass and concrete — but the spirit inside was anything but new. It was old power, the kind that settled into the bones and made people weep without warning.

Inside, the sanctuary buzzed with anticipation. The band was already there, setting up for worship with quick conversations to the audio team and fingers pointing at monitors. Chatter filled the air. And the choir, dressed in deep royal blue, stood poised like soldiers before a holy battle.

• • •

The praise team followed — twelve strong — dressed in ivory, soft teal, and moss green. Not uniform, but unified. Their placement was intentional: sopranos to the right, altos to the left, tenors behind. Each one took their mic, heads held high in prayer and anticipation. They weren't just singers. They were vessels.

And then, *Winds of Glory* — Devotion Heights' dance ministry — began to move. They were the very embodiment of their name.

Six dancers, adorned in flowing electric blue and golden red praise garments, descended the aisles like messengers on assignment. Their garments shimmered in the light, sleeves and sashes catching air like divine fabric. Every movement was reverent — arms extended, feet deliberate, postures low and lifted all at once.

Devotion Heights had always been known for this: worship in every language — word, sound, and motion. They didn't just sing. They hosted glory.

Just then came Tobias "Toby" Cain, one of Devotion Heights' worship leaders. He was edgy, tattooed, a former secular artist now set ablaze for Jesus. He opened the service

• • •

with a booming declaration that rolled through the room like thunder, inviting the saints to rise and engage.

"This is the day that the Lord has made," he cried out. "Let's rejoice and be glad! **HE IS IN THE HOUSE!**"

His voice was powerful — full of praise, soul, gritty but grounded. The congregation responded with thunderous praise.

The band launched into the first song — keys rolling, bass grooving, percussion locking in with authority. The energy hit like a wave. People stood to their feet, hands clapping, feet stomping, voices rising in unison.

And then... she stepped forward.

Novi Noelle Thorne-Jaxson.

At twenty-six, she had already become legend in worship circles — not because she sought it, but because when she sang, people felt God listening back.

The crowd stilled. Even the ones who didn't know her name recognized something shift.

• • •

A vision in all ivory. The dress wasn't extravagant, but on her, it carried weight. Modest, elegant — it hugged her frame with quiet confidence and moved with the kind of grace that made heads tilt without meaning to. Her hair fell in soft waves that shimmered beneath the pulpit lights, framing a face that somehow glowed and trembled all at once.

There was reverence in her posture, yes — but more than that, a quiet ache. The kind of ache that didn't demand attention but drew it anyway.

She was the worship leader. The adopted daughter of Calen and Elenya Thorne, who raised her as their own. Zayven Jaxson's wife. A mother of two. Adored by a church that didn't know her heart still wandered in the wilderness.

To most, she was a vessel of anointing. But inside, Novi was always negotiating away her will to be sanctified and pure. Listening to the call of God and denying the craving of the world.

Her voice, when it came, wasn't just melody. It was balm. A confession wrapped in harmony. A longing that refused to lie still.

• • •

From his place behind the drums, Nolen tapped into the rhythm — not leading but following.

He was listening to her.

Not just musically... spiritually.

Every flick of his wrist, every beat of his kick, responded to something deeper than tempo.

There was no spoken word between them. No visible exchange or cue.

But something passed between them. Something silent. Something sacred.

An unspoken but deeply felt echo.

A frequency only they seemed to hear.

Nolen Jahlil was a man of rhythm. A father of three, a husband in name, and a gifted musician in ministry. To most, he was strength in silence — reliable and unreadable. A leader whose presence carried weight, even when he wasn't speaking.

But behind the drums, with Novi out front, something unspoken stirred in him.

• • •

When she ministered, it didn't feel like accompaniment. It felt like interruption — holy and inconvenient. Like a mirror he hadn't asked for, reflecting the man he might've been if he'd chosen differently. And yet, somehow, it also felt like an invitation. A quiet urge that he could still become more than what life had reduced him to.

Married to Teanir — loyal in motion, absent in spirit — Nolen had long made peace with the silent war between duty and desire. But when Novi worshipped...the silence cracked.
The war got louder.

She sang like she ached in the same places he did. Moved like she understood the rhythm of his restraint.

And though he never said a word, not even to himself, he let his heart follow her voice —
not because he meant to, but because he didn't know how not to.

Novi closed her eyes.

A soft melodic hum left her lips — so faint it barely touched the microphone, but it settled over the room like holy

• • •

14

incense. And when she opened her mouth to sing, the sanctuary shifted.

She didn't perform. She poured.

From every ache she hadn't voiced. From every scar. From every disappointment she couldn't name. From every unanswered question and prayer. From every moment she stayed instead of leaving. From the woman who no longer recognized the man she married.

Her voice wrapped itself around the weary and the watching and pulled them into something holy.

Tears slipped down cheeks across the sanctuary. Hands lifted. Knees buckled. People with hands held high reached toward the rafters. Others crumpled into their pews, lying prostrate, crying in worship.

Winds of Glory slowed — now swaying within the tempo of her worship, like waves caught in a tide. One dancer fell to her knees in tears. Another lifted trembling arms as if caught in a wind only she could feel.

The room entered stillness.

Not silence — just reverent awe.

● ● ●

It wasn't the volume of the moment. It was its weight. And still, she sang. Behind her, Nolen's drumming intensified — not overpowering — but echoing. Echoing *her*. He wasn't playing the beat. He was playing her pulse.

The worship rose... and rose...

And Nolen played as if her voice was the only instrument he needed to hear. His drumming wasn't showy — it was synchronized. Reverent. Anchored to her sound like heartbeat to breath.

They never looked at each other.

They didn't have to. The presence that passed between them reverberated across the platform and into the congregation.

It was unspoken. But it was real.

Zayven, her husband, sat in the second row. Legs crossed, checking his watch, and wondering when his time was coming so he could step up and welcome the guests. He wore his brand-new designer shoes — perfectly matched to his tailored suit, the one he picked out knowing the livestream would catch every angle. His cologne clung to him like intent. He looked like the man of God people expected. Medium-

• • •

brown skin, good looking — beard lined with precision, hair tapered, voice always ready with scripture. He carried himself like a leader in waiting — suited, rehearsed, always in posture.

He loved the idea of being the head. The legacy. The calling that garnered attention. He glanced toward the ministers, hoping worship would wrap on schedule — but they were on their knees.

Novi was ushering heaven into the room.

He shrugged with disappointment. Not just because the time was going over what he felt it should've been but also because the intimacy required to lead her — *really* lead her — eluded him. And under the polish, was an ache. Not for God — but for recognition, for platform, and for purpose he hadn't yet earned.

And as Novi poured out so deeply, and what he could never seem to reach in her, he sat two rows away. Watching.

Ticking off time.

While she sang to the heavens, he counted minutes on earth. He even looked to the back doors to see if anyone else was waiting for it to be over, but when he turned even the ushers had let go of the doors, hands raised in surrender.

● ● ●

She sang until the Lord said, *Enough.*

The congregation erupted — praising, crying, hands lifted in surrender — as she allowed the worship to rest where God desired.

Nolen struck the final crescendo on the cymbal — a ringing, reverent echo, signaling transition as one of the ministers approached the altar to welcome the visitors.

Novi flinched, almost imperceptibly.

Because that sound, that final crescendo and echo… was exactly how she felt inside.

Novi stood near the side exit, removing her ear monitors and placing them carefully into her gold and blue case. She handed her microphone off to one of the audio techs, nodding a quiet thanks. Her hands moved with practiced focus as she adjusted the small wireless pack clipped to her waistband, but her mind had already drifted.

She could still feel it — the resonance in her chest, the tingling in her fingertips, the echo of Nolen's drumming vibrating through her bones.

That final cymbal was still ringing in her spirit.

• • •

"Hey, sis."

Janet Ruiz-Gonzales passed behind her with a polished smile and a tone dipped in just enough sweetness to pass for sincere.

"That was... different," she said, pausing just long enough to make it unclear whether she meant it as praise or critique. *"I mean, you really went somewhere today."*

Janet was another worship leader — junior in title, senior in ambition. Petite, overdressed as usual, bold makeup set like armor. Her natural curls were slicked and sculpted into place. Every detail about her seemed styled for approval. She always said the right things. But with Janet, even the compliments felt... calculated.

Novi met her eyes for the briefest moment. She caught the flicker — that too fast glance that always carried something unsaid.

But peace was a choice. And Novi chose it again.

She offered a soft nod and a small smile, not trusting her voice just yet.

• • •

Wherever I went, she thought, *I didn't go alone.*

Across the sanctuary, Cassia Dandridge, Minister of Music and Creative Arts, was giving direction to the band — gesturing at charts, pointing at Toby, correcting the sound tech with one hand and motioning for a change in vocal cues with the other. Her presence moved through the space like a tide: commanding, firm, but deeply anointed.

She glanced at Novi once, her brow furrowed briefly — then looked away.

Cassia knew.

She didn't know *what*, but she knew *something* had shifted. The atmosphere had been thick with it — not just performance, not just protocol, but something *divine*. Something powerful. Worship services didn't always break open like that. Not like today.

Novi exhaled slowly, catching her breath, and slipped out the side door.

The August sun slapped her skin — hot, thick, and unrelenting. It reminded her she hadn't eaten since the day before. She fasted twice a week before ministering, believing that denying herself something she enjoyed opened a clearer

• • •

channel to hear from the Lord. But now, with the sun pressing down on her shoulders and her spirit still stirred, it was all catching up.

She pressed her fingers to her temples.

It was too hot to think.

"Hey."

She turned sharply.

Nolen stood near the corner of the building, drumsticks in hand, sweat still glistening along his temple. He wasn't looking at her directly, just tapping one of the sticks against his thigh in a slow rhythm.

"My bad — didn't mean to sneak up on you."

"Oh, you didn't," she replied, folding her arms across her chest. "I just didn't know anyone else was out here."

He nodded, eyes scanning the sky for a moment.

"That... was powerful today."

"Yeah."

Her voice came out quieter than she expected.

● ● ●

She wondered if what she had felt — that unspoken connection in the spirit, that sacred pulse between them — had also been real to him. She normally overthought things, second guessed every gesture, every spiritual impression. But not today. She didn't overanalyze it — not yet. That one lingering thought still echoed:

Did he feel it, too?

But she was too full of what God had done in the service to wrap words around it. She stayed silent.

They stood there — not looking at each other, not speaking — but held in the kind of stillness that only came when presence was enough.

Then Nolen stepped a little closer — not close enough to touch, but enough for her to smell the cedar and musk in his cologne. Enough to remember the way his eyes had looked in the shadows of the sanctuary as she sang that final note.

Enough to *feel* it again.

"I heard you hum before you sang," he said, his voice low. "It shook something loose in me."

• • •

She looked up, startled by his honesty. *"I've never played like that before,"* he continued. *"Like... like I wasn't leading anything. Just following something sacred."*

Her throat tightened.

She wasn't ready for this conversation. Not here. Not now. His words confirmed everything she had quietly been turning over in her heart. It was all too much. She couldn't speak about it — not without sounding strange. Not without unraveling.

"We should go back in," she whispered. "Our families are probably looking for us."

Nolen thought of Teanir — his wife — and suddenly felt the weight of obligation again. After everything he'd just felt in worship, returning to her felt like stepping back into confinement.

"Nah. I'm good. But... you go ahead."

He said it lightly, but it landed heavy.

Novi turned to walk back inside. He didn't follow.

• • •

Inside, Zayven was waiting by the exit, shaking hands with a few ministers and checking his reflection in the glass doors. He flashed his usual politician — like smile when he saw her approaching.

"Are you good babe?" he asked, placing a hand at the small of her back.

"You went off today, babe. Whole crowd was crying. That's the kind of stuff that goes viral, you know?"

Novi smiled, tight and forced. "Yeah?"

She cringed inwardly. Everything with him was about image. Fame. Applause. Never about God. Never about what it meant to draw people to the altar — to Him. His focus was always the camera lens, never the cross.

"You see Minister Kendrick try to shout like he caught the Holy Ghost?" Zayven laughed. "Man looked like he was fighting bees." She laughed softly — more out of habit than humor.

"Let's grab the kiddos from children's church," she said, eager to change the subject and just go home.

• • •

"Yeah, you right babe. Let's go get the babies."

As they walked away, her eyes drifted, just briefly, to the window near the sanctuary exit.

Nolen was gone.

•   •   •

CHAPTER 2
Unspoken Fire

When presence becomes pulse. When longing becomes language.

The day after that kind of worship felt... muted. Monday brought routine. Normalcy. Structure. And Novi hated it.

She stood in her kitchen just after 6:00 a.m., barefoot, the hem of her robe brushing her knees. The scent of Earl Grey steeped in the air, but her tea sat untouched. Steam curled upward in lazy tendrils as she stared blankly at the counter.

Her children, Davien and Autumn, were still asleep upstairs. Zayven had already left for his job at the city building, dressed to impress as always, chasing a position no one was offering him yet.

She admired his ambition and drive, sometimes. But more often, it felt like performance.
Even at home.
Especially at home.

She opened her phone and stared at her calendar.

• • •

Worship rehearsal Thursday. Meeting with Cassia Friday. Children's ministry parent check-in. Dance ministry planning call. Doctor's appointment for Davien. Grocery list. Birthday party. Nothing personal. Just tasks. Her whole life, a checklist of what everyone else needed from her.

But her soul?

Her soul had been restless since Sunday.

Something had been stirred — deep. Holy. Electric. And it hadn't been quiet since worship. It wasn't just the weight of God's presence that still lingered in her chest...

She could still feel it — the aftershock deep inside, the breath that caught in her throat. The way her body had responded not just to the presence of God... but to the way *he* played. Or maybe even to *him*.

She couldn't name it — only feel the resonance that echoed through her body every time she remembered that rhythm.

His rhythm.

Across town, Nolen stood in his garage, elbow - deep in his snare drum bag. He wasn't fixing anything. Just unpacking. Repacking. Adjusting. Avoiding.

His oldest, Brandon, had asked for pancakes that morning. Nolen passed the task to Teanir, muttering something about 'gear to clean.'

What he really had?
Was noise in his chest he couldn't turn down.
Because he couldn't stop thinking about her.

It wasn't just the way she looked — though God knows, that ivory dress did something to him. It was her voice. The way it landed. The way it *stayed*.

He'd always thought she was beautiful. That quiet, no - makeup needed kind of beautiful. Her hair - thick, healthy, flowing - the kind of hair a man imagines touching without meaning to.

But it wasn't just her softness.

It was her spirit.

The way it vibrated something sacred inside of him. The way she moved like she'd been sent. And maybe that's

• • •

what made it worse. Because at home? He didn't feel that. Not with Teanir.

He had met Teanir during his college years - back when he left Baltimore to attend Roosevelt University in Chicago. It had been a culture shock, but in the kind of way that made him feel like he'd finally stretched out his limbs.

He was a Roland Park boy — private school, jazz records, Sunday suits, backyard cookouts with linen tablecloths and quiet tension. Roland Park was nice — almost *too* nice. Structured, curated, proper.

His mother, Babette, had raised him with dignity. She placed him weekly at the Boys and Girls Club with kids who were rough around the edges — to give him *that* edge, which he had — and kept just enough distance to keep him from growing soft.

Chicago was a different rhythm. Faster. Bi-polar in some ways. It had a grounding to it — a balance of poverty and wealth that made the city feel like one unit.

But in other ways, it was cold. People didn't speak when they passed you on the street. Didn't acknowledge your

● ● ●

presence and were quick to grab their bags and hold them closer to themselves for fear of it being snatched up.

Unlike back home, where it wasn't unusual for a stranger to hold a conversation with you — or the door you were walking through.

And that's where he met Teanir.

A Park Heights girl from back home, but not from *his* side of the city.

She wasn't Roland Park. She was rowhomes, loud neighbors, and riding the bus alone before she should've had to.

She fit into Chicago life well. He liked that.

She had smooth, dark brown skin, naturally blue-gray eyes that made people stop mid-sentence, and an attitude like armor.

Fine? Absolutely.

But sharp-edged. Unapologetic.

Carried a chip on her shoulder the size of a generational wound.

• • •

Back then, he was with Tanika — his *real* girl. Classy. Beautiful. Wife material.

Teanir? Teanir was a detour.

Something to smash. And he did.

But even detours have a way of turning into destinations when you're not paying attention.

What started as a few late-night linkups turned into a pregnancy. She kept it. Teanir had him cornered.

Tanika was devastated — but gave Nolen another chance.

He tried to make it work. Tried to be a good man. He loved his son — but didn't love his son's mother. The guilt of hurting Tanika... and the weight of Teanir's expectations... it was *too* much.

After falling asleep holding his son, Teanir made her move — and he slipped.

Again. One night. One mistake.

Now another pregnancy.

● ● ●

This time, he didn't chase Tanika. He'd hurt her too much.

Ashamed, he did what was right — what was *honorable* — for his sons.

But deep down, he knew. He hadn't lost her. He gave her away.

Now two kids deep, Tanika long gone, Nolen felt like a prisoner in a life he never chose. He dropped out, took a government job through his mother's connections. Married Teanir — not for love, but for the sake of his sons. Tried to do the "right" thing.

Then came Jordon. Child number three. The final lock on the door.

He built a full house and lived with a hollow heart — until Sunday.

When Novi hummed that note and the Spirit broke through the ceiling like thunder?

It wasn't just worship.

• • •

It was the first time in a long time he didn't feel trapped. The first time something in him felt... *called.* He rubbed his palms on his jeans and shook his head.

It wasn't right.
He had a wife he didn't love — but still, a wife.
A family he hadn't asked for — but still, his family.
He made vows before God.
He honored them.

But this?

This wasn't lust. This was something else. Something sacred. Something rooted.

Like his hands had been playing her heartbeat. Like he could hear her spirit through his bones.

And his body didn't feel convicted.

It felt... connected.

Later that afternoon, Cassia Dandridge sat at her desk, the office door cracked just slightly. A red pen bled across next month's rotation schedule, forgotten mid-stroke.

• • •

She'd replayed the worship service over and over again. She knew the Spirit when it moved. She'd seen it fall in power. But this...

This was something else.

Novi didn't just lead worship — she had been a vessel. And Nolen — his playing had shifted the very atmosphere. It wasn't just skill. It was alignment. A spiritual sync so precise, it was unnerving.

And under it all... was fire.

Quiet. Subtle. But unmistakable.

That night, Zayven sat at the foot of their bed, scrolling sermon notes on his phone. He wasn't preaching anytime soon. No one had asked. But he studied anyway — always ready to stand near Bishop Byrd and "just happen" to drop a few outlines.

Novi stepped out of the bathroom, drying her hands. "What would you like me to cook for dinner?" she asked gently.

He didn't look up. "Already ate. DoorDash."

• • •

She nodded. Her stomach ached from emptiness, but hunger wasn't what haunted her.

She sat at her vanity and removed her earrings. Her eyes caught his reflection — composed, preoccupied.

She wondered when he last looked at her.

Not her voice. Not her performance.

Her.

"You sang good yesterday," he said, still scrolling.

She paused. Half - smiled. "Thanks."

"They were crying. That kind of sound opens doors. You never know who's watching."

And there it was again.
The ambition.
The performance.
The platform chase.

She turned away from the mirror and opened her notebook. Words spilled from her hand before she could stop them.

● ● ●

Unshaken, He looks at me
The God who heals, He
Heals the wounded me
Who....heals the wounded me

He plays away the pain
His sound is my deliverance
She stopped.
Closed the book.

Put it away before she read it twice.

By Friday, rehearsal at Devotion Heights was electric.

Toby led warmups with his usual fire. The team laughed, teased, tossed around ideas. The band locked in.

But when Novi walked in, something shifted.

Nolen looked up.

Just for a second.

Still no words. Still no touch.

But even Janet Ruiz - Gonzales noticed it.

• • •

Cassia cleared her throat. "Let's get serious now. Sunday we have to be ready vocally."

They ran harmonies. The Winds of Glory took their cue. Rehearsal moved like clockwork — until Novi began to hum.

Soft. Unscripted.

And Nolen responded.

Without thinking.

A rhythm flowed from him that wasn't written on any sheet.

It came from someplace deeper.

The room paused.

Cassia blinked. Toby turned. Janet raised a brow.

And from the choir stand, Venus side-eyed — a little too long, and a little too sharp.

She remembered the photo.

A member texted it to her on her phone. The image was: Nolen by the side exit, eyes locked on Novi like she was

more than a worship leader. Nothing overt. Nothing that could get anyone sat down. But intimate enough to make Venus' instinct prickle.
She'd saved it.

Just in case.

Because Venus Johnson didn't confront - she *collected*.

At 50, she had learned that timing was everything. She hadn't survived the fire of church politics, backroom gossip, and a long - dead flirtation with Bishop Byrd by acting too soon.

Besides, she'd seen women like Novi before. Young. Gifted.

Glowing. And too beloved for their own good. She didn't trust it.

Not because she didn't see the anointing - but because she'd lived long enough to know how quickly adoration curdles into accusation.

Venus crossed her legs and smoothed the hem of her designer dress. Her perfume clung to the air like authority.

• • •

She glanced at Nolen again. His head was down. His fingers were alive.

Everyone else may have been swept up in the Spirit — but Venus was watching something else.

A connection.
A current.
No one said anything.
But everyone felt it.

The rhythm.
The ache.
The unspoken fire.

CHAPTER 3
The Space in Between

In the space between longing and restraint, something sacred stirred.

The chords were clean. The harmonies locked in. But something in the room pulsed beneath the music. Novi adjusted her mic stand, eyes focused on the cross in front of her, looking across the sanctuary and directly above the clock the church used to keep time...but her awareness...was elsewhere.

No — not elsewhere.

On him.

Nolen sat behind the drum kit, head low, hands loose on his thighs. The kind of loose that meant he was listening with more than just ears. Feeling the room.

Feeling *her.*
She didn't want to look.
She knew better than to look.
But her body wasn't in agreement with her spirit.

• • •

She reached for her water bottle just as he raised his head. Their eyes met.

For a second.
Not even a full breath.
But something in her body… opened.

She looked away first. Quickly. But not quickly enough. He didn't smile. Didn't nod. Just looked. Still. Quiet. But intense.

His fingers drummed lightly on his thigh — off tempo from the song the team was running. Something else was playing in his head. Something syncopated. Something dangerous.

She tried to focus on Toby's direction — something about the bridge needing to build more — but her mind couldn't land.

Not with him watching her like that. Not with her body remembering what it felt like on Sunday to sing while he played — like they were breathing from the same place.

Like the music wasn't on the charts. It was in them.

Cassia walked by, humming harmony parts under her breath.

"Alright, I want to run that again with the bgv's, and y'all sing out — no more falsetto. I gotta hear what it really sounds like. Y'all be up here on Sundays singing strong and wrong."

Venus whispered something to Janet, who gave a half - smirk but didn't bite.

Venus didn't miss anything. Especially not how often Nolen's gaze found Novi when he wasn't even supposed to be looking up.

But Novi didn't see her. She couldn't see anything but what was happening in her body.

In her chest. In her breath.

This ache that didn't feel like lust... and didn't feel like sin either, although she was starting to wonder if maybe it was.

They started the run again. She opened her mouth to sing — and there it was.

His rhythm.

Matching her phrasing.

• • •

Following her breath before she even released it.
He was in her timing.
Again.

Not like a musician.
Like a man learning the map of her.

She closed her eyes and pulled back — just slightly and trying to create a barrier in her own spirit. But it was too late.

There was no barrier.

Not anymore.

Her voice dipped, shifted… danced.

And Nolen answered without a word.

A soft fill. Not flashy. Just… *felt.*
Like a *yes.*

Venus's head tilted.

Janet raised an eyebrow again, but she was half into the song and half into her alto part.

Cassia loved it — loved this intuitiveness she thought was from the whole band and Novi. She said, "Y'all tapped in,"

• • •

not realizing it was just Novi and Nolen. Maybe she wanted to encourage the band to tap in more…

Or maybe she really didn't see what was happening. Because she was too busy writing notes.

But Nolen saw Novi's shoulders stiffen. He saw her exhale. And he felt something move in his gut that he hadn't felt in years.

It wasn't attraction.

It wasn't fantasy.
It was *recognition*.
And that was more dangerous than lust.

He leaned forward, elbows on his knees, drumsticks loose in his hands as the song reached its climax.

Novi's voice made a run at the top — soft, controlled — and he caught her. Matched the energy like her voice was wind and he was riding it.

She felt it.
All the way in her spine.

He was with her.

• • •

In a way her husband had never been.

In a way she hadn't felt since she was a teenager singing alone in her bedroom, pretending someone could feel her even when no one was listening.

She finished the run and stepped back from the mic, breath shallow.

Not from the vocal.
From the tension.
From *him.*
She didn't look over.

She didn't need to.
She could *feel* him.
And he was feeling her *back.*

Rehearsal continued like nothing had happened. Toby cracked a joke. Janet laughed. Venus narrowed her eyes. Cassia scribbled down transitions and tempo cues.

But between Nolen and Novi?

Something had shifted again.

It was still unspoken.
Still sacred.

● ● ●

Still too early to name.

But it was coming closer.

Whatever it was.

Nolen sat in his car for almost fifteen minutes after rehearsal ended. The air conditioning was off. Windows up. Heat and memory pressed against his skin like sweat.

He couldn't breathe right.

Not because the music was off. Not because he missed a cue. But because she sang… and he followed. And whatever they had done on that stage didn't belong to the rehearsal room anymore.

It was intimate.

Not sexual.

But something just as charged.

Maybe worse.

He drummed his fingers on the steering wheel, trying to shake it off. But his hands remembered the weight of it. The way her voice moved through the room like incense. The way it curled around in his thoughts.

• • •

He'd played behind hundreds of singers. From old-school saints to stage-hungry sopranos. But with her? It wasn't just music. It was language.

And he understood it before she spoke it.

What the hell is happening to me?

He leaned back, rubbing a hand down his face. This wasn't like him. He didn't catch feelings. Not even curiosity. He lived at arm's length now - from joy, from spontaneity, from desire.

It was safer there.

And yet, here he was, breathing heavy in his truck because a woman he barely spoke to had shifted his entire center of gravity.

And it wasn't just the worship.

It was her.

The way her voice broke mid-run. The way she didn't reach for attention. The way she carried grief in her tone and glory in her phrasing.

● ● ●

He knew what she sounded like when she was pouring out. But tonight?

Tonight, he started to learn what she sounded like when she wasn't sure she should be pouring at all.

That uncertainty did something to him.

It softened his chest.

It made him ache in a way he didn't have language for.

And when her shoulders stiffened and her breath held, he felt it in his *gut*.

He thought to himself... . 'You can't afford this. You've got a wife. You've got kids. You've got a whole life you already signed up for.'

He sat there and said those words to himself like a mantra. Over and over, and over again until he couldn't say it anymore.

But when he finally opened his door, stepped out into the muggy evening air, and caught a glimpse of Novi by the far side of the lot, wearing a maxi dress and sandals...

• • •

He didn't turn away.

Novi moved quietly against the pavement as she made her way to her car. The streetlamps buzzed above her, moths orbiting around the light like tiny planets. The night was thick with humidity and too much adrenaline. She just needed to get home.

To sit still.

To pray this thing out of her body once and for all.

She opened the car door, closed her eyes, and exhaled — long and slow.

And then —

"Hey."

She turned, startled.

Nolen was walking toward her, his hands shoved into his pockets, moving like he hadn't meant to catch up with her... but did.

She didn't say anything.
He didn't stop until he was a few feet away. Not too close.

Not too far.

Just... close enough.

• • •

"You alright?" he asked, his voice low.

She nodded, gripping the door handle a little tighter.

"Yeah, Just… a long day."

"Mmhmm."
He looked down at the asphalt. Then back at her.

"You sang like something was chasing you."

She swallowed.
"It was."

Silence settled between them.
Not awkward. But heavy. He nodded slowly, like he understood more than he should. Then he broke the silence with a need to speak to her, to hear her voice outside of her singing.

"Was I… outta pocket in there?"

She blinked.
"What do you mean?"

He looked off into the darkness beyond the church. "I don't know. Just… felt like we hit something. Not planned. Not… rehearsed."

• • •

She looked at him fully now.

And for a second, she didn't see a drummer. Or a husband. Or a man she should've avoided weeks ago. She saw someone who had also been open.

"No," she said quietly. "You weren't out of pocket."

He nodded.

They stood like that for a moment — in the thick night air, in the unspoken mess of it all. And then he smiled. Just a little.

"Alright. Goodnight, Sista Jaxson."

"Goodnight."

She watched him walk away.

And this time, she didn't breathe until she got in the car and closed the door.

• • •

Reflections

Zayven

The kitchen lights were dim, casting long shadows across the marble countertops. Zayven sat at the breakfast bar, scrolling through real estate listings on his iPad with the same intensity most people reserved for prayer.

The man was always looking.
For the next opportunity.
The next stage.
The next platform.

He'd been networking with some of the deacons after rehearsal — dropping his vision for "family centered initiatives" at the church. Emphasis on *his*. He wasn't on the preaching schedule. Not even on the radar. But he believed in favor by proximity. If he stayed close enough to the Bishop, eventually the oil would trickle down.

He glanced toward the hallway, listening for Novi. She was quiet tonight. Again.

• • •

She had that edge in her voice when she came in — not irritated, just… distant.

He told himself it was probably just exhaustion.

Or hormones.

Or the weight of ministry.

He didn't ask.

Instead, he opened his Notes app and jotted down a sermon title:

"When the Spotlight Finds You."

Teanir

Teanir sat on the edge of the bathtub, wrapping her hair in a silk scarf as the shower steam began to fade. The boys were down — finally — and her feet were sore from chasing the boys around all day.

But Nolen hadn't come home yet.
And he hadn't texted.
Again.

• • •

She bit the inside of her cheek.

Not enough to bleed.

Just enough to keep from screaming.

He'd been distant for weeks now. Not cold, just… removed.

His hugs were more like obligations.

His "love you's" felt like habit. And that silence in his eyes — the kind that used to mean he was thinking deeply about something — now just felt like absence.

She'd asked once.

"You okay?"

He just kissed her forehead and said, "Tired."

But she wasn't stupid.

She knew that kind of tired.

She'd seen it in many women's faces on soap operas and then the man shows up smelling like someone else's perfume.

• • •

Teanir tightened the knot on her scarf. She wasn't about to play stupid. If something was going on, she'd find it. And if she'd stumble upon it?

She'd make sure whoever it was regretted it.

CHAPTER 4
The Breaker Note

When presence becomes pulse and longing becomes sound.

It began before the music even started. Before Novi stepped on stage. Before the congregation had even fully filled in. The atmosphere was thick. The kind of thick that wrapped around your ankles when you walked in.

The kind of thick that made the ushers exchange glances and say, *'The Spirit of the Lord is heavy in the atmosphere, breakthrough is coming!'*

The kind that made people weep before the first chord was even played — while the intercessors were praying to prepare the place for worship that morning.

Devotion Heights was full — standing room only. It wasn't a holiday. It wasn't friends and family Sunday. Not even an anniversary service. But people showed up expecting something. The word had spread — *this was the place to be for Sunday worship.* And members could hardly get parking spaces because the lot was already full.

. . .

Cassia Dandridge stood near the organ, rubbing her lips together as she adjusted her lipstick. She felt it too. She didn't know what God was about to do... But she knew it was coming fast.

She whispered a prayer under her breath — low and urgent. Nolen tapped his sticks on the edge of his snare, warming up his wrists. But his eyes were on the center mic.

She wasn't there yet. He felt ridiculous for how much his body had been humming all morning. Like every nerve was on edge.

Like anticipation lived in his bones.

He hadn't texted her. Hadn't spoken to her since that night outside rehearsal.

But she was in his spirit. And now, she was walking up the steps to the stage. She wore royal blue with gold trim. Her dress kissed her ankles as she moved.

Flowing. Regal. Holy.

● ● ●

Her hair was pulled back in a soft twist, curls pinned behind her ear, revealing her neck and shoulders — nothing suggestive, but so vulnerable it made him swallow hard.

She was elegance. Covered. Stillness with fire underneath. And when she stepped to the mic and whispered, "Good morning, family," the room shifted.

He gripped his sticks tighter.
This wasn't just another service.
This was about to be something else.

Toby opened worship with the team.
Energy. Fire. Movement.

The praise was loud — tambourines, stomping feet, hands clapping. People shouted their way to breakthrough, and Winds of Glory descended the aisles, electric blue and golden -red fabric flowing behind them like flames.

It was high.
It was good.
But it wasn't *there* yet.

Then Novi stepped forward again. She looked at the band - just briefly.

• • •

And then — right at Nolen. One second. Maybe two. Nothing said. Nothing signaled. But something passed between them.

And he knew what she was about to do. She didn't say the song title. Didn't announce the key.

She just hummed.
Soft.
That sound.
That rhythmic hum.
The same one from rehearsal. From last Sunday.

From somewhere deep in her that had nothing to do with music and everything to do with release.

Nolen leaned into the snare. And answered her. Low. Controlled. A beat that was built from nothing. A pulse and a prayer that reverberated inside of her.

She began to sing.

Not with power. Not yet.

With need.

● ● ●

"I will wait for You... I will wait for You... I will wait for You... Holy Spirit, come again..."

Her voice wrapped around the rafters like oil down an altar. And Nolen was right there — heartbeat to her breath, rhythm to her ache.

The congregation began to lean in. Some stood. Some knelt. Others wept quietly, undone by something they couldn't explain. Cassia whispered, *"My God,"* and stepped back, letting it happen.

Even plotting Venus forgot to watch.
Because the Spirit had entered.
Not casually. Not gently.
It had rushed in like wind and whisper all at once.
And Novi... she opened.

Not just her mouth.
Her heart.
Her pain.
Her whole self.

• • •

Her voice broke mid-verse, but she didn't stop. She sang through it.

And that break was the very sound that turned the sanctuary inside out. People came running. Collapsing at the altar. Laid out like spiritual casualties of a war they didn't even know they were fighting.

The musicians stopped playing — except Nolen.

He kept going.

Not driving the sound — but carrying the warfare that drums carried into battle.

And her voice was the song, and he was the net underneath it.

She sobbed between lines now, feeling all of what she'd felt last Sunday — and more.

With all of this happening, the melody never fell apart.

Nolen kept her safe.

She kept him connected.

She never had to worry if he would follow where the Lord was taking her — not like other musicians who might question or give her that look when she shifted mid-song.

Nolen was the ebb to her flow. Together, they were something no one could name. And when she finally dropped to her knees — mic still in hand, voice trembling — the band built one last time behind her.

Nolen hit the cymbals.

Once. Twice.

And as many times as the Lord spoke in his ears, and as He had spoken to Novi, it was holy.

He hit them again.

And again.

And again — until one final strike.

It was the sound of something breaking.

Breaking in the spirit.

Breaking inside of the people spread across the floor.

Inside of Novi, crying out to God.

• • •

Inside of the musicians, hands raised in surrender.

And that's when the room exploded into
full surrender and worship.

Later That Night it was an impromptu Creative Arts Meeting

It was late — later than it should've been. The sanctuary lights were dim, and church had been over for hours — even after the Creative Arts department had been asked to stay for a last minute meeting with Bishop Byrd. It was the only time he could guarantee everyone would be there, since they were already at church anyway.

It had been hot that day, and most of the praise team had long since filtered into the night — filled with hunger and conversation about how the Spirit moved, but even more eager to get home.

But Novi had stayed behind, sorting through lyric sheets left in the rehearsal room.

She told herself she was just being helpful. Organized. But the real reason she lingered sat heavy in her chest.

• • •

Nolen.

He was still here.

He always stayed back to break down his drum kit, moving slowly like he didn't want the night to end either.

When Novi finally stepped out into the warm evening air, she found him standing near his truck, leaning against the driver-side door like he'd been waiting all his life.

"I forgot to give you something," she said, voice catching slightly. She held up his black drumsticks. "You left them."

He smiled, stepping forward.

"You picked up my sticks for me. Thank you."

She laughed a bit, holding them out. "I happen to have a great memory. I saw you forgot them."

But he didn't take them right away. Instead, his fingers brushed hers. Warm. Slow.

Holding her hand there longer than necessary. And that was when it happened — The shift.

• • •

The silence between them, heavy with something louder than worship.

A flicker of light caught her eye — across the street, the coffee shop still had one small light glowing above the window. Most nights, the musicians would swing there after rehearsal, grabbing donuts or espresso before heading home.

But tonight?

It was empty.

Quiet.

Soft.

He nodded toward it.

"Walk with me for a minute."

Novi hesitated.

"I should head home."

"I know," he said. "I just... need to breathe. With someone who sees me."

That was all it took.

• • •

They walked quietly past the dark storefront and stopped beneath the hanging lantern at the back patio. No one else around. Just them. The hum of the city in the distance.

He turned to her, voice low.

"You feel it too, don't you?"

She didn't answer.

Couldn't.

Her heart pounded. Her fingers trembled.

One wrong word, and everything would spill out.

He stepped closer.

"Novi…"

The sound of her name, in his mouth was like — a call, divine.

"I know your mind is racing, I feel it. Mine is too," he said, voice steady. "You wanna know why I asked you to walk over here… why I waited for you today after church."

She *had* wondered that. But truth be told?

She didn't care.

• • •

Any chance to confirm — to *name* — the connection she felt in her spirit, she'd take it. She needed to see if it was real. Needed to feel it up close.

The scent of his cologne reached her before he did, but it wasn't just that. His presence carried weight, the kind you couldn't bottle — like the air shifted when he stepped closer. She swallowed hard, afraid she might faint... or fall... or say something reckless.

What is this man doing to me? she thought. The feeling was amplified here, in this quiet space with just the two of them — no choir, no congregation, no noise to hide behind.

Her stomach fluttered. Butterflies she hadn't felt in years. Butterflies she'd never felt with Zayven.

She didn't answer. But her eyes said everything.

And he caught it. His gaze locked with hers, steady, searching, like he was reading every unspoken word, every confession she was too afraid to let slip from her lips.

His jaw flexed. He drew in a breath, sharp and quiet.

Then he stepped in closer.

• • •

And she swore he could feel her heart pounding.

His hands cupped her face — gently. Slowly.

And then he kissed her.

It wasn't rushed or hungry. Not yet.

It was reverent, worshipful and intimate.

Like a whispered prayer between twin souls.

His lips moved against hers with a tenderness that broke something open inside her. Then came the hunger — not just his, but hers, the same ache that had kept her awake at night, imagining him. He met her hunger with need, and together they kissed like time itself had surrendered, stretching into hours.

Her hands clutched his arms — muscular, warm, real. Arms she'd watched drumming for years, never once imagining she'd hold them this way.

And now, she was.

She anchored herself to the moment.

To him.

• • •

When they finally pulled apart — breathless — neither spoke.

There was nothing left to say. But Nolen smiled, a smile that confirmed everything he'd been holding in. A smile that said, *I see you. I feel you.*

The kiss, the brush of his hand in her hair, the grip of her fingers on his arms — it had said everything for them.

For the first time, they both felt completely, utterly... seen.

Because in that moment, outside a quiet coffee shop, lit only by one flickering light...They both knew..

This wasn't just temptation.

Not anymore.

● ● ●

CHAPTER 4: PART II
The Watcher's Eye

No glance is ever hidden, when the unseen is looking back.

Sunday evening flashback

Church had been over for hours.

The sanctuary had emptied slowly — waves of high heeled feet and shouting voices carried out into the summer air. A Sunday like that didn't end quickly. People lingered. Crying. Hugging. Kneeling at the altar long after the music stopped.

But the moment Bishop Byrd dismissed the congregation with his signature "Go in peace, but stay in power," Venus had made sure her heels clicked a little louder down the aisle than they needed to. Let them know who ran the room.

Still, even she couldn't ignore what had just happened in worship. Something had opened. The room had thundered with something raw and holy. But Venus wasn't sure it was all Spirit.

• • •

Some of it felt like something else.

Someone else.

Now, Creative Arts had been called to stay for a last-minute meeting with Bishop Byrd. They'd gathered in the overflow room — hot, packed, and full of tired folk ready to be home. Bishop could be winded but even he was ready to state the point and go home.

Zayven left before the meeting wrapped, claiming something about prepping for a guest speaker at another church. Teanir too, with her usual side-eye and matte red lipstick, muttering that *"the kids were hungry and ready to go home."*

But Venus stayed.
Of course she stayed.

And as Bishop Byrd dismissed the meeting well past nine, Venus stepped into the sanctuary again — just to *"check the lights,"* she told her husband, Kendrick.

He followed close behind, still in his suit jacket, carrying her purse like he always did.

Good man. Loyal. Predictable.

● ● ●

She loved him, sure. Loved his steadiness. Loved the way he kept a pen in his jacket pocket and scripture in his mouth. But sometimes... sometimes loyalty just wasn't exciting.

Kendrick Johnson was respected in every room he entered — a man of quiet power. A gentleman. Twice widowed, now devoted. The kind of man women said they wanted... until they realized he didn't argue to be seen.

He paused a few steps behind her, adjusting his tie and scanning the sanctuary with quiet patience. He didn't ask why she lingered.

He already knew.
And there, across the stage?
Nolen Jahlil was still packing up his drums.

Lord, have mercy.

That boy moved like rhythm was inside of him. She could see the strength in his forearms even from here. It made her shift a little in her heels, then she'd scold herself silently.

Get your mind right, Venus. That's a married man. A young married man.

• • •

But that didn't stop her from watching. Didn't stop the memory of the photo tucked away in her inbox. She had told Kendrick it was nothing — just someone sharing a moment from a recent service. But she hadn't deleted it. Nolen, standing by the side exit, eyes fixed on Novi like she was more than a worship leader.

Nothing scandalous.
But intimate.
Too intimate.

Venus had filed it away. Just in case.

Kendrick moved beside her now, placing her purse gently on the pew and glancing toward the stage. He didn't say a word. Just looked at her, then at Nolen.

Venus straightened her spine, forced a small smile, and folded her arms like she wasn't thinking what she was thinking.

But it didn't stop her from watching.

She knew Teanir. Had seen her rolling her eyes during rehearsal, always looking tired or snappy.

• • •

Didn't seem grateful. Didn't seem soft. A man *needs soft. You blessed, little sis,* Venus thought. *You don't even know what you got.*

She glanced sideways at Kendrick who was still talking about the bishop's notes, and offered a quick, disinterested "Mmhm."

That's when she noticed something else. Novi was still here too.

Venus narrowed her eyes. She hadn't seen her come out of the Creative Arts Meeting. Maybe she slipped out early. Maybe she was avoiding the group. Or maybe… she was doing exactly what Venus *thought* she was doing.

She watched as Novi came down the side aisle, slow, like she didn't want to leave just yet. Holding something in her hands.

And then — there it was. Nolen walked toward the doors then outside. And Novi met him there, running with drumsticks in hand.

Right at the edge of the parking lot. Venus lifted her keys, waving them dramatically as she called out, "Let's go, Kendrick! I'm not standing here all night."

• • •

He followed her out like always. But once she reached their car and he buckled himself in, she leaned over, kissed him on the cheek, and said, "Babe, I think I left my notebook in the choir stand. Can you go grab it for me real quick?"

He looked tired, but nodded. "You sure?"

"Positive."

She waited until he disappeared back inside. Then she pulled off. Or at least she made it look that way.

Venus circled the lot, headlights low, and parked two rows down in the staff section — out of view, but still with a perfect angle toward the coffee shop across the street.

And just like she thought... they didn't go to their cars.

They walked.
Together.
Not rushed.
Not discreet either.

Straight toward the coffee shop patio, where a single flickering lantern buzzed above the window like it had been waiting for them.

• • •

She couldn't see what happened behind the shop. Not clearly. The hedges blocked the patio view.

But she saw enough.

The closeness.
The pause in conversation.
The way Novi tilted her face up when she thought no one was watching.

The way Nolen leaned in with that same smirk he used to give the altos when they came in on cue and sang down their parts — but this time?

It was different.
This time, it looked personal.

Venus gripped her steering wheel tighter. *'Mmhm. I knew it.'* She said out loud to herself. She didn't have the full picture.

But she had enough.

Enough to know that whatever *that* was — it wasn't prayer. It wasn't rehearsal. And it *sure as hell* wasn't ministry protocol.

• • •

She reached over and tapped her phone screen. No messages. No missed calls. She clicked it off again, sat back in the seat, and stared at the soft orange glow coming from behind the shop.

'You think you're slick, Novi Jaxson.' She spoke out loud again to herself with a slight chuckle.

She wasn't surprised.

Beautiful voice.
Beautiful young face.
Always *"humble,"* always *"set apart."*

But Venus had been in ministry too long not to recognize emotional entanglement dressed up as spiritual synergy.

She should know.

She'd mastered the art herself — back before Devotion Heights, back before she learned how to package holiness in high heels and a soprano register. She had wrangled plenty of men who were *interested in the anointing* but wanted something far more flesh than Spirit.

It always starts on stage.

• • •

Always starts with harmony, a shared chord, a look across the mic stand.

By the time the scandal breaks, it's already been happening in the shadows for months.

I'm watching, she thought, her nails tapping lightly on the wheel.

I'm always watching.

Because sometimes you have to protect the altar.

Even when the ones on it don't realize they need protection from themselves.

CHAPTER 5
The Morning After

Conviction doesn't always come like thunder. Sometimes, it's a whisper.

Novi woke before the sun.

She didn't know what time she'd finally fallen asleep. But her eyes opened in that fragile space between dream and memory, the part of the morning where the world is still quiet and your body hasn't yet figured out what's real.

And then she remembered.

His lips.

His hands.

The way her name sounded in his mouth.

She sat up in bed, sheets tangled around her legs, her throat dry and her chest aching like she'd been running in her sleep.

The house was silent.

Davien and Autumn were still asleep down the hall. Zayven had left early again — probably at the gym or somewhere networking with someone who didn't matter. His

• • •

cologne still hung in the air faintly, like a memory she wasn't trying to remember.

She reached for her Bible. Then pulled her hand back. Not because she didn't want the Word, but because she was scared of what it would say.

She stood up, walked to the mirror, and stared at herself.

There were no signs of sin on her face. No fire, no brimstone. No scarlet letter burned into her forehead.

But her body… her body remembered everything.

The press of Nolen's hands on her cheeks. The reverence in his kiss. The way it had unlocked something ancient in her. Not lust. Not a mistake.

It had felt like prayer.

Like longing answered.

She pressed her fingers to her lips, then dropped her hand, ashamed.

God, what did I just do? She thought.

• • •

She didn't know if she wanted to repent or run.

Across town, Nolen stood in the shower, hot water pouring over his skin like punishment.

He hadn't slept.

Every time he closed his eyes, he felt it again.

Her voice under the moonlight. The softness in her eyes. The moment her breath caught just before he kissed her. And worse — the way his soul had said yes.

He tilted his head back into the stream and whispered, *"God... please."* But he didn't finish the prayer. Because he didn't know what he was praying for.

Forgiveness?
Clarity?
Strength to stay away?
Or grace to see her again?

He punched the water off, grabbed a towel, and leaned against the sink.

He had crossed a line.

* * *

But the crazy thing was... it hadn't felt like crossing a line at all.

It felt like coming home.

Back at Novi's house, the morning moved on without her. The kids were awake now — cartoons humming in the background and cereal bowls half-finished. She moved on autopilot: ponytails, toothpaste, shoelaces, hugs and kisses.

But her insides were scrambled. She kept replaying it. The way he asked her to walk. The quiet space between them. The moment the world disappeared, and it was just him.

And the truth?

She hadn't wanted it to end.

She still didn't.

She looked at the time and realized she was late.

Staff meeting.

She hurried into a quick shower, then while still wet, she put on jeans and a cardigan, mascara barely dry before she

• • •

ran out the door. Her mother stopped by to grab the kids, thank God.

But as she pulled out of the driveway, she saw it.

Her hands. Shaking.

The church was quiet when she arrived.

Too quiet.

The kind of quiet that made her nervous - not because of gossip, but because silence always had a way of exposing your thoughts. She slipped into the staff meeting ten minutes late. Cassia gave her a nod. Bishop Byrd glanced but said nothing. Toby smiled.

Venus?

Venus didn't even look up from her notebook.

Which, for some reason, made Novi more nervous than if she had. The meeting moved. Budgets. Calendar planning. Upcoming youth service. Nothing about what happened on that stage yesterday. No mention of the spiritual detonation that shook the whole church.

• • •

But Nolen wasn't there.

She noticed that too.

Too fast — too clearly.

She pulled out her phone and typed out a message.

Then deleted it.

Then typed it again.

I was wondering…

Delete.

We need to talk.

Delete.

She shoved the phone back in her purse… 'breathe' she told herself. But her hands wouldn't stop shaking.

Novi sat frozen in her seat.

Cassia was talking about stage design for the youth explosion service. Venus was flipping pages in her notebook with intentional quiet. Everyone else seemed normal. Moving on.

• • •

But Novi's heart was still trapped in last night.

She pulled her cardigan tighter, as if it could hide the ache underneath her ribs.

Then —

Buzz.

Her phone lit up against her thigh. Unknown number. Her stomach flipped. She swiped it open.

NOLEN:
I tried not to text this - but I needed you to know
I don't regret it.
Kissing you felt like
I could breathe again.
On the real, I felt like I'd been
holding my breath for years.

I know that we shouldn't have.
But nothing about last night felt like a mistake
Not to me.

I feel connected to you enough to know you
tripping about it.

I'm not asking for anything. I don't expect anything.
I just need you to know... I feel you

If we never get that close again
That kiss changed my life.

• • •

Her vision blurred.

She blinked hard.

Read it again.

Her fingers hovered over the keyboard of her phone. Backspace. Stop. Think.

But the truth?

She felt it too.

And that was the part she wasn't ready to confess.

Not to anyone.

Not even herself.

She slipped the phone face — down onto her lap and folded her hands over it like prayer.

Because whatever this was?

It wasn't over.

It had just begun.

CHAPTER 6:
Sunday's Shadow

Contentment wasn't the same as love, and he could feel the difference.

The kitchen smelled like cinnamon and maple syrup — the kind of sweet that clung to your skin and your memory. Brandon stood on a chair near the counter, flipping pancakes with too much enthusiasm and not enough wrist control. Nolen kept a watchful eye while Dewaun drummed his fingers on the table, mimicking his father's rhythm with a butter knife. Jordon, the youngest, was running in circles around the kitchen island with a superhero cape made from an old church banner.

It was chaos. Beautiful, noisy, syrup — sticky chaos. And Nolen wouldn't trade it for anything in the world. "Yo, Bran — slow down before you burn the next one," Nolen said, ruffling his son's curls.

Brandon grinned. "It's not burnt! It's crispy."

"Crispy is how I like my bacon. Not my pancakes."

• • •

Jordon jumped on his back and yelled, *"DADDY HORSE!"* before sliding off and nearly knocking over the juice pitcher.

Nolen grabbed it just in time.

This was the part of fatherhood he lived for.

Not the bills. Not the strained mornings trying to keep the house from unraveling.

But this — syrup fights and drumstick tap battles. He loved his sons more than his own breath.

They kept him grounded in a life he hadn't chosen but refused to run from. His whole life might've been a storm, but they were the eye in the center of it. And maybe that's why the guilt cut so deep now.

Because even in this perfect moment... his mind drifted.

To her.

To that kiss.

To the feel of Novi's lips — soft, slow, trembling — like something prayed for and finally found.

• • •

He blinked it away and turned back to the griddle.

But upstairs, the water was running.

And it had been far too long.

Teanir sat on the bathroom floor, back against the tub, legs tucked under her oversized T-shirt.

She stared at the running water in the sink, eyes unfocused.

The mirror was fogged, but she hadn't taken a shower yet. She just needed the sound. Needed the steam. Needed a space where no one would ask her anything.

It was her hiding place. Her escape from the loudness of being invisible. Downstairs, she could hear them laughing. Nolen's voice. The boys' squeals. The sizzle of pancakes.

And she hated how much she loved that sound.

She hated how good of a father he was — how easily he poured into them. She used to think if she gave him everything — her body, her loyalty, her obedience — that one day, he'd see her.

• • •

Really see her.

That he'd love her.

But now, even that closeness — the quick sex that used to at least tether them for a moment — was gone. He hadn't touched her in weeks. He hadn't kissed her in months. He hadn't made love to her.…Well, never.

Not in the way she imagined love should feel.

But she took what she could get.

She always had. And now there wasn't even that.

A tear slid down her cheek, and she wiped it fast, like it disrespected her.

"I'm not gon' cry," she whispered. But the ache didn't care.

The silence wrapped around her like a sheet she never asked to be covered in.

She wanted him.
Not just his presence.
His heart.
Even just a piece.
Even if it was tired. Even if it came late.

• • •

She'd take crumbs if it meant it could someday turn to a feast. But deep down… she knew.

Something had shifted.

Back downstairs, Nolen threw a dish towel over his shoulder and leaned against the counter while the boys argued over who got the last pancake.

"Y'all better split that like brothers," he warned, chuckling.

Buzz

One new message.
From her.
He didn't open it. Not yet.

He shoved it in his pocket, heart already thudding.

He glanced up the stairs. The water had stopped. Teanir would be coming down soon, pretending she was okay. She always did. And he would smile and carry the weight. But something was breaking inside him, slowly.

And that kiss?

• • •

That kiss didn't feel like a betrayal.

It felt like truth.

A truth he'd have to deal with — one way or another.

But not today. Today, he'd feed his boys. And pretend the house he built wasn't made of pieces already breaking.

The boys had eaten. The kitchen was halfway clean. And Nolen felt like he was holding his breath. He didn't hear Teanir come down at first — not until her bare feet tapped gently against the hardwood floor, like she was trying not to interrupt the air.

She stood at the kitchen entrance, hair pulled back in a ponytail, oversized T-shirt hanging off one shoulder, eyes dark underneath, face washed but tired. Always tired.

"You made breakfast," she said, her voice flat but soft.

"Smells good."

"Yeah," he said. "The boys asked for it."

She nodded, walked over to grab a mug from the cabinet, poured herself coffee. No sugar. Just hazelnut cream.

• • •

No longer black. Just something to hold.

She leaned against the counter, staring at the floor while he rinsed a plate in the sink.

The silence thickened.

"You used to make me breakfast," she said without looking at him.

He exhaled hard through his nose. "Tea…"

"I'm just sayin'. It's fine. I get it. I'm not mad." But she was. And he could hear it in the way her voice stretched around the word 'fine' like it was begging to mean something else.

"You ain't touched me in weeks," she added. "And don't lie, cause I counted."

"Teanir"

"I get it. You tired. You busy. I just wanna know…" She finally looked up at him. "Am I still your wife? Or am I just the one keeping your kids fed?"

He dried his hands and turned around. "You're the mother of my boys."

• • •

"Right," she said, laughing without humor. "That's it, huh?"

"Here we go again, so you want me to say, what you want me to do?"

"I want you to stop treating me like I ain't here!" Her voice angry when she meant it to come out softer, but she had no control over it. That happened when she talked to him, a lot. Maybe it was a because of where she was raised, or maybe it was because she was just angry with him because she felt she always had to fight for his attention, even at home... .even from their boys.

She turned now facing him.

"You treat me like I'm some girl you just knocked up. I'm your *wife*, Nolen. I may not be what you wanted, but I was who you chose. I didn't beg you to marry me, YOU decided that, and I said yes."

He opened his mouth to respond but his phone rang. His mother's name flashed on the screen.

Sen. Babette Jahlil.

He let it ring twice, then picked up.

• • •

"Ma."

"You sound winded. What's going on over there?"

"Nothing, I'm fine."

"I've been calling. You didn't answer last night."

He looked over at Teanir. She stared at him with folded arms.

"I'm sorry Mama, I was busy. We had service."

"Mm - hmm. I'm glad you're still doing that over there at that big church. Make sure to tell Bishop Bryd and First Lady Jacquiline I said hello next time."

He could hear Teanir in the background saying something about him being disrespectful and rude answering the phone while they were in the middle of a conversation, then something about his mother. Babette, his mother, is one of the few Black women to serve in the Maryland Senate — a graceful force shaped by generations of political legacy and the privileges of an affluent lineage.

He closed his eyes.

• • •

"Tea, please I'm talking to my mother."

"I was calling to see if you'd be willing to take a call with the Mayor on another position I think you'd be great at but let me hold off for now. I keep hoping that Teanir would get herself together, be the politician's wife in training but I'm always reminded that we might be pushing our luck. I bet she's still sitting around in your house, while you carry the weight. Is she even looking for a job yet?"

He didn't respond.

"She's the mother of your children, yes, I know. But that doesn't mean she has to be the end of you. Think about your legacy son."

"I gotta go," he said sharply.

"Nolen -"

He hung up.

Teanir was watching him.

"She talking shit about me again?"

He didn't answer.

● ● ●

"You let her, don't you? Let her say whatever she want cause she got money and a name. She still mad you didn't marry that bougie ass girl with the pearls. What was her name again? Tahini? Teflon? Tanika?"

Nolen's jaw flexed.
Teanir clocked it. "Yeah. That's still in you I see. Don't matter *how* many years ago it was."

"I'm going out," he said, grabbing his keys.

"Oh, of course you are. Like always."

He didn't answer her.

Didn't even slam the door.

Just left

❦

The Spot.
It wasn't much.

Just an abandoned lookout over Liberty Reservoir. No signs. No tourists. Just cracked concrete, tree roots, and silence.

• • •

He called it "The Spot" because it had always been his place to go when he needed to hear himself think. And right now, his thoughts were screaming.

He sat on the hood of his truck, hoodie pulled over his head, the scent of pine and wet earth filling his lungs. His phone sat beside him, Novi's text still unread.

He finally opened it.

NOVI:
I felt it too. I feel crazy to even admit that.
I still feel it. And I know we can't do this
but I've never felt closer to anyone.
I felt you in my spirit even when you weren't
Around me. I feel you now.

He closed his eyes.

He should delete it. He knew that.

Instead, he typed.

NOLEN:
You're not crazy. I felt it too.
I felt you in my bones in a way
I've never felt another woman before
And I've never even touched you.
I don't regret kissing you.
I never will.

• • •

He hovered his finger over the send button.

Paused.

And hit it.

Tanika's Ghost

For some reason, as the message sent, her face flashed in his memory.

Tanika.

Laughing on the quad.

Taking notes with her left hand, holding his palm under the table with the right.

She was it.
Smart. Poised. Light. Deep.
And he ruined it.

She had gone on to do everything she said she would — anchorwoman, then field reporter, then CNN correspondent with her name on a book deal. He'd seen her a lot on TV. Eyes bright. Braids pinned up. Voice like authority.

• • •

She was everything he didn't fight for.
Everything he let slip.
And now he was here.

Divided between the woman he never loved...
and the one he could no longer pretend not to feel.

Novi sat at her vanity, the glow of her lamp casting long shadows on the wall behind her. The house was silent - Zayven had fallen asleep watching ESPN reruns, the kids curled up in their beds with stuffed animals and soft lullabies humming from their white noise machines.

But she was awake.

Wide awake.

Hands ready and heart pounding.

His message was still open on her phone.

You're not crazy. I felt it too.
I felt you in my bones in a way
I've never felt another woman before
And I've never even touched you.
I don't regret kissing you.

• • •

I never will.

Her chest rose slowly. Fell slower. Noelle. He'd called her by her middle name. Only her mother did that. Sometimes her husband, when he was trying to impress church folk. But coming from Nolen?

It landed like prophecy.

She stood, robe cinched at the waist, bare feet pressed to the floor. She paced once, twice. Then sat down again.

She wanted to say, *Stop. Please. This can't happen.*
But that would be a lie.
Because it already had.
And because she didn't want to stop.

Not really.

Instead, she typed:

NOVI:
I told myself I imagined it. That maybe I was tired,
overwhelmed, misreading the moment.
But I wasn't.
I felt it.
In my body.
In my chest.

In the part of me that only wakes up when I'm singing.

• • •

And you were already there.
I know this is dangerous.
I know it's wrong.

But I'd be lying if I said I didn't feel like that kiss -
was the first time someone touched me
without taking from me.

I don't know what this is.
I just know...I don't want to pretend
I didn't feel it too.

She held the phone to her chest.

Closed her eyes. Then hit send.

The moment the message disappeared, her whole body exhaled.

Not relief.
But surrender.

And just then — soft footsteps behind her. Zayven stirred in the doorway, blurry-eyed. "You coming to bed?" he mumbled.

She nodded. "Yeah. I just needed a second."

"Is everything okay?"

• • •

She smiled, the kind you practice when you've got too much spirit in your body to admit what's real.

"Yeah," she said. "Just tired."

He disappeared again.
She stared at her phone once more.
Nolen hadn't read the message yet.
But he would.

And when he did… she wasn't sure what would break first. The silence?

Or her?

CHAPTER 7
Familiar Fires

Some truths don't need to be spoken to be understood.

Starbucks at Harbor East was packed, as it usually was on Saturday morning — young professionals with laptops, joggers refueling, and couples laughing over oat milk lattes. Novi sat by the window, her fingers wrapped around a caramel macchiato she barely sipped.

She hadn't looked at her phone in ten minutes. Which, for her — this morning, felt like a year.

He still hadn't texted back.

She kept the screen face — down on the table to keep herself from checking again. From obsessing. From waiting.

Across from her, Odessa Lancaster stirred her Americano with slow, thoughtful hands. She anointed herself Novi's big sister and they met weekly for coffee to talk about the next move of God, or which new televangelist had the *real* oil. She looked good today — skin glowing, makeup soft, her tight curls brushed up into a chic puff that gave her cheekbones center stage. Dressed in all black but with fire-red

• • •

nails, she was the type of woman who could command any room without ever raising her voice.

Once, Odessa had been known for her warmth — for the way she filled a space with grace and praise, even as life hollowed her out behind closed doors. She had done everything the right way: married young, served faithfully, raised four boys with more tenderness than she ever received. The church called her virtuous. But virtue had a cost.

And today, there was a stillness to her. Like she was bracing herself to say something that couldn't be unsaid.

"I need to tell you something," Odessa said finally. Her voice was quiet but clear. "And before you say anything, just… hear me first."

Novi sat up straighter.

"It's Don," Odessa said. "He and I… we're involved."

Novi blinked. "Don as in"

"The organist. Yeah."

Don Shepherd wasn't the kind of man you barely noticed all at once. He knew music — fluid, unobtrusive, always in the background until suddenly he filled the whole

• • •

atmosphere. He always tried to be charismatic and to some women, he had a way of saying just the right thing at just the right time — words like warm honey, soothing and sweet, even when they didn't mean much past the moment.

He'd been playing keys at Devotion Heights for years, slipping between Sunday sets and Saturday night jazz gigs in smoky bars on the east side of town. No wife. No drama. Just a rented apartment, an old car that coughed when it started, and fingers that could make you feel like God was still listening.

He noticed Odessa long before anyone else did. Not for her voice or her beauty, though she had both.

It was the sadness.

The way her smile never quite reached her eyes. She reminded him of women he'd known before — his mother, maybe — women who gave and gave until nothing was left but the shell of who they used to be.

With Odessa, he didn't offer promises. Just presence. Poetry. A softness she'd forgotten she deserved. What started as conversations after choir rehearsal turned into walks, and into whispered jokes and knowing glances across pews. Then

• • •

came late-night phone calls, a poem tucked into her Bible, a ride home when Phillip couldn't make it.

Then picnics. Then hotel keys tucked discreetly into palms. What Don offered wasn't just romance — it was resurrection.

"Is he married? " Novi asked right away.

"Married? No. He's not," Odessa cut in quickly. "That's what makes it worse in some ways. Because I can't even use that as a reason to say no."

Novi blinked. "Okay…"

"I am seeing Don, and Don is seeing me." She said it in a sing- song sort of way. Almost to convince herself that it's actually happening.

Novi nearly choked on her sip.

"Don?" she whispered. "Don who plays the organ?"

Odessa gave her a look. The one that said, Don't play dumb, girl. "You know exactly which Don."

Novi leaned in. "Wait…Don *is* single."

• • •

"I know." She sipped again, cool as ever.

"You are a *married* woman."

"I know." She felt shame and contradiction all at once and let out a big laugh. Not only at herself but the dichotomy of what she knew, felt and that she was with him.

A long silence stretched between them. Behind it, the espresso machines hissed, steam swirling through the air like unspoken sins.

Odessa sighed. "You ever been in a marriage where your body is present, but your soul has to lie down just to survive it?"

Novi didn't answer. But her chest ached. She understood that. She felt that was a norm in all marriages.

Odessa continued. "My husband stopped seeing me years ago. I mean really seeing me. I was a calendar item. A status boost. A body he thanked God for in public and ignored in private. Then Don came along."

Novi's face softened. "But you and Don...?"

"It started with music."

• • •

Odessa said, her voice distant now, like she was narrating a movie she still wasn't sure she was starring in.

"Late-night rehearsals. Feedback sessions. Songwriting turned into poetry. Poetry turned into long walks. Secret picnics. Out-of-town church conferences where we just so happened to be booked in the same hotel. Eventually... the line just disappeared."

"Odessa... " Novi whispered, half-conviction, half-concern.

"I'm not proud of it. But I'm not broken over it either," Odessa replied. "And that's the scary part. Because Don — he sees me. Every note. Every mood. Every key I try to hide in. He sees all of it. And he doesn't run from it."

She paused.

"I know it ain't right. But it feels... real."

Odessa looked out the window for a beat before turning back.

"Don is... complicated. But he's kind. Gentle in ways I forgot I liked. When I'm around him, I don't feel like I'm begging to be noticed. I feel...held. I feel like a woman again."

• • •

Novi stared at her hands. Quiet. Wounded. Confused. Because in Odessa's story, she heard echoes of her own.

"And I know what you're thinking," Odessa said. "You think you're strong enough to avoid this. That what you felt with Nolen was just a moment in the Spirit. A worship high."

Novi looked up, eyes wide.

"Oh yes, baby," Odessa said, crossing her legs. "I saw it."

"You what?"

"I been watching that boy since before Teanir got pregnant with his third. That man plays with his soul. He plays like he's working something out every time he sits behind those drums. But lately?"

Odessa tilted her head, eyes narrowing just slightly.
"Lately, he only watches you."
Novi's stomach dropped.
Odessa leaned in, voice barely above a whisper. "And if I see it, others will too."

"I haven't done anything…" Novi whispered.

"Yet," Odessa replied, not judging. Just honest.

• • •

"You think I should walk away?"

Odessa didn't answer immediately. She sipped her coffee, eyes drifting out the window as though the right words were written somewhere in the sky.

"I think you should know what fire you're playing with," she said finally. "And decide if the warmth is worth the burn."

Novi swallowed hard, her mouth suddenly dry.

"I'm not saying this to push you into guilt," Odessa added quickly, her bracelets sliding as she adjusted them on her wrist.

"I'm saying it because I know the ache of not being seen or feeling enough in the eyes of your man. The temptation of being felt — and it mean something. And I don't want you to find out too late that your peace — being loved or unloved — comes too late."

Novi watched her carefully. The advice wasn't coming from a place of judgment. It was lived. Worn. Heavy with years Odessa had never spoken of in detail but carried in every glance, every sigh.

• • •

And Novi remembered.

She remembered the nights after church when Odessa lingered in the parking lot, her voice breaking as she whispered about the man waiting at home. Phillip Lancaster — one of Bishop Byrd's proud Armor Bearers. A man praised in public, but feared in private.

Phillip was hard, not loud. He didn't need to be. His power lived in what he withheld — love, apology, warmth, presence. He grew up in Alabama under a father who taught him silence was strength, control was a man's duty, and women were meant to fall in line. When Phillip met Odessa, she was young, insecure, grateful to be chosen. He chose *her*, but his choosing always came with conditions.

They married fast. And when Odessa found her own confidence — in motherhood, in ministry, in her own voice — Phillip resented it. Resentment that turned to fists in the early years. He grabbed, shoved, slapped. Enough to bruise. Enough to remind her she was his. That stopped when he became an Armor Bearer. The church gave him structure, image, power.

He couldn't afford to be sloppy.

• • •

But the bruises only went inward. The abuse became colder. Calculated. He ruled with suspicion, with absence, with silence that cut sharper than words. The church called him reformed. Odessa knew he was only rebranded.

And now, as she sat across from Novi, her voice low but steady, Novi could hear the truth behind her warning. Odessa wasn't speaking against love. She was speaking against chains. Against cages wrapped in scripture. Against losing yourself in a man who only sees what he wants, never who you are.

Novi blinked. And in that moment, she understood why Odessa reached for Don. Why she let herself be touched, be seen, by someone outside the walls of her marriage. It wasn't about lust. It was about survival. About being reminded she was still a woman, not just a wife to Phillip's rule and pride.

Odessa leaned back in her chair, coffee cup in hand, eyes tired but fierce.

"This fire with Don... feels good," Odessa said softly.

Novi shifted in her seat thinking about Nolen and looked down at her cup. Why did she feel this way about him? This wasn't some shallow temptation, like sneaking glances at a man she shouldn't want. This was deeper. Unexplainable.

● ● ●

Like her spirit recognized him before her mind could catch up. She thought about Nolen and felt him even when she wasn't in his presence.

At the dinner table.

In the sanctuary.

And especially in his presence. She *felt* him.

There was an unspoken current between them — silent, invisible, but strong enough to rattle her inside.

And the terrifying part? She believed he felt it too.

Maybe she was imagining it. Maybe he was just a man taking advantage of something fragile in her, something she hadn't recognized yet. Before she could stop herself, the words spilled out. "Odessa, I think I might be falling in love with him."

Odessa laughed softly, not mocking but aching, the way women do when they see their younger selves reflected back.

"Baby, years ago I would've *scolded* you. I would've told you to fast and pray, to get on your knees until that feeling left. But I know better now."

• • •

Her bracelets jingled as she adjusted them, her eyes heavy with truths she rarely spoke. "I spent years with Phillip — years being unseen, unheard, untouched. And when he *did* touch me, it left me with black eyes and bruises. The church crowned him faithful, but at home he starved me of love. And you know what happens when a woman starves too long?"

She paused, gaze locking on Novi's.

"She starts reaching for bread wherever she can find it. That's how Don happened."

The admission sat thick in the air.

"I'm not proud of it. But I won't lie either. Don sees me. Feels me. Reminds me I'm still alive. Never raised a hand to me except to hold my face when he kissed me. And for the first time in decades, I remembered what love feels like — real love, not duty dressed up as devotion."

Her eyes bore into Novi's now, her voice steady, almost pleading.

"Don't wait until your hair is gray and your children are grown to admit you've been dying inside. Don't waste your years proving to people in pews that you're holy while your heart is starving. The mistake isn't in love finding you where

• • •

it shouldn't. *The mistake is ignoring love when it calls* — and spending your life being loyal to something that only *looked* like love and respect to everyone else, while you sacrificed what you needed for people who wouldn't give a damn about you in the end."

She softened, her tone matter of fact again. "So I won't tell you to run from it, though maybe I should. What you feel? I know it. I've lived it. Just… be careful, Novi. Fire warms, and it's beautiful, but it also burns. And once it burns, nothing ever goes back to the way it was — for good or for bad."

Novi sat in silence, blinking back the sting rising behind her lashes.

Buzz.

She flipped it over.

• • •

NOLEN:
I don't have the words for what
last night was.
But I know what it wasn't.
It wasn't fake.
It was real, and that felt good.
Thank you for putting a smile
On my face.
I would love to return the favor
One day.

She stared at the message.

"Was that him?" Odessa asked, eyes locked on her face.

Novi didn't answer.
She didn't have to.

Odessa giggled, reached across the table, and gave her shoulder a gentle push.

Novi smiled faintly, but inside she was tangled — conflicted, though *not* convicted. Grateful, at least, to have someone like Odessa. Someone she could talk to without judgment. Most church conversations were just recycled gossip about who was doing what, with whom, and where.

Now, she realized *she* had become one of those whispered stories. A topic Odessa had seen with her own eyes.

• • •

And God only knew who else had noticed.

She sipped her coffee, savoring Odessa's presence, but silently prayed for a solution to the feelings she couldn't shake.

CHAPTER 8
The Echo and the Veil

It is not always the fire that burns. Sometimes it's the shadow it casts.

After Sunday service the sanctuary still held the heat of revival. Not from temperature but from presence.

Even hours after Sunday service had ended, there was a residue of something holy that clung to the space. A vibration still living in the air, almost like a hum under the floorboards.

The kind of energy that made you lower your voice without knowing why. That made the air feel thicker. That made grown men cry and seasoned saints stay seated after the benediction, just breathing it in.

Cassia Dandridge sat on the front pew, her red pen idle between her fingers, notepad open on her lap. She hadn't written anything down. Not yet. Her mind wasn't on transitions or setlists.

Her spirit was circling something deeper. Something troubling.

• • •

She'd been in worship long enough to know when the atmosphere shifted because of glory... and when something else was braided into it.

Something between Novi and Nolen had pulled the sanctuary into another realm.

It was powerful.

Undeniable.

But it wasn't pure. At least, not completely. There was something else under the surface. Something charged.

Something tethered.

She had just closed her notebook when she heard the soft click of heels behind her.

Venus and Janet.

They moved carefully, like women approaching a prophet, their eyes watchful, respectful, but also heavy with purpose.

"Cassia," Janet said gently. "Can we talk a minute?"

Cassia turned, chin lifted. "Of course, baby. What's going on?"

• • •

Janet was dressed like always — a crisp black pantsuit, tailored sharp, with a powder blue blouse buttoned to the collar. Her natural curls were clipped short and slicked low, sharp lines defining her edges. Her makeup was full — bold lip, contour tight, lashes thick — but the rest of her? All control. All armor. All curated.

Venus was more understated, but her presence was thick. The kind of woman who remembered everything and spoke only what she wanted you to hear.

"It's about Nolen and Novi," Venus said.

Cassia didn't react outwardly. But her chest tightened.

Janet folded her arms. "We know you love them. We do too. But… something's shifted. And we didn't want the whispers to get to you before the truth did."

Cassia nodded slowly. "I've seen it. Felt it. But I haven't looked too close." She hadn't wanted to. Not at them. Not at what felt like a divine misfire — holy, but not heaven sent.

"They been locked in lately," Venus said, "but not like praise team tight. Like… *soul* tight. It's real subtle. But it's there."

● ● ●

Janet's tone was light, but her eyes were sharp. "The congregation notices things. Even when they don't know what they're looking at. That kind of energy? On a platform? It ripples. Even when no lines are crossed."

Cassia let out a breath.

"You think it's gotten that far?"

Janet tilted her head, calm. "I think it's already started. Even if they haven't touched."

Cassia tapped her pen lightly on the notebook before setting both aside.

"Thank you for telling me. I'll handle it."

She didn't say how.
And they didn't press.

But behind her eyes, Cassia was already praying.

Later That Afternoon

The sanctuary had emptied out hours ago. Most of the Mountain Top Praise Team had filtered out. The rest of the

• • •

creative arts team had met with Bishop Byrd in a meeting that ran long — and quiet tension still hung in the air.

Janet had watched it all.

Watching the way Nolen stayed behind. Watched the way Novi lingered — supposedly reorganizing lyric sheets. She'd made sure to be nearby, but not too close. Speaking softly with

Venus. Hovering.

Janet had learned how to see things without making herself seen. She adjusted her gloss in a compact mirror. She never sweat. Never broke form. But something about the way Novi carried herself lately made her teeth clench behind her smile.

It was an effortless holiness.

The humble glow.

The way people leaned in when Novi opened her mouth to sing, like the Lord Himself, used her voice to unlock hearts. Janet hated how easy it came for her. How she didn't need to belt the loudest run or wear the boldest outfit — and still, people wept.

• • •

Still, Cassia glowed whenever Novi ministered.

Still, Nolen watched her like she was something sacred. And Janet saw it. All of it.

She watched from the wings of rehearsal. From the back row of the sanctuary. From the group texts she always managed to exit right before anything got real.

She saw the glances.
She saw the hunger.

She'd even seen the way Nolen's entire body shifted when Novi opened her mouth. How his drumming bent toward her timing. How he anticipated her breath.

And maybe that's why Janet couldn't look away.

Because somewhere in her still lived a curiosity. A question about what it would feel like to be desired like that — by a man or a woman — with no shame.

But she swallowed that thought like she always did.

Nolen stayed behind as usual, wiping down his snare, re-stacking his sticks like ritual.

Cassia didn't announce herself.

He turned — and there she was.

"Hey, baby," she said, voice low. "You got a minute?"

He nodded. "Always."

She walked down the steps slowly, her heels tapping out a rhythm of their own.

"I need to ask you something," she said. "I love you like a son."

He nodded once. Braced himself.

"Is something going on between you and Novi?"

He blinked. Didn't flinch. Didn't lie right away either.

"I'm not accusing you," she continued. "I'm asking because it's been brought to my attention."

"No," he said. "Not like that. We haven't — "

"But something's there," she finished for him.

• • •

He sighed. "Yeah. There is. I can't explain it. It ain't lust. It's... alignment. When she sings, I *feel* her in my chest. I hear her in my hands. It's like we're synced on something deeper than music. I know it might not look right. But it don't feel wrong either."

Cassia held his gaze. "I know what kind of marriage you're in, Nolen. And I know what you gave up for it. But that girl? She's anointed. And fragile. And so are you."

"I know."

"She looks at you like you're the only anchor she has."

"I know."

"And you be looking right back."

He didn't deny it — he let out a little smile and a chuckle.

Cassia softened, just slightly.

"I'm not pulling you off the drums. But I am pulling you into accountability."

He nodded.

She turned, walked away — not cold. Just clear.

* * *

She wasn't preparing punishment.

She was preparing for what might come next.

Novi stood at her kitchen sink. Lights dimmed. Dishes ignored. The house still. Her fingers wrapped around her phone, unmoving. A text message came through.

Buzz.

NOLEN:
You'd never imagine what just happened.
Cassia asked if something was going on
between us. I didn't tell her the truth.

Her stomach flipped.

NOVI:
Did she say someone saw us kissing?

NOLEN:
Nah. Nothing like that.
If she saw it, she'd have said so.
We're good.

● ● ●

She breathed. Not relief. Just… stillness.

Buzz.

NOLEN:
When I kissed you,
I felt something deep in me.
I don't regret it.
It wasn't just feeling you.
It felt like revelation to me.
This might be wrong, Noelle
but every part of me says it's right.

Novi didn't reply.

Couldn't.

The guilt she expected *never* showed up.

Only the knowing.

Only the ache.

Only the memory of the moment when his lips met hers like a whispered answer to every question she didn't even know she'd asked.

• • •

And in that silence…The aftershock still lived.

Not in her body.

In her soul.

CHAPTER 9
Breathing Under Water

It's not drowning that kills you. Sometimes, it's holding breath too long.

The Monday after Sunday revival service didn't feel like coming down.

It felt like being held under.

The sky over Baltimore was a pale, moody gray. Rain teased the edge of the morning — never falling, just threatening. The kind of day that sat heavy on your skin. The kind that dared you to hope but reminded you where you were.

Novi sat in her car outside Davien's daycare, forehead resting on the steering wheel. The gospel playlist she'd queued up that morning had looped twice already. She hadn't heard a word of it.

Not really.

Buzz.

• • •

Not him.

Just another calendar alert:

She exhaled.

The text from Nolen still lived in her body like breath she hadn't released.

It wasn't just desire. It was revelation.

"This might be wrong, Noelle... but every part of me says it's right."

She hadn't answered.
Not yet.
But not because she didn't want to.

She did, and that was the problem.

Meanwhile: Nolen's House

Nolen stood in the hallway, towel slung low on his hips, steam still clinging to his chest from the hot shower. Jordon tore past him, chasing Dewaun with a Nerf gun. Both boys screamed.

• • •

"Not in the hallway!" he barked, already too tired to mean it. Brandon sat in the living room, headphones on, eyes locked on his Switch.

The house was loud. Alive. Normal.

Teanir stood in the kitchen, back turned, washing dishes. Hair in a messy bun under a bonnet, wearing one of his old T-shirts and leggings — what used to turn him on years ago. But now? Now it just made him ache in a different way. He watched her. The way she scrubbed. The force in it. The silence.

He stepped in slowly.

"You alright?"

She didn't turn. "Why wouldn't I be?"

"Just asking."

More silence.

She rinsed a plate like it had insulted her.

"You been quiet," he said. "Since yesterday."

• • •

She turned finally. Her face was bare — no makeup, no warmth. "You ever wonder what it's like to be picked?" she asked.

He blinked. "What you mean?"

"Chosen. Not by accident. Not because of babies. Not because your *real* girl walked away. But because somebody looked at *you* and said, 'You. I want *you*.'"

He rubbed his face.

"Come on, Tea. Don't do this."

"I'm not fighting with you," she said evenly. "I'm just... tired of pretending you ever loved *me*."

"I never said I didn't — "

"You didn't have to."

He looked down. He knew where this was going. He knew she wasn't wrong either.

Teanir took a breath. "You don't even touch me no more."

He didn't answer.

• • •

"I never liked sex that much," she said quietly. "But if it meant you'd hold me after? I'd do it. Every time. Just to feel you see me."

Her voice broke, just a little. But enough.

Nolen walked into the living room and sat down. His phone rang. His mother.

"Hey, son. How's everyone?"

"Just chillin'. What's up?"

"I called Teanir earlier. She didn't sound right. Maybe she could use a break from the boys. You want me to get them this weekend?"

He thought about his mentor and godfather, Pastor Sandiford, who had been married for more than forty years. Whenever people joked about the grass being greener on the other side, Pastor Sandiford would always say, *"The grass is greener where you water it."*

Nolen didn't regret Novi.

But maybe he'd let his own grass go dry. Maybe that's why he couldn't connect with Teanir. Not anymore.

• • •

"I think that'd be cool, Ma. What time you coming by?"

"I can come and pick them up tonight. Just make sure they got everything they need. Love you, son."

"Love you too, Ma."

He hung up and sat there, thinking.

He had to try. For *real* this time. He needed to know if he could still feel something for his wife — or if he was just chasing ghosts.

His phone buzzed.

Novi.

Terrible timing.

Buzz.

NOVI:
I'm not proud of what we did.
But I'm not sorry either.
I've never felt more seen in my life.

He stared at the message, shook his head, and stood. Walked back to the kitchen.

• • •

"My mom's coming to get the boys," he said.

Teanir looked confused.

"Okay... Was I supposed to have them over there?"

She knew Babette didn't care for her. That relationship had always been tense.

"I'll pack their bags," she said quickly.

He watched her head up the stairs. Then he called out after her.

"Pack a bag for yourself, too. We're leaving soon — going away for the weekend."

That flutter in her chest — undeniable. A hope so alive, it scared her. God had heard her. Her prayers were working. Her marriage was being restored.

While she packed, he booked them a two — night stay at *The Ivy Hotel in Mount Vernon.* Five stars. Luxury. Quiet.

She packed fast. Face done, hair combed, and two lingerie sets she knew he might love tucked inside. In the beginning, just slipping on his shirt or a pair of lace panties could fix everything. She thought about that time a few weeks

• • •

ago when she tried, and he just turned over and said he was tired.

But this time? This time he offered. That mattered.

When Babette pulled up in her sleek, top of the line — Cadillac Escalade EV, the boys ran to her screaming "Gigi!". She was too young, too flawless to be called Grandma. That name was for Teanir's mom.

They left. Nolen and Teanir got in his truck.

He was going to water his grass. Best he could.

The suite was beautiful. Rose petals on the bed. Candles lit. A warm bath drawn, bubbles rising under the soft flicker of tea lights. Teanir stepped out in deep red lace, her curls falling down her shoulders.

She turned slowly.

He smiled. She really did look beautiful — especially when she tried. Since their sons were born, those moments had been rare. But tonight, she'd put in the effort. And for that, he was willing to try too.

•••

They sipped wine. Laughed — just for a moment about the boys. He lit the last candle, and when the flame steadied, she looked up at him like it meant something.

Maybe it did.

Still, all he could feel — deep in his chest — was Novi. Like her soul was crying out to him from miles away. He forced it down. He was good at that — compartmentalizing. Tonight *had* to be about his wife, about figuring out if there was still anything left worth saving. He'd learned to love her once. Maybe he could learn again. At least, he had to try.

But when he kissed her, it felt empty. That one kiss with Novi still burned inside him — electric, unforgettable. Nothing else compared. And the shame of knowing that sat heavy on him.

He shut it out and kissed Teanir harder. With so much force she pulled back, visibly angry and insulted. And honestly? She should have been. Because he didn't kiss her like his wife. He kissed her like she was a woman he'd dragged home from the club after too many drinks — no love, no tenderness — just the raw need for pressure and release.

• • •

Nolen apologized, then lied — said she brought out a passion in him, that he'd just gotten carried away. She smiled, a little relief softening her face, and they moved to the bed.

But he wasn't making love.
He was just fucking.
No caress. No breath held between kisses.
Just motion.
Flesh.
Pressure.

She clung to what she could. In her mind, she replayed his words about passion. Maybe this was it. Maybe this was the passion *needed* to save her marriage. And she was willing to do whatever it took. If this was what restoration looked like in the beginning, then she would endure it until it was built back up again.

He looked into her eyes — the same eyes that used to mesmerize him back in college — searching for connection.
Nothing. She told herself it was good enough.

She smiled.

It's a start.

• • •

But for him? It was effort. All effort.

Even when she whispered *"I love you,"* it felt like a test.

Afterward, she rolled into his arms, eyes fluttering shut with a small, content sigh.

But he just stared at the ceiling feeling….empty.

That night, he dreamed about her.

Novi.

Laughing — soft and wild. Lips brushing his ear. Her mouth on his chest. The way her breath caught when she kissed him.

In the dream, she was his and he was full.

Alive.

He woke up hard as a rock.

Teanir stirred beside him, slid her hand across his stomach, misreading it. She smiled, kissed his neck, and climbed on top of him slowly.

He let it happen.

• • •

After all, this was his wife.

He was trying — watering his own garden, tending to his own grass. But why didn't it *feel* like enough?

He closed his eyes.

And in his mind — Novi.

Teanir's body moved on top of him, rhythm steady, warm, pulling him in. But what he saw — what he felt — was *Novi*. The taste of her kiss. The scent of her perfume, still trapped in his memory.

He thrusted deeper (*Novi*).

His grip tightened on Teanir's hips, dragging her closer. Every shiver, every moan, he imagined belonged to Novi. His body betrayed him, growing harder inside of Teanir thinking about…. (*ahh, Novi*).

Teanir arched, grateful, soaking up his sudden urgency. For a moment, she had him — his drive, his fire — the same intensity she remembered from their college days. She smiled through her moans, believing love had finally come back to them.

● ● ●

But when he opened his eyes, her face pulled him into the present. Unwilling to lose momentum — or Novi, he flipped Teanir over and pressed her into the sheets. She gasped at the force. He leaned over her shoulder, eyes shut tight, refusing to let reality take her place.

In his head — only Novi.

What it would be like to be inside her.

He thrusted harder and his breath broke, and a guttural sound ripped out of him — *"Rrrghhh..."* — as he drove deeper. (*Novi!*)

Bitterness followed instantly.

And anger at how much effort it takes to force connection. He hated that he had to think of another woman just to finish, while his wife was right here, giving all of herself.

Teanir moaned — breathless, grateful. In her heart, she believed this was restoration — that they were finally back. Nolen opened his eyes. And beneath it all, there was only disappointment.

• • •

Nolen rolled to the side of Teanir, heart pounding. He shouldn't have given Teanir that kind of hope.

And somehow...

It already felt ruined.

Sunday Morning

They made it back just in time for church Sunday morning. Teanir wore a new dress. She smiled, glowing. Held his hand. She believed. He stood beside her, suit pressed, eyes cast low. He'd tried to water his grass. But all he could think about... was another garden entirely.

The sanctuary hummed with energy. Malik Drayton, one of the young adult worship leaders, led worship that morning. It was vibrant and full — but felt muted somehow. Ushers guided latecomers to their seats. The Spirit was moving, but Nolen couldn't feel a thing.

He sat beside Teanir in the third row, close enough to be seen, far enough not to be called out by Pastor directly. Her hand rested lightly on his knee. Her nails were done. She looked... happy. Radiant, even.

● ● ●

She brushed her dress — a deep plum wrap style that hugged her waist and dipped just low enough to hint, not holler. Her face was made, her smile soft and steady. She'd gotten up early, curled her hair, laid her edges like it was Easter Sunday.

To anyone watching, they looked... whole.

But Nolen's chest was tight. He hadn't prayed all morning. Not really. He tried during the drive over. Tried while buttoning his shirt and tying his tie. But his mind kept drifting — back to that text from Novi, to her voice in his dream, to the way he had touched his wife last night... while imagining someone — *her* — instead.

He adjusted in his seat.

Bishop Robert Byrd stood at the pulpit, voice thick with conviction. "God is not just a restorer — He is a revealer."

Nolen flinched.

He felt exposed. Like somehow, everyone knew.

Teanir leaned in, whispering, "You okay, babe?"

He nodded. "Yeah."

• • •

She squeezed his hand and smiled. Like her prayers were working. Like they were walking into a new season together.

Zayven and Novi came in late that Sunday. She wasn't scheduled to sing, so Zay didn't understand why they had to be there early. And truthfully? They didn't. But she'd spent too long in the mirror, staring at herself, adjusting, re- adjusting . and doubting. They were late. And she was frustrated.

Nolen hadn't responded to her text — and in his defense, she hadn't tripped. She took days to respond to his message too. Sometimes she just needed a bit of time to process — but still, it stung.

She slid into the last row during praise and worship, Davien on her hip, diaper bag slung over her shoulder like a badge of war. Her eyes scanned the sanctuary out of habit. She knew exactly where to look.

There he was.

Nolen.

With his wife.

• • •

She caught herself holding her breath again.

He looked... present. Suit pressed, posture straight. She hated how fine he looked in the sanctuary.

She hated that she missed him.

They had only shared one kiss — but that kiss was *everything.* The way they connected in worship? That was *everything.* And now, looking at the radiance and satisfaction on Teanir's face, it felt like somehow... she'd *lost everything.*

Her chest tightened. Not just with desire — but with grief. Because she knew, deep down, she had never really been his. And maybe she never would be. And that was a good thing, she reminded herself. She needed to be focused — on bringing in souls, on healing wounds, on letting the Lord move through her music. Not thinking about a man that wasn't her husband.

Davien tugged at her dress. "Mommy, sing!"

She forced a smile and stood, swaying gently as the choir lifted *"You Made a Way."* But her voice cracked on the lyrics. Because God *had* made a way. She might not have liked the way... but she was still standing. Still breathing. Still here.

• • •

"Don't know why, but I'm grateful," she sang, repeating it like a invocation— trying to convince her ears of what her heart refused to believe.

And in the pulpit, Bishop Byrd thundered in preaching the word this morning. "Sometimes the enemy ain't chasing you," He thundered. "Sometimes it's God *pushing* you out of what's comfortable — because He's tired of you playing house in Egypt." People stood. Hands lifted. A few shouted.

Nolen felt Teanir's fingers brush his. He glanced down at their hands, now interlaced.

She closed her eyes, swaying, tears pooling at the corners. Worshiping because she believed again. Believed they were back. That their marriage was on track — because he'd taken her away, because he'd touched her again, because she could feel his breath on her neck.

And maybe that should've meant something.

But Nolen?

All he felt... was guilt.

He wanted to believe it could work.

* * *

Wanted to believe she was enough.

But even in church — even in the presence of God — he couldn't stop thinking about the wrong woman.

As service came to an end, and the benediction was finished, people began hugging, collecting kids, heading to brunch or Sunday or heading home.

Nolen walked out with Teanir by his side, holding her hand because that's what a good husband does.

Novi moved toward the exit, avoiding eye contact. But she felt *his* eyes on her and she saw the way he paused mid-step. She heard the breath hitch in his chest.

She walked faster, Davien's little body bouncing with every step she took.

And Nolen?

He didn't call out.

Didn't follow.

Didn't look back.

But he wanted to.

• • •

CHAPTER 10
When It All Breaks

Not everything that breaks leaves pieces you can gather.

Teanir was glowing again. Moving through the house like prayers had been answered. Laughing with the boys, cooking more than usual, even humming while folding clothes. To her, their weekend getaway meant something. It meant hope. Restoration. Reconnection.

To Nolen?

It meant guilt.

She noticed the shift. He hadn't touched her since they got back. Not even a brush on the shoulder. And the silence pressed in until she couldn't take it anymore. Folding laundry one night on the couch, she decided to finally confront it. To call it out. To get the devil out of the way and her husband back on track.

The weekend they had was almost perfect. He had made love to her with so much passion and desire, she felt like a new woman. She wasn't about to let the enemy steal that

• • •

from her. She *saw* what God had done — and she was angry that the devil was trying to undo it.

"We just gotta keep trying," she said firmly, "no matter how hard it gets."

He didn't respond. Just kept scrolling his phone.

"You hear *me?*" she pressed.

He sighed, set the phone down. "Yeah. I heard you."

She studied his face. "So what's the problem then? We had a good weekend. You don't feel that?"

"I'm trying, Tea."

"Well, damn try harder. I can't be the only one in this marriage doing it!"

That was it. The last straw. He'd tried to keep it buried, let it simmer beneath the surface. But now — it broke.

He stood up from the couch, eyes burning into her. All he could think was why did he have to fight so damn hard just to love her? His boys were no issue — they were his heart. But *her?* No matter how hard he tried, he kept circling back to the

• • •

same thought: how did he even end up here? With her. How this family even happened. And what he gave up because of it.

"You want the truth?" His voice was low, sharp. Dangerous. "You really wanna know why it's hard for me to try?"

She crossed her arms tight across her chest. "Yeah. Tell me."

"You planned this. *All of this,*" he snapped. "You knew I had a girl. You knew where I came from. You knew what my future looked like. And you saw an opportunity."

Her mouth dropped open. "Excuse me?"

"You saw me — a kid from an affluent family. With a name. With a future. And you trapped me."

"Trapped you?!" she shot back, voice rising. "Are you serious? Ain't nobody trap you!"

"Did you — or did you not — tell me you were on birth control?" His voice cracked through the room like thunder. "Every time. And I was young and dumb enough to believe you."

• • •

Her face flushed red beneath her dark brown skin. Her arms dropped, fists at her sides. "I didn't get pregnant by myself! I wasn't *sleeping* with myself, Nolen!"

"Nah, but you sure as hell made sure it happened. And you know what hurt me most? I didn't even *want* to be with you like that. I never did."

Teanir's voice shook. "So why'd you sleep with me, Nolen? Huh? Why'd you keep coming back again and again and again?"

"Because it was easy — YOU were easy."
He said it like a slap. She froze, mouth open, breath caught.

"I was a horny college kid who was only thinking with my dick. I wasn't trying to build a life with *you* — I was trying to get away from one."

Her face crumbled. "Wow."

But he didn't stop. Couldn't. The years of biting his tongue were finally bleeding out.

"You came from Park Heights. Hood girl with a scholarship and a chip on her shoulder. You *knew* you didn't belong in my world, and my mother knew it too. She told me

• • •

don't bring home no girl from the hood. And what I do? Went digging in the gutter. Brought home a whole pregnancy from a chick I didn't even love from the ghetto."

She was bitter now, rage spilling out. "So now you digging in the *gutter* to be with me? Now I'm ghetto trash?"

"Don't play dumb — I'm saying you knew what it was. You hung on to it like it meant something. We was just smashing, Tea. Just what college kids do. That's all it was supposed to be. Don't act like this was some romance and I was wining and dining you, bringing you flowers, movies, trips, taking you to meet my folks. You wouldn't even be here if you weren't on a mission to make me your husband."

"You married me," she shot back, her voice low, trembling with loathing.

"Because I'm a man. I wasn't about to let my sons grow up with a mama from the hood leading them in God knows what kind of life. So yeah, I married the mother of my kids — not the love of my life."

"And your legacy," she said, eyes filling with tears. She hated crying, hated the weakness of it, but now she couldn't

• • •

hold them back. "Because of what your stupid-ass family thinks?"

"Exactly," he spat. "You knew I didn't have my father and that I was *never* gonna let another man raise my boys. That's not negotiable."

Her voice cracked. "Then just fucking say it, Nolen. You're still thinking about her."

He blinked. "What?"

"Tanika," she hissed. "That's who you can't let go of, ain't it? You've been in denial this WHOLE time — acting like you moved on, when you never really did."

His jaw clenched. He stayed silent.

"You still got that picture of y'all from college saved in your iCloud," she scoffed. "Still act like *we're* the mistake and *she* was the plan."

He didn't correct her. Didn't say no. Didn't tell her the real reason he couldn't breathe at night, couldn't sleep right, couldn't stop remembering softness in another woman's eyes.

● ● ●

154

She stepped into his face and yelled. "Man the fuck up and say something then, nigga!"

He looked at her with disgust. This was the part of the hood that never left her. The reason she never knew how to be soft in any way that mattered. Every time she felt cornered, it was like going head-to-head with a man instead of his wife.

He stepped back, voice low and sharp. "I don't owe you no explanation, but I'm not thinking about Tanika."

"Liar," she snapped.

The tension snapped in two.

"Bottom line, I was clear — to you," he said. "I did what I had to do. I raised my sons. I dropped out. Got married. Played the role, still playing it. I provide for this house and you. You don't work. Don't want to work. You ain't got no ambition."

She trembled, her body betraying the ache of hearing him say it all out loud, cruel and cold.

"But you knew from the beginning, didn't you?" he pressed, voice biting. "You knew I had a girl. You knew I wasn't staying. And you *still* planned it. You weren't trying to

● ● ●

build a home — you were just trying to get out of Park Heights."

"I was in love with you!" she screamed.

"Nah. You wanted me. That's a difference. You never loved me. Because if you did, you wouldn't have lied to me and manipulated me. You used the fact that you didn't have a father, and I didn't have one, to make me obligated to stay. And you won. You were right."

Her eyes filled, but she held back the tears — except for one that slipped down her cheek, offering no softness to the blow.

"All I thought about was what my mama said," he bit out. "You know how it felt to disappoint her? Walking into her house having to tell her the Park Heights chick was having her grandchild?"

Teanir screamed, her whole body shaking. "And you think I didn't have dreams? You think I wanted to be a wife you pitied? You think I didn't want more than being the girl who got pregnant without being married — twice?!"

He said nothing.

• • •

"You a coward, Nol," she spat, her voice breaking. "You hide behind fatherhood, so you don't have to admit you're miserable in the skin you're in. You blame me for the choices THAT YOU MADE. And for the weak ass man that you *really* are."

He didn't move. Didn't speak. Just stood there, breathing hard — the silence heavier than any word.

It cut him like a knife.

He gave a nod, *not* in agreement but in saying that he was done with the conversation… and he was done with her.

He grabbed his keys off the counter, chest heaving.

"Where the fuck you going now?" she yelled.

"Anywhere but here."

"Yep run back to yo mama, mama's boy," she shouted after him. "But nothings gonna fix what's broken in you!"

But he didn't turn around.

He walked out, slamming the door behind him.

• • •

He was clear now. If he had never been clear before,
he was clear tonight.

He needed to see her.

It was late. And he didn't care.

CHAPTER 11
The Spot

Some places are found and not everything sacred lives in a church.

The keys felt like they were burning in his hand.

Nolen didn't even remember starting the engine — just the heavy slam of the door, the heat in his chest, and the sound of his tires skidding against concrete as he pulled away from the house.

He couldn't go back home.

The one he built from the ground up because Tea wanted to be and have everything she never had before. And he couldn't go to his mama's house, because he didn't feel like hearing her tell him 'I told you so'.

He didn't have a home. Just walls he shared with a woman who had planned her way into his life and called it love. His mind wasn't on Tanika. And it sure as hell wasn't on Teanir.

It was her.

• • •

Novi.

The softness in her voice.

The way she saw straight through him and didn't flinch. He pulled over on a quiet stretch of road near the water, his fingers tapping the screen before he could talk himself out of it.

NOLEN:
I need to see you.
Are you busy?
Just... can we talk?

He stared at it for a second. Then hit send. The typing dots appeared almost immediately.

NOVI:
Hey, Not at all.
Zay's out.
Kids are with my mom.
Where should I meet you?

No one knew about this place. Just him. He hesitated for a moment. *Do I share this with her? My place?* The hesitation lasted only a breath. Trust wasn't something he gave easily, but with her, it felt natural. Certain. This wasn't just a hiding spot — it was a piece of himself, a sanctuary carved out of silence.

• • •

One he'd never shared with anyone. And somehow, he knew she was the only one he could trust to hold it... and him.

> NOLEN:
> It's a spot around the
> Liberty Reservoir.
> I'll send you a GPS ping.
> Drive safe.

Liberty Reservoir | 10:04 PM

The Spot lived up to its name. Hidden. Still. Unbothered. An abandoned lookout that had once been a scenic rest stop before time and tree roots cracked it open.

The sun was gone now, leaving only the violet bruises of dusk smeared across the horizon. The trees whispered. The air was warm, but not heavy.

He stood next to his truck, hands in his pockets, trying to calm his breathing.

Then her headlights crept into view.

Novi pulled up slow.

• • •

Soft sundress. Flip-flops. Hair pulled up in a messy bun that somehow made her look even more stunning. No makeup. Just her. Just *Novi.*

She stepped out, and their eyes locked.
No words. Just gravity.

She walked up, not stopping. And the moment she was close enough, he grabbed her waist, pulled her in, and kissed her like he'd been dying of thirst.

Their mouths crashed — fast, open, *needy.*
It wasn't polite. It wasn't controlled.
It was *oxygen* — and they both needed to breathe.

His hands found her hips. Her thighs. The soft curve of her backside. He groaned into her mouth as she pressed against him, breathless.

Her body melted into his, and for a second, the world stopped.

He slid one hand beneath her dress, fingertips brushing the inside of her thigh.

She gasped and pulled back. "Nolen…"

• • •

He leaned in and bent down so his forehead pressed against hers, breathing heavy.

"I want to taste you," he whispered, voice low with restraint.

Her eyes widened.

She opened her mouth to protest — again — but he was already guiding her down gently, laying her on her back against the earth.

Grass curled around them. Stars blinked above. The cracked concrete platform beneath them glowed silver in the moonlight.

He lifted her dress, slow, deliberate.

Her skin was soft.

Warm.

Glowing like honey. She arched her hips, fighting the need rising in her.

"*Nolen…*" she whispered, trying to breathe.

But it was too late.

His lips met the inside of her thigh. Then higher.

• • •

Then —

He kissed her like it was holy.

Like *she* was holy.

In reverence.
Tongue deep.
Intentional.
Starving.

She moaned, hands gripping the grass, chest rising with every flick, every stroke.

He groaned into her, the taste of her driving him crazy. He reached up, and their fingers laced — tight, pulsing.

She tried to scoot back, breath catching, overwhelmed by the sensation.

But his hands held her steady, firm yet tender, his eyes locked on hers — steadying her, grounding her. "Don't," he whispered, voice low and aching. "Stay with me. Let me have this… let me have you."

Her resistance melted. She was already unraveling, but in his arms, it felt like surrendering to something bigger than either of them.

● ● ●

He pressed in deeper, buried his face between her legs, tongue moving in rhythm with the way she writhed beneath him.

He *devoured* her.

Not politely. Not gently.
Hungrily.

She gasped, reaching for his shoulders, for something to hold onto — but he didn't stop. He *liked* the mess. The soaking. The shaking. The surrender.

The way she tried to hold it back — and couldn't.

She was unraveling beneath him — trembling in his mouth, crying out his name like it had always been written on her tongue.

He groaned with satisfaction, tasting every drop. Her surrender surged through him like fire and reverence, like he'd been entrusted with something sacred. His jaw flexed. His hands gripped her thighs like prayer. It made him need her — and it stitched him back together.

● ● ●

Her moans echoed into the trees, raw and unrestrained, marking the moment like a confession neither of them could ever take back.

When they were spent, he slowly kissed his way up her belly, chest, and neck. Then collapsed beside her, heart pounding.

They lay there, tangled in sweat and starlight.

She turned toward him. Her lips were swollen — bitten from trying to stay restrained. But she couldn't. He made her unable. Her chest *still* heaving. "I... I wasn't expecting that." She said breathless.

"I was," he said softly. "Been thinking about that since the first moment I saw you sing."

She didn't speak.

She inhaled him deeply and leaned into his chest.

The scent of his sweat — earthy, warm — intoxicating. Better than any cologne.

She wanted to live in that smell. In this moment.

He wrapped an arm around her. Pulled her close.

● ● ●

And under the stars, they both fell asleep.

No guilt.

No answers.

Just silence.

CHAPTER 12
Before the Light

Some truths only come out in the dark, just before the world wakes.

Novi woke just after 3 a.m.

The sky above was still deep navy, stars barely clinging to their place. A soft breeze rustled the leaves, brushing cool air across her skin.

She blinked slowly, adjusting to the dark, and moved just enough to feel the warmth of Nolen's chest still pressed against her back.

He stirred almost immediately, like he could feel the shift inside her.

His arm slid tighter around her waist. "You okay?" he murmured, voice still heavy with sleep.

She nodded against him. "Just... woke up."

He let a few moments pass before whispering, "You wanna talk?"

• • •

She did.

She didn't know where to begin.

So she just let herself breathe.

"It's strange," she said softly, "how quiet the world is when you're not pretending."

He didn't respond at first - just nodded, chin resting lightly against her head.

"I don't get this kind of peace," she continued. "At home. Not really."

"You feel like you're always in motion," he said.

"Yeah." She exhaled. "Always working. Always holding it together."

"You don't have to here."

She paused. Swallowed. "I don't even remember what it feels like to be seen. Really seen."

He leaned up on one elbow, looked at her in the faint moonlight.

"You're seen, Novi," he said gently. "*I* see you."

• • •

Her throat tightened. She didn't expect that to hit as hard as it did.

She looked at him. "Zayven… he's got a way of making it seem like I'm doing too much. But I have to. I work two jobs. Not even counting what I do at church."

"You pay most of the bills?" Nolen asked.

"*All* of them," she said flatly. "He's always quitting jobs, chasing some hustle. Keeps saying something will pop off eventually. But in the meantime, it's me. Mortgage, food, kids, gas, daycare. And his sneakers."

Nolen scoffed under his breath. "Sounds like a real provider."

She let out a tired laugh. "Right?"

Then her voice grew soft again. "But I stay. Because of the kids. Because it looks good. Because… I thought God was gonna fix it."

He nodded, and for a while, neither of them spoke. The weight of their unspoken truths pressed gently between them.

• • •

Nolen finally spoke, voice low and tight. "Sometimes I feel like I'm crumbling under the pressure of being everything for everyone."

She turned toward him.

"I love my sons," he said. "But I'm with a woman I never wanted. Never loved. And every time I walk into that house, it feels like I'm suffocating. Like I'm dying slowly... in jeans and responsibility."

Her heart twisted.

"And the thing is," he continued, "I keep showing up. For them. For my house. For the marriage. But it's like I've had to erase me to make it work."

She blinked through the silence, then whispered, "That's what I've been doing too."

His eyes locked with hers. "We're both sacrificing our souls for appearances."

They didn't move. Just looked at each other.

"Do you ever feel like... love isn't supposed to hurt like this?" she asked.

• • •

He nodded slowly. "Yeah. And last night? With you?" He reached for her hand. "That didn't hurt. That healed."

She took a shaky breath. "You make me feel -"

She hesitated. " — like I'm more than what I do. Like I'm not just surviving."

"You are more," he said. "And being here with you... it reminded me I'm not too gone to feel something real again."

She stared at him, eyes glossy. "I didn't think I'd ever feel anything like this."

"I thought I'd hardened up. Thought it was too late for me."

His voice broke slightly. "But you... Novi, you pulled something alive out of me."

She leaned her forehead into his chest. His arms wrapped around her again. She inhaled his scent again, a scent she'd remember in her memory always.

They lay like that as the sky began to shift.

Dark blue gave way to violet. Violet to amber.

The light of dawn spilled over the trees.

• • •

He looked at her, eyes soft, face kissed by sunlight.
She had never looked more beautiful.

"I feel… full," he said. "For the first time in years."

Her heart swelled, then opened. She closed her eyes.

"I feel seen by you, appreciated by you," she whispered. "And I'm afraid to admit… I don't feel guilty for it. And I know that I *should*."

He didn't respond right away. He just held her.

"I know this isn't what's supposed to happen," she said. "I'm married. You're married. I should be praying, repenting. I should be —"

She stopped.
Tears welled in her eyes.

"— but I feel my heart is full, Nolen. Full of you."

He closed his eyes. Kissed her forehead.

Neither of them said the word.

But they didn't have to.

Her phone buzzed, breaking the moment.

She looked down.

Zayven.

Then another buzz — a text from her mom.

MAMA:
Hey baby, Zay called looking for you.
I didn't tell him anything.
Just said you probably needed a break.
Are you okay?

She closed her eyes.

"I have to go," she said quietly. He nodded, slowly sitting up.

She stood, smoothing her dress, the ache in her chest almost unbearable. "You good?" he asked.

"No," she admitted. "But I'm grateful."

He walked her to her car, neither of them ready to let go.

She turned to him at the door. "I'll carry this. Whatever happens next. I don't regret it."

● ● ●

He reached for her hand, kissed her knuckles. "Me either."

He smiled, and so did she.

He leaned into her and kissed her gently before opening the door for her.

She got in, started the car, and drove off slowly.

Nolen stood there long after she disappeared.
Alone. Still.
Letting the silence return.

He looked out over the water, hands in his pockets. And for the first time in a long time, he thanked God. Not because he was being reckless or rebellious. But because he realized — he could still *feel.*

Still love.

Still hope.

And even if it was all wrong...

It was real.

• • •

CHAPTER 13
Shifts

The shift wasn't in what they did, but what they could no longer ignore

---

The sun was already high when Novi pulled into her driveway. She parked slowly, her heart pounding. The glow of the morning now felt like a spotlight - too bright, too revealing.

Her skin still hummed from the night before. But her spirit?

Fractured.

She unlocked the door to the quiet house. The moment she stepped inside, the silence felt wrong. Too clean. Too cold.

Her phone buzzed again.
Zayven.

ZAYVEN:
Where you been?
Ma said you stayed out.
You back now?

No *"Are you okay?"*

• • •

No *"I was worried."*

Just suspicion, laced in performative concern.
She typed back:

NOVI:
Yeah.
Just needed a breather.
I'm back.

It wasn't a lie. Not entirely. She did need to breathe.
She just didn't expect to breathe *with someone else.*

Zayven's response came quick:

ZAYVEN:
Cool. Don't forget my shoot's at 3.
I need you to iron my jacket &
have my slides in the car this time.

That was it.
No *"I missed you."*
No *"I love you."*
Not even a question about where she really was.

Just: serve me. Show up for me. Look the part.

• • •

She stared at the screen, then tossed the phone on the couch. She hadn't even changed clothes. Her sundress still carried the scent of him.

Of Nolen.

She caught her reflection in the mirror.

Same woman.

Different eyes.

Teanir was already in the kitchen when he got back. She looked refreshed, even cheerful — like peace had come over her in his absence. She'd made breakfast: pancakes, turkey bacon, eggs with cheese the way he liked them.

She didn't greet him immediately. Just slid the plate in his direction.

"You were out late," she finally said, casual but pointed.

He nodded. "Yeah. Took a drive. Needed space."

"Mmm." She stirred her coffee, not looking up. "You used to talk to me when you needed space."

• • •

He didn't answer.

I mean," she added, "before it started feeling like *I* was the space you were running from."

He sighed, hands tightening around his fork. "Teanir, not this morning."

"I'm just saying," she shrugged, "you've been different since we got back from the hotel. Distant. Detached."

She turned, eyes narrowing slightly. "I know you think you good at hiding it, but I feel it. Something ain't right."

Nolen met her eyes for a beat longer than he should've.

"I told you," he said evenly, "I'm just tired."

She stepped closer now. Not angry. Not yet. Just... suspicious. "Is it her?"

He blinked. "Who?"

"Tanika."

He nearly choked on his eggs. "What?"

● ● ●

"You still holding a torch for her? You still think that was supposed to be your happy ending? Because if that's what this is, just say it."

His voice dropped. "You're projecting."

"No, I'm watching. And I see how your face changes when I talk about her — or when I try to talk to *you*."

He pushed back from the table.

"That's what this is? You think I'm cheating with someone who hasn't been in my life for almost a decade?"

She stepped forward, voice rising. "I think you phony! You play perfect at church, act like you this pillar of strength — but you a weak ass nigga. You still stuck on what could've been instead of what *is*. God is trying to restore us and you out here chasing ghosts."

Nolen stood now, fists clenched. "Don't talk to me about ghosts. You're the one that haunted me."

"Oh please —"

"Nah. You wanna know the truth? I know you planned this. You got pregnant on purpose, you knew what having a

● ● ●

child with someone like me meant. My family. My legacy. You *know* you trapped me!"

She froze.

He said it again, just like the night before. She had hoped that was only anger — that he didn't really believe that was the truth. Because in fact, at least in part... it *was* the truth. She just never said it out loud.

But not because of legacy.
Because of family.

She knew that a man who didn't have a father knew what having a family divided felt like — and that he, like her, would hold on to that family no matter what. Be there for his kids, no matter what.

And now she was surprised that he didn't see it the way she did. He saw it as a trap of what it *was* and not the beautiful thing that it *could* be... that it *should* be.

"And I was never gonna let another man raise my sons. You know that's why I stayed. Not because I loved you. Not because I wanted *you*."

• • •

Her mouth parted, shocked. "So that's it? That's what you think this all is? A trap?"

He didn't soften. "You wanted the name. You wanted the ring. You got it."

Her voice cracked. "And you think she does?"

He didn't answer.

"Whoever *she* is," she hissed, "you think *she* wants you without the name, the ring, the platform?"

He grabbed his keys off the counter.

"Wow," she said bitterly. "Run, then. That's all you do anyway. Just don't forget that your sons are watching you. So, what kind of man you showing them that you are — and who they should be?"

He paused.
That hit harder than anything else she'd said.

But he didn't turn back.

Not this time.

* * *

Novi folded Zayven's jacket like he asked. Pressed it. Hung it on the back door for his convenience.

But her chest felt tight the whole time.
Her mother texted again:

MAMA:
You sure you're okay baby?

NOVI:
Yeah, just tired.

And it was true.

But not the kind of tired a nap could fix.

She stared at the jacket, suddenly realizing that she didn't even recognize herself anymore.

Not the version of her that served while starving. Not the version who gave everything while feeling nothing. Not the version who bent to stay married while her soul stretched toward something that felt like love.

Real love.
And she couldn't pray.

Couldn't even fake it right now.

• • •

Because her heart was already full.

And broken.

At the same time.

CHAPTER 14
The Truth We Can't Say

Some truths aren't hidden; they are unspoken and undeniable

"Girl, sit down before your nerves melt into that tile."

Velani's voice floated from the kitchen as Novi paced slow circles across the floor, one sandal off, curls falling from the messy bun she hadn't fixed since she got home.

Velani Morgan had always been the one who knew how to hold people together while they unraveled. Smooth-skinned and sharp-tongued, she carried the kind of wisdom that came from living through the fire, not just reading about it. The bohemian wide legged pants — the earth bangles, the way her presence filled a room like a sermon... it all said the same thing: I've been broken, but I don't break easy anymore.

She was Novi's best friend, spiritual compass, and emotional bodyguard — all rolled into one. They'd met back in grammar school once Novi was adopted. She introduced her to church and they were just two church girls with cracked pasts and heavy futures, but even then, Velani was already part grown. Already a mother. Already learning that love could be

• • •

a battlefield. Now, at 26, she'd traded survival for sovereignty, and she didn't flinch for anybody's drama. Except Novi's.

Always Novi's.

"I can't sit. I'll come apart if I sit."

"Then fall apart standing," Velani said, calm as ever. "Just don't act like you're not breaking. I see it all over you."

Novi collapsed onto the couch, fingers tugging at a loose thread on her dress. Her voice was low. "I did something, Vee."

Velani walked in slowly, two mugs in her hand, a look on her face like she already knew. She set one down in front of Novi and took a long sip from her own, her eyes steady.

This wasn't new territory. Velani had spent hours on the phone months ago, biting back every scream while Novi spiraled through a half-whispered confession about Nolen. The voice messages, the prayers, the little glances that lasted too long. Velani had shut it down early. Hard. He's married, Novi. And so are you.

After that, Novi stopped bringing him up. Carefully tiptoed around his name like it might detonate everything between them. Velani didn't press. She knew her best friend.

● ● ●

Knew that silence wasn't peace, it was proof something was simmering just beneath the surface.

Now, the pot was boiling over.

"Don't tell me," Velani said finally. "Tell you."

Novi's eyes brimmed but didn't spill. "I think I'm in love with him."

Velani blinked once. "Nolen?"

She nodded slowly. "It wasn't just the sex. That was… insane. But it's more than that. He sees me. We talk. We pray. He listens. He — "

Velani raised a brow. "He's married."

"I know."

"And so are you."

"I know that too."

Silence.

"He's not like Zay," Novi continued. "He's not performative. He's not chasing applause. He's just… real and honest. Like me."

● ● ●

Velani said nothing, only watching her. Letting her go deeper.

Novi hesitated, then exhaled sharply, like the truth had been pressing against her ribs all morning. "It happened last night."

Velani narrowed her eyes. "Y'all hooked up?"

Novi gave a faint, guilty nod. "Yeah."

Velani leaned back slowly, blinking once. "Y'all had sex?"

"Not... all the way," Novi said, voice catching. "It was — oral. But it was... real. Intimate. All of it."

Velani stared at her a beat longer, then let out a dry little laugh and sipped her coffee. "Girl. That's sex... Was it *good?* Did you grab that nigga's head?"

"Vee!" Novi laughed out loud. Velani always had a way of turning a conversation into a 'did you at least get off because if you did, it was worth it' regardless if she agreed with you or not.

"I know, so yes we had sex..."

• • •

"I mean, well..." she added with a smirk. "..not technically," "Y'all just played hard."

Novi groaned and dropped her face into her hands. "Vee..."

"I'm not judging you girl," Velani said, softer now. "But I told you the first time you brought that man up that he's dangerous. Not 'cause he's evil. But because he makes you feel seen in a season where you feel invisible. That's a setup. And I know it's easy for me to sit here and say don't do it when that man is giving you everything you lacking."

Novi peeked at her through her fingers. "I tried not to talk to you about him anymore."

"I noticed," Velani said. "Which is how I really knew it was getting deep."

"And Zay? Girl, I just found out he quit another job. That's four in a year, Vee. Four! And we just got a notice from the mortgage company that we're six months behind. I don't know how that happened when all of my checks are directly deposited into the bank. He's supposed to be paying the bills. But every time I ask, he gets defensive or flips it back on me.

• • •

And now I gotta figure out how to come up with extra money — again just to keep us in that house."

Velani leaned forward. "You working two jobs already."

"And church. Which is another job in itself."

Novi's voice broke. "I believed in submission. I believed that if I followed God and followed my husband, we'd be covered. But I'm drowning. I'm submitting to someone who's not even standing."

Velani reached across the table and squeezed her hand. "That ain't submission, sis. That's survival. And that *ain't* God."

Novi started to cry. A cry that came from her soul. She could be real with Velani. They'd been best friends since fourth grade. She knew being vulnerable in front of her was okay.

"I can't even say anything at church. Zay would *die* if the elders knew we were broke. He walks around like he's building something, branding something, being something. But I'm the one holding it all together. Quietly. Behind the scenes. Dying inside."

• • •

Velani walked over and gave her the biggest sisterly hug.

"It's okay, sis. I always said I thought he was a joke when you got with him, but you was all dick-matized since he was your first."

They both let out a laugh that made the tension in the room break for a moment. She always knew how to make Novi laugh, even when she was sad, and even when everything else was breaking.

"Girl, you a mess — but you're not lying."

"So, sis, what about Nolen?" Velani asked gently. "What is he giving you beside the obvious?"

Novi smiled. "*Peace*. A break from pretending. He listens to me. He asks about me — not what I can do, not how I can help. Just me. He challenges me. He remembers things I say. He asks what he can do for me."

"Damn, sis," Velani said. "Now, that's what a real man's supposed to do." She shifted in her seat. "I don't know, sis. I wanna be like 'Girl, leave that negro alone,' but if he doing all that? I can't even fix my mouth to tell you that. He doing the thang, honey."

• • •

Novi got more tissues and looked at her best friend and said "You think I'm crazy for even being on this path I know."

Velani sat back. "You're not crazy, Novi. I think you're just *tired* of starving and calling it fasting."

A tear fell down Novi's cheek again. She wiped it quick. "But how do I go back to him now, Vee? To Zay? To that life?"

"You don't, sis. You go forward. That might mean going back home physically but not spiritually. Not emotionally. You keep your heart facing forward. Toward truth. Toward healing. Not toward guilt."

Novi looked down at her cup. Whispered, "It wasn't supposed to *be* like this. I loved Zay, sis. You know I did. I gave everything and got nothing in return... well, except for my kids."

"I know," Velani said. "But you're here now. So be honest with yourself first. And don't let anybody shame you for what grew in that dark place.

Just figure out what you need to come back to the light."

• • •

Office of Associate Pastor Ernest Sandiford

Nolen needed the council of someone tried and true. That knew what it meant to be married and have a family. He had thoughts about his fight with Teanir and wasn't even home a full hour yet before another fight had started and he was in his truck driving off from the place that didn't feel like home.

As we walked into the study, it smelled like old books and frankincense. Shelves of theology texts lined the walls, and the soft ticking of a vintage clock filled the silence while Pastor Ernest listened.

He didn't interrupt. Just let Nolen speak.

"I'm trying, Uncle Ern. I really am. But it's like... every day I wake up and I feel more trapped. Teanir, the house, the schedule, the responsibilities - it's like I'm buried in expectations I never asked for."

Pastor Ernest Sandiford had made a life out of listening to storms like this. Not the loud, public kind but the quiet, internal kind that brewed inside men who never learned how to name their pain.

• • •

He wasn't flashy like Bishop Byrd or trendy like the youth ministers. Ernest was the kind of shepherd who remembered everyone's birthday, knew when your mother passed, and had a marked-up Bible and banana bread ready before you even knew you needed it.

Late sixties, earth-toned skin, close-shaved silver hair, and a limp that came and went with the weather. He carried decades of wisdom like a cloak. He didn't need a platform to be powerful. Just a chair across from you and the truth spoken in love.

To Nolen, he wasn't just the associate pastor. He was a father in every way that mattered. The man who pulled him aside when his temper flared. Who looked him in the eyes when he was a kid playing on the drums and said, "Now play that again when it's just you and God listening."

Ernest folded his hands across his lap, nodding slowly. "And the retreat?"

Nolen laughed, humorless. "She loved it. Of course. Anytime she gets all the attention, she's a different person. Softer. Sweeter. But it didn't fix anything. It didn't change the fact that when I touched her, I didn't feel anything. Not a spark. Not a flicker. Just... duty."

● ● ●

"You been holding this in too long."

"I didn't know where to put it. How to say it without sounding like I'm the villain. I'm a father. A provider. But I'm not a husband in the way she wants. And I haven't been for a long time."

Pastor Ernest leaned forward, elbows resting on worn knees. "You ever wonder if the weight you're carrying ain't yours to carry?"

Nolen blinked. "Say more."

"Responsibility without relationship will always feel like punishment. And punishment will harden your spirit. You're not an evil man, son. You're exhausted. But that space? The one you're in now? It's dangerous. That kind of frustration leaves the door cracked for the enemy to slip in."

Nolen swallowed. Hard.

"I'm not saying you're weak," Ernest continued. "But I am saying you're vulnerable. *Any* man would be in your position. And temptation? It can look like red lips and short skirts… or anything that can take you away from what you promised your wife before God when you took that oath. And if you're not careful, you'll confuse relief with release."

• • •

Nolen nodded slowly. "I just want out, man. Out of the lie. Out of the pressure. She always dropping hints about what she wants from me — even got her mama in on it. She'll call the house and say stuff like, 'It'd be nice if you do this for your wife. I know Teanir would love that.'"

"And you can get out," Ernest said gently. "But you gotta do it God's way. The Word says He'll make a way of escape. But you have to take it when He shows it. That's your test."

Nolen looked down at his hands. "Man, I don't even know who I am anymore. I know the type of man I could be."

He had to stop himself right there. He was about to tell Pastor Ernest about the man he is when he's with Novi. How he's respected. Admired. Loved — not for what he has or what his family name means, but for who he is. She's not combative. She listens. She gives. She loves. She nurtures.

All of that makes him not only feel like a man... but feel like the man he knew he could've always been— if he hadn't gotten caught up with the babies and Teanir early on.

• • •

"You're still God's man, son," Ernest said, standing. "Even when you're unsure. Even when you fall. You're still *His*."

A knock at the door signaled Sheila had brought sweet potato pie and coffee. She stepped in, warm smile and kind eyes, and set it down beside Nolen.

"You staying for dinner?" she asked softly.

Nolen managed a weak smile. "I might need to."

She nodded. "Good. You always have a seat at our table. And I made fried country steak, collard greens, yams, cornbread, and some sweet tea."

And for the first time that day, Nolen felt the smallest piece of himself exhale.

• • •

CHAPTER 15
Louder Than Worship

He was on the other side of the room and felt closer than God.

It wasn't the same anymore.

Not when they stepped onto the altar.
Not when she picked up the mic.
Not when he picked up his sticks.
Not when the lights dimmed and the sanctuary quieted, expectant and full of eyes.

There had always been chemistry between them on the platform. But now, it hummed like electricity in the walls. Every note she hit, he followed. Every breath she took, he anticipated.

Every song became a confession.

That Sunday, Devotion Heights was packed again — third service. Pastor had gone over in the 9 a.m. worship service, and people were already restless, whispering in the pews.

• • •

But when Novi began to sing, a soft, aching lead on *Build My Life* — the room fell into reverent silence.

Nolen felt it before he even touched the drums. The way her voice trembled, not from fear, but from the weight of the song.

The way her fingers curled around the mic like a lifeline. The way her body swayed with the Spirit— and maybe with memory, too.

Because earlier that week, in a hidden place, she had cried out in his arms in a way no man had ever touched her. And now, she was standing here like nothing had happened.

Like everything hadn't changed.

He counted her in gently with the hi-hat, tapping just enough to carry her voice —never overpowering.

But Kara noticed.
She always did.

She watched Nolen too closely now. Watched Novi even harder.

• • •

199

She clapped when others clapped. Raised her hand in worship.

But her eyes? Cold.

Janet, standing behind Novi, didn't even pretend to hide it with her arms folded across her chest, jaw set tight with mic in hand.

Venus in the soprano section on the pulpit, head tilted, lips curled into a smile like she knew something the others didn't.

Only Jeff Casen, the new Praise & Worship Director, stood unreadable. Bible in hand. Signature Bluetooth in one ear. Nodding in rhythm, but offering nothing else. His lips didn't part. His eyes didn't waver. He was calculating.

When Novi reached the final chorus, her voice soared – vulnerable, raw, deeply anointed.

The congregation erupted. Not just claps. Shouts. Tears. People standing to their feet.

Because that sound wasn't performance.
It was confession.
It was longing.

• • •

It was *her*.

After service in the dressing room, the air was different there. Thicker. Cassia walked past with a warm smile and a side hug. "That was beautiful, baby girl."

"Aww Praise God," Novi whispered, still catching her breath.

Jeff leaned in from the hallway. "Great job today," he said, polite and professional. "Real strong finish."

"Thanks."

Then he turned. "You too, Nolen. Tight playing."

Nolen nodded, grunted his thanks.

Jeff paused. His voice light. Casual. "People really feel y'all when you flow together like that."

It was a compliment.
And a clue.

Novi's stomach twisted.

She glanced toward Kara, who was watching like she'd

• • •

just found ammunition.

Across the room, Venus caught her eye and smirked. Novi looked away, heart pounding.

Still, nothing could touch the way he played for her. Or how she sang when he was behind her. And no matter who noticed…

She wasn't ready to let it go.

They were all leaving out and by this time the crowd thinned. Families gathered their children. Ushers reset the offering envelopes.

Two new lay ministers stood chatting by the side aisle, sipping lukewarm coffee from paper cups.

"That worship today?" one of them said, nodding toward the front. "Incredible. That Novi and Nolen pairing? Whew. How long have they been married?"

A woman in a floral blazer blinked. "Oh, no… Novi's married to Minister Zayven Jaxson. That's her husband."

• • •

The minister raised an eyebrow. "Oh... my mistake. They sure don't move like it."

Unfortunately...

Zayven overheard every word.

He had doubled back to grab a misplaced Bible from the front pew and caught the tail end of the conversation.

His steps slowed. His jaw locked.

Not because he was hurt.

But because it hit him — his image was slipping. If people believed *that* — if whispers started, if appearances cracked — it wouldn't just be about Novi.

It would be about *him*. His platform. His ministry trajectory. His brand.
And that?

He couldn't afford.

Not when he was building something.

Not when he had plans.

● ● ●

His fingers tightened around the Bible spine, his face a blank mask.

But something in his chest turned cold.

Because if the *people* were seeing it…

Then it meant *something* was being shown.

And Zayven Jaxson didn't like being blindsided.

Not on stage.

Not at church.

And definitely not by his own wife.

• • •

CHAPTER 16
The Unmaking

His question didn't start the unraveling — it finished it.

"So… how long have y'all been married?"

Novi blinked. "Excuse me?"

"You and Nolen."

He didn't smile. Didn't flinch.

"That's what they're saying, right? Y'all look so perfect on stage that people assume you're together."

She froze, heart pounding.

"Zayven, I'm married to you."

"I'm asking a question. As the man of THIS house, I expect you to answer better than that"

She scoffed.

Thinking about how he's so quick to say he's the man of the house and yet had never actually acted like it.

• • •

He performed outside the home and expected her to fall for it inside the home.

"Don't."

He stood slowly, folding his arms. "You thinking about cheating on me?"

Her mouth parted. Heat rushed to her face.

"Or are you already betraying me?"

The words hung in the air like ash.

She wanted to come clean, out of respect for their union — but his word was a reminder to her that their entire marriage was a betrayal, him as a man, a husband, a father, and a provider.

And something inside her snapped.

"YOU wanna talk about betrayal?" she fired back. "How about the fact that I got a letter from the mortgage company last week? We're four months behind."

He shifted. "That's not what we're talking about — "

"Oh, it is now," she snapped, stepping toward him. "Because I work two jobs, Zayven. TWO. Not counting what

• • •

I do at the church. There's more than enough money in that account to cover the mortgage, the utilities, the car — everything."

He rubbed his chin, eyes darting.

"So, where's the money going, Zayven?"

He didn't answer.

"New sneakers? More branding photoshoots? Another logo for a ministry you haven't even launched?"

"I'm building something, Novi. You wouldn't understand you're not the man of this house and — "

"No," she cut him off. "What I don't understand is how long I have to carry this entire family by myself? You promised to be the priest, provider, and protector" her voice broke, "But you haven't been any of those things to me."

Zayven got quiet. Too quiet.

Then he did what he always did when cornered — Quoted scripture.

"A wise woman builds her house, Novi. But a foolish one..."

• • •

"Don't DARE throw Proverbs at me right now," she hissed.

"Not while I'm bleeding from the foundation cracks you caused in this marriage."

He opened his mouth to speak again —

Buzz.
Group text.
She read it aloud.

WORSHIP TEAM CHAT:
Hey team! Exciting news!! 'Fresh Oil' is taking off!
We've got a 5-day promotional tour opportunity.
Travel, hotel, food — all covered. $3,500 stipend
for each worship leader. Novi, we especially want
you because you are leading the single.
Please send availability!

Novi stared at the message.

That money could help them keep the utilities on while she paid the late fees and the past-due mortgage.

It could cover groceries. Pay for daycare. And more than anything, it could buy her time.

A break from him.

• • •

She looked up at Zayven.

"I'm going," she said flatly.

"Wait — what?"

"I would normally ask," she said calmly, "but I'm not asking you for anything. I'm providing for my children, as always, *again*.

You aren't the priest of this house.

You're not the provider.

And you definitely haven't protected me."

"Novi, come on."

"I wish I had known what kind of man your father was," she whispered. "If I had, I would've never married you."

That hit.

Hard.

He stepped back like she'd slapped him.

"Novi, please. Don't say that. You didn't make a mistake. The enemy is just attacking us. That's *all* this is baby.

• • •

He's trying to destroy our marriage before God can solidify our brand."

She gave him a hollow look.

"You're more worried about your brand than your home."

Then she turned and walked upstairs.

Later That Night

Zayven came into the bedroom after midnight, breath steady but movements too careful.

She was lying on her side, eyes closed, body still. He slipped into bed behind her, hand resting on her hip. Slowly, he slid beneath the sheets.

She didn't move.

His breath hitched as he shifted lower.

Tongue searching. Mouth moving.

But all she could think about... was Nolen.

• • •

The way his hands held her.

The way his voice filled her ear.

The way he made her feel known.

Loved.

Open.

Zayven's rhythm had always been rough. Mechanical. She never enjoyed oral sex with him. In fact, she'd convinced herself her body just wasn't built for it. Like some people didn't like certain foods… maybe she just didn't like that part of sex.

But then came Nolen.

He didn't just go down on her. He worshiped her. With focus. With patience. With intention. And for the first time in her life, she came from it. Fully. Shaken. Undone.

She hadn't even known that was possible.

How had she even let him go there?

She hadn't guided him. Hadn't instructed. Zayven was her only partner before this — eager, aimless, always rushing to prove something. Nolen had been… present. Tuned in. Like he was listening to her body breathe.

● ● ●

She grimaced suddenly and pulled away.

"I can't," she muttered.

He paused. "What?"

"How do you expect me to get turned on for a man who refuses to be accountable for his *own* house."

That silenced him.

She turned her back to him and pulled the sheet over her shoulder. Within minutes, her breathing slowed. Sleep claimed her.

But Zayven lay wide awake.

Eyes on the ceiling.
Heart pounding.
Not with conviction.
But with calculation.

Because if he couldn't win her heart back with truth... He'd find a way to win her image back with show.

Whatever it took.

• • •

CHAPTER 17
The Engagement Tour
Not every kind of surrender happens on the Altar.

The praise team's new single, "Fresh Oil," had exploded across streaming platforms within weeks. What began as a spontaneous worship moment at Devotion Heights was now a full-blown movement, radio airplay, guest invitations, and a statewide tour that was equal parts ministry and pressure.

Cassia was ecstatic.

Jeff Casen, strategic as ever, made sure to capitalize on the moment. "This is bigger than a single," he'd said. "This is a sound. We have to steward it."

For Novi, it was something else entirely.

Another burden. Another long stretch away from her kids. Another season of smiling through the exhaustion while Zayven spent his days in front of church folks, shaking hands and preaching his way into circles he hadn't earned.

• • •

Zayven didn't fight her decision to go on the tour — not because he supported her, or because he knew it made him look good, but because they were broke and needed the money.

"My wife is out there singing the heavens open," he told anyone who would listen. "We just trying to win souls."

He hadn't held a steady job in 4 years, and after the argument she had with Zay earlier in the week, she didn't have the luxury of saying no.

Nolen was elated.
He sent a quick text to Novi.

NOLEN:
Hey... I'm glad you said yes. I thought you were staying home.

NOVI:
I had to — I didn't really have a choice.
I have bills to pay...so....yeah I'm going

The tour schedule was tight: five cities, seven days, two Sunday appearances, and a live radio interview. Cassia traveled with them for appearances. Jeff managed the flow.

● ● ●

Kara and Janet whispered in the back of the sprinter van. And Nolen?

Nolen watched her every chance he got.

He sat across from her on the ride to Philadelphia, pretending to doze off while secretly watching the way her hands fidgeted with her necklace. On the platform, he stood behind her during soundcheck, playing softer when she sang lead, pushing harder when she broke into a run.

They were separated by responsibility, surrounded by people, but more in sync than ever.

What killed them was the nearness.

Sleeping in the same hotel and being unable to speak openly as they would on the phone. And also being unable to speak on the phone because everyone was always listening. Walking the same hotel hallways at night.

Sharing meals in greenrooms under fluorescent lights and too much noise.

And still — no time. No real intimacy.

Not since The Spot.

● ● ●

Nolen couldn't get her out of his mind — not that he wanted to. He *craved* her. And nothing he did, not even brief sexual encounters with his own wife, came close to satisfying what he *had* to have with her.

He had wanted to taste her. And he did — finally.
But now?
He wanted more. No, he needed more.

He wanted to know her. Not just her body, but her inward parts. Her fears, her rhythm, her edges. He wanted to solidify the bond that had already taken root and grown into something undeniable.

In a way, he secretly hoped the sex will be bad. That maybe it would dull the ache. Maybe then he and Teanir could finally work things out. He's had bad sex before. He knew how to push past that kind of disappointment.

But this?

This wasn't disappointment.

This was obsession. Connection. Worship.

● ● ●

Maybe it was a dream — some intense, flesh-fueled fantasy. But even if it was, this closeness without claiming, this proximity without possession… It was torture.

Being near her, seeing her across stages and pews, hearing her voice but not being able to touch her… it was too much.

He felt like he would burst from the weight of wanting her. They stole glances. Fleeting touches.

One whispered joke by the coffee machine that made her hide her smile behind a bottle of water.

But no privacy.
No release.
And it was killing them both.
Especially Nolen.

Every night, he looked for a crack in the wall. A moment alone. A signal.

He texted her more than usual. They'd both shifted from phone calls and FaceTime to texts, a silent rule they never discussed but instinctively honored.

NOLEN:
You good?.

• • •

NOVI:
Yes...

NOLEN:
You eat?

NOVI:
Lol, yes...

NOLEN:
What room you in?

NOVI:
Are you coming up?! LOL

She always answered. But never initiated. That was her last line of defense. The one thread of control she still clung to. She couldn't risk it.

Not with Kara hovering like a shadow, Jeff observing like a silent judge, Janet documenting with her eyes, and Venus?

Well... Venus was just *waiting* for something to use. Venus walked like her footsteps meant something. Always in heels, even in rehearsal. Early 50s, still wearing the kind of dresses that said "I still got it" — even if nobody asked. She used to be something. And in her mind, still was. She hated the light Novi carried. Not because it was fake, but because it was real, and Venus hadn't felt real in years. Her smile was

• • •

slow and sour. Her compliments came with edges. The kind of woman who offered to "pray for you" while waiting to see you fall. Still, by night five…

The dam was breaking.

When they reached the last city, Novi found herself rooming with Odessa. Sweet, funny, sharp-tongued Odessa.

The kind of woman who didn't mince words and didn't miss signs.

On the bus, Odessa had been chatting about Don, the same organist she'd secretly been in a relationship with for months.

By that evening, she was grinning like a teenager.

"I *finally* let him get it, girl," Odessa whispered, eyes wide. "Let that man see all this glory."

Novi nearly dropped her Earl Grey tea.

"You didn't!"

"I did," Odessa giggled. "And now I can die a happy woman. He had me singing notes that the Lord himself hasn't released in the earth realm."

• • •

They both howled with laughter.

But inside, Novi's thoughts drifted.

She hadn't told a soul about The Spot — other than Velani.

Not about the stars. Not about the way Nolen had touched her.

Worshipped her. Opened her like a prayer.

By the time they got to the hotel, Odessa was out cold. Snoring like thunder. Sleeping like a stone.

Novi laid there, eyes open, pulse racing.

The silence made the longing for him worse.

She thought of the gift shop. Maybe they had earplugs. Maybe a soda would help.

She slipped out quietly, still in her blouse and skirt, hair barely pinned, make-up gone.

She didn't care.

As she passed the vending machines, the hotel lobby was still and low-lit, bathed in blue from the machines and the

● ● ●

sound from the flatscreen TV playing basketball highlights in the lobby.

She paused at the drinks. Ginger ale or cranberry juice. She wasn't really thirsty. Her body was lying.

Buzz.

NOLEN:
You up?

She didn't answer. She didn't need to. Because the elevator dinged. And there he was.

Nolen.

He stepped out like he'd been summoned. Calm on the outside, but carrying a storm underneath.

His black joggers hung low on his hips. His t-shirt clung to his chest in all the right ways. Skin warm and golden from the soft light above. His hair was brushed low, his chain peeking from his collar. A fresh lineup. The scent of his cologne lingering even before he got close.

She almost dropped her bottle.

He didn't speak.

• • •

Just looked at her like he had been waiting five days to breathe.

"You coming down?" she asked, voice lower than she meant, praying no one else was close enough to hear.

"No," he said, the corners of his mouth lifting. "I'm hungry. But they ain't got what I wanna eat."

His eyes held hers as he dragged his lower lip slowly between his teeth, then released it with a deliberate lick. Heat rushed through her — low between her thighs. She dropped her gaze, burning with embarrassment... and desire.

The elevator doors started to close. He blocked them with one arm. She stepped aside. He stepped in.

They stood side by side in silence, breath shallow, the space between them electric with restraint until the doors closed.

Then suddenly — He grabbed her. His hand on her waist. His lips colliding against hers.

The kiss was fire and frustration, wild and full of need. So much passion it shocked even him. She gasped, her hands curling into his shirt as he pulled her closer, deeper.

• • •

He groaned softly against her mouth.

Five days.

Five cities.

Five nights of pretending.

And now...

He couldn't pretend another second.

They didn't say a word as they stepped off the elevator.

Just a shared look.

A quiet knowing.

The hallway was hushed, carpeted in silence, lined with numbered doors that all suddenly felt too loud for what they were about to do. Nolen walked ahead, not too fast, glancing back just once to make sure she was still behind him.

She was.

When he reached the door, he slid the key card in slowly, listening for the soft click. Then he turned to her, leaned in close — closer to her right ear, and spoke low, deep, and hungry.

"I wanna taste you again."

• • •

223

Then he bit her ear gently, his breath hot — like it was speaking everything his mouth didn't say.

She didn't answer.

She didn't need to.

He walked in.

She followed.

The lights were low. One bed was rumpled and occupied with his roommate sprawled out, snoring like a freight train, dead to the world.

Nolen shut the door behind them, leaning back against it for a beat, eyes locked on her.

It was quiet.

Dark.

Electric.

And now, finally, they were alone.

CHAPTER 18
Room 318

It was never meant to happen. And yet, it felt like it always would.

The room was dark and quiet, except for a sliver of city light slipping through the blinds. On one bed, Nolen's roommate lay sprawled, snoring faintly.

Novi sat on the edge of the second bed, her back to Nolen. Her heartbeat thudded like a drum — a rhythm only he could play.

"I can't believe we're doing this here," she whispered, eyes fixed on the flickering skyline.

Nolen stood behind her, close enough that his breath stirred the strands of hair at her neck.

"It was killing me not to touch you," He murmured, voice low and rough, "I wasn't going to wait another night. Five nights is too damn long."

Her lips parted to respond — but she gasped instead, his hands sliding around her waist, fingers dipping just

• • •

beneath the hem of her shirt. His touch was slow, deliberate, almost testing the silence, testing her resolve.

All he could think about were her legs. How long he had waited to touch them again.

"We have to be really….quiet," she breathed, arching slightly as his mouth grazed the curve of her neck. "He's right there."

"I know," Nolen said, voice deep.

He lifted her right thigh onto the bed's edge, trailing his fingers up and inside — slow, reverent — before slipping into her folds. One finger. Then two. Thick. Deep. Wet.

She closed her eyes, a small gasp escaping.

"Shhhhh," he whispered slowly into her ear while thrusting gently and deep — he groaned low as her juices ran down his hand. He withdrew his fingers and slid them into his mouth, groaning with need.

"Damn girl," he muttered. "Taste like everything I've been craving."

• • •

Her back arched as his hand moved beneath her shirt, palms cupping her breasts, thumbs brushing over her nipples until they hardened beneath his touch. Then his mouth replaced his hands — warm, hungry, claiming.

She was his.

With one fluid motion, he turned her gently and laid her across the bed.

"I need this," he said, voice thick with desire. "I said I was hungry... so let me eat."

She whimpered as his mouth moved down her body, kissing her stomach, her hips, her thighs — until he buried his face between her legs.

His tongue was the deepest worship, sin, and salvation. Long, deep strokes blended with quick flicks that made her shake. His fingers slid into her mouth — not just for sound, but because he needed to feel her there, too.

"Open wider," he growled. "Take it like that."

She obeyed.

• • •

He was lost in her — her scent, her taste, the way her thighs trembled around him. She moaned, gripped the sheets, clenched. Her orgasm ripped through her like a storm.

But he didn't stop.

When he finally came up, lips wet, eyes locked on hers, he stripped in seconds.

She watched his thick length spring free... full, heavy, already dripping with need.

Her hands explored the warm, sculpted muscle of his body. She was soaked. Ready. There was no turning back now.

He moved over her, kissing her breathless, the head of his arousal pressing against her entrance.

And then he slid inside.

Slow.
Deliberate.
Worshipful.

Stretching her in the most perfect way. He took his time, never rushed, never careless. He was big, and he knew it. But this wasn't about power. It was about claiming her as she was claiming him.

● ● ●

"You want me to stop?" he whispered.

She didn't and shook her head, no.

He sank deeper, and she gasped with her body adjusting, her mouth falling open. He pinched her nipples gently, then slid in a little more.

"You feel that?" he murmured. "That's mine." She cried out in soft muffled moans, hands clutching his back as he reached depths no man ever had, both physically and emotionally.

He drove deeper.
Steady.
Slow and rhythmic now.

"Baby...look at me," he said, his voice filled with need.

She lifted her eyes to his.

His hardness throbbed inside her, his hands slipping beneath her shoulders holding her close. His gaze pinning her in place — holding her body, holding her soul. He filled her completely.

She smelled like heaven. Sweet. Intoxicating.

• • •

He was hooked. Addicted. It wasn't just lust, it was biology. Divine design. She was made for him.

Her eyes widened, then shut... her face etched with rapture. If he could've frozen that moment, he would've.

It was the face of a woman undone.

Their rhythm built — slow and dominant. Her body clenched around him with every pull, every thrust. Novi turned her head, biting her lip, glancing toward the other bed.

Nolen was hitting her spot with precision. Like her body had always been written in his language.

Tears slipped from her eyes.

He growled low and threw both her legs over his shoulders, angling himself deeper. She bit down on her moan. He kissed her shoulder, her throat, her lips — until her entire body trembled beneath him.

He explored every hidden place inside her.

Curious. Reverent. Relentless.

"You gonna come again for me?" he asked her.

• • •

She shook her head, breathless. She already had. He smiled like he knew a secret and whispered in her ear.

And then he hit it — that spot in the back, angled just right, holding her leg in one hand. She came again. And again. And again.

Her body betrayed her gloriously.

She cried.
Clung to him.
Undone.

No man had ever taken her apart like this.

The pleasure was overwhelming — sacred even — peeling her open in ways she hadn't known she could be. And Nolen knew. He understood and he wasn't done.

The sheets rustled softly. Her moans, though *muffled*, filled the room. Nolen kissed her deeply to quiet her when he knew she would orgasm. He loved the discovery of her. And what he felt for Novi, no other woman had *ever* had him like this — not fully, not completely. She felt unreal — physically, emotionally, and spiritually.

This wasn't *just* sex.

• • •

This was a reckoning.

A becoming.

A love story unfolding in sweat, silence, and fire.

For the first time in a long time, he was making love to a woman who checked all his boxes. He groaned into her skin and closed his eyes, her body gipping him tighter with each orgasm. Soft, warm, soaking, and holding him like she never wanted him to leave.

His thrusts came faster now, intentional, commanding.

Their breaths were tangled in rhythm, rising at the same pace. Her fists twisted tight in the sheets. He caught both legs, lifting them onto his shoulders — they trembled against his chest. Holding them firm, he slipped her toes into his mouth, eyes closing as he savored her.

He collapsed beside her, arms circling her waist, lips brushing her temple. They laid tangled in the sheets, the world muted in the aftermath.

"You good babe?" he whispered.

● ● ●

She nodded, her lips grazing his shoulder.

From the other bed, his roommate snored on, undisturbed.

Nolen stifled a laugh. "Next time — my own room. Promise."

Novi sat up slowly, gathering her clothes. He watched her like a man waking from a dream he didn't want to end.

As she reached for her bra, he snatched it.

"I'm keeping this," he said, grinning.

She raised a brow. "Excuse me?"

"Something to remember tonight by."

She smirked. "Please, I need it." He handed it over with a shrug. "Fine. For now."

She slipped it on, but he pulled her back in for one last kiss, deep, tender, still hungry. She melted into him.

And felt him rock hard again.

Her eyes widened. "Again?" she whispered, stunned. "After four hours?"

• • •

He gestured toward his shorts. "Look what you keep doing to me."

She laughed, soft and breathless. "You're insatiable."

"You love it."

She smiled — cheeks flushed. "But that's exactly why I have to leave. I have to shower and get ready."

He kissed her again, slow and sweet.

"I'll see you in the lobby," she whispered, fingers brushing his jaw before she slipped out the door.

He watched her leave, still aching, already counting down the minutes until he could feel her again.

CHAPTER 19
The Silk Robe

Not all longing is real — and not all restraint is empty.

The promotional tour was a huge success.

Devotion Heights Church was buzzing. The praise team had just returned, and though spirits were high publicly, tension rippled just beneath the surface. Novi and Nolen hadn't had a moment alone since the hotel. Every touch, every look had been stolen under scrutiny. The afterglow was fading. Pressure was mounting.

And then came the check.

Nolen had been promised a stipend for leading and coordinating the music ministry during the engagement tour — a generous one. But when the finance department claimed the check had already been picked up, he learned it had been "accidentally" taken home by Venus Johnson.

Venus. Always conveniently in control of the narrative.

• • •

It started with a text:

VENUS:
Heeey Honey! I accidentally grabbed your
ministry check from Cassia's folder this
afternoon. You probably need it
before the weekend, right?
You can swing by if you're out.

NOLEN:
Aight

The address followed.

Nolen wasn't thrilled. But he didn't ask questions.

Venus was older. You could tell she worked out — her body was in perfect shape, toned yet soft. She carried her athletic curves in fitted, classy attire, the kind that always looked good on a woman her age. In the church, she carried weight. And above all, she had a gift: she knew how to frame her invitations as concern… never manipulation. So he told her he'd swing by on his way home.

The neighborhood was quiet with well-kept lawns, porch lights glowing like suburban halos. He parked in front of her townhome and walked up slowly, something in him already regretting the trip.

• • •

She opened the door before he could knock.

"Hey, suga," she said, leaning against the frame with an easy smile. "Right on time."

He stepped inside. The scent of vanilla and something floral clung to the air. It smelled like expensive lotion and desperate effort. He stopped in the foyer, glancing around. Dim lights. Jazz playing low from a speaker in the corner. Her place was clean, curated. Everything in place.

"Appreciate you holding that," he said. "Cassia didn't mention nothing about the check, but I was gonna hit her up tomorrow."

"Well, now you don't have to." She smiled wider. "I think I left it in the living room or maybe my bedroom. Come sit while I find it. You want something to drink?"

"Nah. I'm good, for real. I won't be long."

She disappeared down the hall without responding.

Nolen stood in the living room, eyes scanning the photo frames on the mantel. Venus and her husband Kendrick. Church photos. Gala shots. Always dressed to the nines. Always smiling.

• • •

But something about the house felt... hollow. Like it was trying too hard.

He heard her footsteps before he saw her again.

When she returned, she wasn't holding the check.

She was holding the belt of a silk robe.

It was black lace at the top and silk towards the bottom... with her breasts barely contained, tied loosely around her waist. She moved like she'd rehearsed the moment — like she'd walked this hallway a thousand times in her mind, each time a little slower, a little softer.

"Found it," she said, holding on to it like it was a piece of lingerie.

He didn't move.

"Venus."

She came a little closer. "You've been looking heavy lately, Nolen. I know what a man looks like when he's carrying too much and getting too little. And I know your wife ain't the one easing that pressure."

He blinked. Once.

• • •

"I know what you need," she said, her voice dropping to a sultry hush. "And it's not all that ministry noise baby. It's... release. Something... soft."

She paced toward him with a slow, sexy stride. "Something... real."

Her eyes fluttered shut. "Something... wet."

She loosened the robe, letting the belt slip and dangle from the loops at her sides. Her hand trailed slowly down her neck, her eyes locked on Nolen's, before sliding across her breasts as her breath came hard, heavy, and full of desire.

Venus set his check on the side table, moving closer as she slipped one side of her robe off her shoulder.

"Nah... I have to get home," he said.

"You sure, baby?" Her voice dropped lower. "You deserve to be taken care of."

She slowly licked her lips and closed the space between them. Too close.

This time, he stepped back, snatching the check off the table.

• • •

"You... " He shook the check in his right hand, almost pointing it at her. "You really invited me here over a church check?" His voice stayed low, flat. He shook his head, more in disappointment than anger. "Nah. This ain't that."

Her face froze in surprise. She didn't respond. Men never turned her down. She was beautiful, and she knew her way around the bedroom. She couldn't believe he wouldn't even consider it.

When Nolen looked at her, Venus saw no hunger in his eyes — only the echo of a man who'd tasted something real and knew this wasn't it.

"Venus," he said flatly. "I'm out."

She blinked, caught off guard. "If you change your mind — "

"I'm not interested," he cut in. "You're beautiful. You know that. But I'm not that man. Not tonight. Not for you."

He exhaled hard through his nose and shook his head. "Don't do this again. Ken's a cool dude."

• • •

Her smile faltered, just before she turned away. He didn't wait for her to walk him out. He walked toward the door, opened it, and left. The click of it closing behind him was louder than any slap. And in the quiet of her living room, Venus stood in a silk robe — alone.

Her seduction unraveled before it ever touched skin. The ride home was quiet. Nolen didn't even turn the music on.

Venus' perfume still clung faintly to his jacket. That heavy, musky kind women wore when they were trying to rewrite time. He rolled down the window. Let the wind strip it from him.

He wasn't angry.

He wasn't even surprised.

He was just tired.

Tired of performances. Of people touching him to satisfy their own narratives. Of being desired for the wrong reasons. He didn't need flattery. He didn't need seduction wrapped in silk.

What he needed was honesty. Presence.

• • •

The kind that didn't ask for anything more than truth. His hands gripped the wheel tighter.

And then he thought of her.

Novi.

The weight of her eyes. The ache in her breath. The sound of her voice when she stopped pretending, she wasn't hungry too.

He shouldn't go.

He knew that. But he also knew that Zayven was out of town and wouldn't be returning until Saturday.

But as his turn signal clicked and the light changed — He wasn't driving home.

Later that night...

Novi's house was dimly lit. She stood in the kitchen, barefoot, wearing jeans and an oversized tee. Nolen stood behind her, recounting what had happened.

"... She was in a silk robe. No panties. Heels. Talking about 'You *deserve* to be taken care of."

• • •

Novi blinked, shocked. "You're lying." She let out a laugh so loud she thought it would've woken up her children sleeping upstairs.

"I wish I was. I was so mad babe. This old woman had the audacity to — "

He stopped, turning to look her up and down. "And you standing here with jeans on?"

She narrowed her eyes. "What?"

"You heard me." He stepped closer. He pulled Novi's jeans to look inside. "Pants. And panties Novi?"

She crossed her arms. "You want me to take them off?"

His silence was answer enough.

She unbuttoned her jeans slowly. Slid them down. He watched.

She reached for the waistband of her panties.

"These too?"

"Nah," he growled. "Leave them on. I think you need to be punished."

• • •

Then suddenly, he was kissing her — hard, desperate, full of tension and fire.

He turned her, pressed her against the island counter. In one fluid motion, he yanked her panties down — tearing them off.

She gasped, wide — eyed.

He smirked, with need and hunger. Lifted them to his face. Inhaled deeply.

"Damn," he whispered. "You don't even know what you do to me."

She was breathless, gripping the counter, already trembling. He entered her from behind — slow, deep, deliberate.

The island shook. Her moans were stifled only by the sound of skin meeting skin.

She came hard — dripping, shaking, unable to hold herself up. He chuckled low, one strong arm wrapped around her waist, holding her steady.

Then he dropped to his knees behind her, tasting her again. Thoroughly. Hungrily.

• • •

She came again, gasping his name like a prayer.

When it was over, her legs weak — she collapsed onto the floor — undone, dazed.

He stood over her, chest rising, smiling like a man who knew he was unforgettable.

Then he leaned down, kissed her mouth, and whispered: "Don't ever let me catch you in pants or panties again."

CHAPTER 20
Backseat Betrayal

Desire made them bold. But boldness has a price.

The next few days were a blur of rehearsals, midweek services, and practiced smiles. For Novi and Nolen, every second in public was monitored. Every whispered word between them carried the weight of scandal. And yet, the hunger only deepened.

They hadn't touched since the night in the kitchen. Time was a thief, and church life felt like a prison. But passion has a way of finding its own exit route.

The praise team had just finished an evening worship engagement across town. Novi had driven herself which was a rare blessing, while most rode in the church sprinter van. The parking lot was nearly empty when she noticed his truck still parked under a low lamp.

She hesitated, glanced around... and walked over. When she opened the door, he didn't speak — just pulled her into the truck and kissed her like a man lost at sea.

• • •

The cab was dim. The windows fogged within seconds. She slid onto his lap, straddling him, their mouths colliding again and again. Her hands roamed beneath his shirt. His unfastened jeans pressed against her — hard, pulsing.

"I've missed you," she whispered.

"Seven days," he muttered against her throat. "It's too damn long."

Clothes shifted. Breathing thickened. His fingers found her, wet and waiting, and she nearly cried out.

"Shhh," he warned, eyes motioning toward the church doors. "They're still inside."

She buried her face in his neck as he slid into her — one slow, aching inch at a time.

She rocked on him carefully, desperate to moan but stifling every gasp. It was frantic. Sacred. Her nails dug into his shoulders as he thrust upward, matching her rhythm with need of his own.

Neither noticed the flicker of a camera lens from a nearby car.

• • •

Or the red recording light hidden inside the truck — planted weeks earlier by Teanir, who had been trying to catch him talking with Tanika.

Across the parking lot, tucked inconspicuously under a broken streetlamp, a private investigator lowered his camera, a grim smile stretching across his face. He adjusted the mic, catching Nolen's whispered confession between ragged breaths:

"No-vi… I love you… I can't live without you… You feel so good, mama… I need you to come hard for me, babe…"

Click.

"No, baby… I have to walk back to my car," she said in a breathless protest.

Snap.

"Aww, baby… You think you have a choice?" He let out a low, knowing chuckle. "You feel so good mama, I need you all over me… right now."

Click. Click.

• • •

His hands gripped her hips, holding her still as he stroked — deep, deliberate and hitting every place inside her that unraveled her. She gushed uncontrollably, the warmth rising to his chest, sliding down her thighs, soaking into the seat beneath them. He knew *exactly* what to do.

And though she thought she was guiding the ship, he was the one charting the course — determining how slow, how rough, how soon she would come.

Click. Click. Click.

Proof - now in hand.

Later that night, Novi lay in her bed-bliss-drunk and dazed. She had no idea what had been captured. All she knew was that her body still trembled from his touch. And her heart.... her foolish, reckless heart...

was too full to beat properly.

Far across town, the next day, Teanir's mother, Elisse Scandri, reviewed the photographs and pressed play on the audio recording.

• • •

She was enraged. Enraged for her daughter. Enraged at the man who'd vowed to forsake all others. But what shocked her most wasn't just the betrayal. It was the identity of the woman. It wasn't CNN news anchor Tanika Vaughn like Teanir had feared.

It was Novi Jaxson.

Devotion Heights' anointed worship leader.

The one who laid hands on her daughter in prayer. The one riding her son-in-law like a $2 hoe in the front seat of his truck.

And being from the hood, Elisse knew how to fight. She knew what needed to be done. She knew how to win. You best believe that the war had officially begun.

● ● ●

CHAPTER 21
The Pictures on the Table

Truth laid bare on the table, colder than the lies before it.

Teanir pulled into her mother's quiet cul-de-sac just after dropping the boys at school and daycare. She hadn't planned to come and didn't want to. But the text from her mother, Elisse, had been clipped and urgent:

ELISSE:
Come by after drop-off.
Alone.
I have something you need to see.

When she stepped into the foyer, Elisse didn't greet her with a hug. She just motioned toward the dining table. A manila envelope lay waiting. Thick. Unassuming. Teanir hesitated. "Mama?"

Her mother pointed firmly to the seat at the table. No coffee. No homemade croissants with brown sugar honey sauce like usual. Just silence and that envelope. Teanir already felt it in her gut that this was about Nolen.

"Open it," Elisse said, her voice sharp.

• • •

Teanir sat slowly and pulled back the flap. The first photo landed in her lap like a slap.

Novi.

Straddling Nolen in his truck. One hand on his shoulder. The other gripping the back of his head.

Teanir's lips parted but no sound came out. She flipped to the next photo. And the next. All taken from a distance, but close enough to capture everything — the expressions on their faces said it all.

Euphoria. Abandon. *Love.*

Her stomach turned. A wave of nausea hit her fast — like she needed to vomit. Then came the audio. Elisse pressed play on her phone and turned the volume low.

"Novi... I *love* you... I can't live without you..."

Teanir's face twisted.

"You feel so good mama, I need you all over me... right now."
She slammed the phone off, her hands trembling, but her eyes were hard.

● ● ●

"Maaaaamaaaa!" she cried out with a gut-wrenching wail, somewhere between a scream and the sound of something breaking beyond repair. Her marriage was over. Her chest felt tight. She couldn't catch her breath. "Why??" she repeated, over and over.

Elisse didn't interrupt. She let her daughter grieve.

She'd always taught her to never let them see you cry, never let them see you weak. But now, at this moment, just the two of them in that quiet kitchen, she gave her permission to break.

Tears poured from Teanir's eyes — tears she'd been collecting her whole life. From the fights she fought as a pretty chocolate girl with striking blue-gray eyes, to the hurt of a father who wanted nothing to do with her. Tears she had collected like souvenirs, now no longer kept contained but broken from all the times she didn't flinch. All the times she stayed strong.

Finally, she wiped her face and caught her breath.

"Mama...when was this?" she whispered, her voice hoarse, eyes bloodshot.

● ● ●

"Five days ago baby," Elisse replied. "I had someone tailing him. After all the stuff you told me, I wanted to know for sure. Thought it was still that CNN news anchor he was obsessed with — Tanika. But turns out, he found a closer distraction."

Teanir stood slowly, photos still clutched in her hand.

"I should've known. Should've trusted what I felt. Mama, I KNEW IT!" she screamed, her rage shattering through the room.

Elisse leaned against the counter, arms folded. "You said her name was Novi, right?"

Teanir nodded.

"She played you sweet. All that worship. All that humility. A damn wolf in sheep's clothing. Usherin' folks in worship and spreadin' her legs for your husband."

Teanir looked back down at the photos. Her jaw clenched. Her heart physically hurt.

She now knew that this is what heartbreak feels like. "Tea... don't say nothin' yet," Elisse warned. "You need a plan, not just rage."

● ● ●

But Teanir was already walking out the door.

And in her fist, the pictures.

Teanir back at home in her kitchen. It was quiet when Nolen walked in. The boys were gone. The sun hung low.

He was exhausted — emotionally wrung out, mentally shut down. And then he saw her. Teanir. At the kitchen island.

A stack of photographs spread like spades.

She didn't speak. Just picked up a photo and tossed it at him. It landed face-up. Him. In the truck. Novi straddling him. Head thrown back.

"You *smell* like her," she said, lip curled in disgust.

He didn't respond. Another photo. "I'm supposed to be a dumb bitch, huh?" Another. "And crazy?" Another.

"And full of the Holy Ghost — like I'm too devoted to notice you changing up on me?"

Her voice was flat. No tears. No begging.

• • •

She wasn't numb. She was drained — all cried out from nights of wondering, praying, waiting. All she had left was cold, accusatory silence. She wanted him to hold her. Say sorry. Promise to try. She wanted him to *see* her.

Instead, she threw another photo.

Each one hit the floor like a blade. His face. Novi's body. Their betrayal, frame by frame.

"I. TRUSTED. YOU!!"

The words cracked sharp. Still, he said nothing.

"You slept next to me. I prayed for *you.* Anointed *you.* And you gave away what belonged to *me... to her.*"

He looked at the photos. No defense. No lies. A part of him felt... relieved. The truth was out. The mask was off. His next thought went to his sons. What would this mean for them?

But Teanir?

He didn't feel guilt. Not for loving Novi. Not even for the pain he saw now. In some twisted way, he felt she finally knew what it was like to be shattered. As far as he was concerned, the marriage was a free gift with purchase.

• • •

The boys were the only part he'd ever truly loved.

"I heard the audio, Nolen."

That surprised him. He thought it was just photos.

He couldn't recall exactly what he'd said... but if anything was captured, it was probably his love for Novi. And he didn't regret it.

"Even knowing this I want my family," she said.

She thought about how, whenever they were intimate, she kept herself quiet, contained. Passion was private. Loud moaning, wild expressions? That was for white women — not her. She was a sister through and through. But hearing Novi with her husband — the raw, unashamed cries, the sounds of pleasure he'd never drawn from her — it cut deep. It wasn't just a surprise.

It was humiliation.

"If you end it with her... I can open my legs and scream real loud too. Do it *every* night, if that's what it takes to make you stay."

He looked at her. Not with judgment — with clarity. Her desperation turned him off even more. For the first time,

• • •

he saw how her identity lived in being his wife. She had no drive. No ambition. She wanted to be kept — but she wasn't even good at that. Didn't cook much and she wasn't good at it. Didn't clean well. Didn't grow. It made his stomach turn.

He scoffed. "You're not serious, right?"

"Of course I am! I want *my* husband. I want *my* family. I'm not gonna let that bitch steal you away. So, if all you want is loud moans and screaming sex, I'll give you that."

He sat down slowly, voice low.

"It's not *just* sex Tea, and even if it was you don't even *like* sex like that. You complained if I touched you twice in a day. Remember you told me that I had a problem? That I needed help? And now *you* want sex.."

Her voice cracked. "I never liked how it felt when it didn't come with love. You never made me feel like I was more than a body you were using to forget someone else."

He shook his head. "Now I was using *you* to forget someone else." That wasn't entirely untrue. But there was a time he really had tried. Still, every time she opened her mouth, she reminded him: She was always what she seemed. Surface. Shallow. Empty.

• • •

He remembered when she dropped out of Roosevelt University. Full ride. Math major. Gave it all up — for him. No dreams. No goals. Just him. *Unlike* Tanika. And now, *unlike* Novi.

Novi had depth. Vision. Fire. Grace. She was nurturing. Ambitious. Anointed. A bona fide freak in the bed. Anything he wanted to try she was down for it — and loved it. She *saw* him. Loved him for who he was. Never tried to tame his fire, never discouraged him, and even in disagreements, she was poised and sought resolution with him — never degraded him. From day one, their connection had been spiritual. Their timing was just off. Now, Teanir was still talking. Demanding answers. But he had none left to give.

The air between them fractured. He reached for his keys.

"I'm out."

She didn't yell. Didn't cry. Didn't slam anything. Just said "Maybe we both need time. You can go stay with your mama for all I care."

And he didn't argue. He walked out.

• • •

That night, Nolen drove to his mother's house. He always kept a key. The place was massive — 6,108 square feet of polished prestige in the hills of Roland Park, nestled behind manicured hedges and a discreet wrought-iron gate. Five bedrooms. Five bathrooms. It felt more like a boutique retreat than a family home. But Senator, Babette Jahlil never did anything halfway.

The house was silent, except for the soft clicking of Bucky Mae's paws on the marble. The Cane Corso raised her head from her spot near the stairs, sniffed, then laid it back down. She knew who he was. Knew he was part of the pack.

Babette was away — traveling abroad on a Congressional Delegation. A CODEL, she called it, as she often did for high-level diplomatic meetings. The house was his for now. Quiet. Unbothered.

He wandered into the great room — his mom's favorite space. The room opened like a breath: vast, luminous, curated with warmth and quiet opulence. A deep sapphire velvet sectional curved in the center of the room, punctuated by white and gray throw pillows that softened its bold geometry. In front of it sat a minimalist acrylic coffee table and cube ottoman, resting atop a plush taupe area rug.

● ● ●

The far wall was a work of art — a Moroccan-inspired accent wall in soft, hand-painted tile, framing an enormous flat-screen television. Skylights above filtered in slivers of moonlight, illuminating the room in silver and shadow.

To his right, the floor-to-ceiling glass sliders revealed a pristine backyard: manicured grass, a trimmed bonsai hedge, a water feature that whispered more than it trickled.

The vaulted ceilings carried the faint scent of sage and eucalyptus from a distant reed diffuser. Above him, a black iron chandelier hung like a crown beneath the beams, quietly majestic.

Two plush blush-pink velvet armchairs sat to the left, positioned for conversation. Next to them, a slim side table held a candle, unlit, and a closed book of poetry.

Everything in its place. Curated. Clean. Peaceful. He thought of Novi. What her laugh would sound in a room like this. Or how her body would move barefoot across the wood. Or what it would mean to build a life with her — to not just steal moments but make memories. She had once asked him what kind of house they'd have if they were ever married. And now... in the glow of his mother's quiet empire, he could see it. Not just a house. A home. With her.

• • •

He didn't need noise. He needed her. No more pretending. No more guilt. No more shrinking from the truth. He picked up his phone.

Typed slowly.

Deliberately.

NOLEN:
Pack a bag. Three nights.
Just us. I need to wake up to you.

Send.

Novi stood at the foot of the stairs, her bag already packed. "I'm going to LA," she said flatly. "I'm staying with my sister for a few days. I need a break — from all this. From you." Zayven looked up from the couch, remote still in his hand. "A break? For what?"

She blinked slowly. "The fact that you have to ask that speaks volumes."

He sat up, defensive. "Here you go again."

"We're behind on the mortgage, Zayven. Behind. I had to leave my children for five days because *you* fumbled our finances. Not once did you say you were going to do whatever you needed to do to provide. I had to step up and do it. One of our cars got repossessed — and you still haven't done anything except buy yourself new clothes, shoes, and quote scripture."

He raised his hands. "The Lord will provide."

She scoffed. "With what? A better car falling out of the sky?" She took a breath, then fired back with scripture of her own. "You know what the Word says, Zay?"

He crossed his arms, jaw set, defiance in his posture.

She quoted it slowly, each word like a hammer: "First Timothy 5:8, KJV — 'But if *any man* provide *not* for his own, and especially for those of his *own house*, he hath denied the faith, and is worse than an infidel.'"

His face darkened.

To him, her calling him out like that was disrespect. Never mind the truth. He was a man — that should be enough. He was in ministry — that should be enough. He stayed in the home — that should be enough. In his mind, making her look good was his primary job.

• • •

"You're being disrespectful," he snapped. "I'm *STILL* a man. And I'm *STILL* the man of *this* house — regardless of who's bringing in the money."

She shook her head, pity flooding her eyes. She kissed the children goodbye, told them mommy was going to stay with Auntie Nicole for a few days. They hugged her, kissed her, and said their goodbyes.

Zayven stood waiting for a hug too.

She looked at him. "You've got to be kidding."

His posture straightened. "When you get back, you'll see. You'll see what I've been working on."

"You're always working on something, Zayven," she said. "But where's the fruit? Where's the reward? All I ever see from what you're working on is a bill — for me to pay."

She rolled her bag to the door, pulled out her phone. "I'm calling an Uber."

"I'll take you," he offered quickly.

She shook her head, not even glancing his way. "I can't even stand the sight of you right now."

• • •

He followed her toward the front door. "What about the kids?"

"You're their father," she said, tone clipped. "That's the *least* you can do."

He didn't argue. But in his mind, the solution was easy — drop the kids off at her mother's house as he always did when he needed to be alone with them, and pick them up when she got back. Problem solved.

Novi didn't wait for a goodbye. The Uber arrived within minutes. She slid into the back seat without looking back once. The car pulled away from their modest neighborhood, heading toward the hills of Roland Park.

She arrived at 4502 Roland Avenue — a sprawling, gated estate that belonged to Nolen's mother. It stood quiet, regal, hidden behind pristine hedges and a wrought-iron gate.

Nolen was already waiting in the driveway in a sleek black BMW — the same one from his college days in Chicago. Babette had kept it stored for him in the garage. He didn't want his truck recognized.

● ● ●

As soon as she stepped out of the Uber, he was there. No words. Just the kind of silence that held history and understanding.

He opened the passenger door.

"Ready?" he asked.

She nodded.

They drove off together, quiet at first, their hands finding each other between the seats like muscle memory.

By the time they reached BWI Airport, the flight was already confirmed— two tickets, first class, nonstop to Napa, California.

Nolen had booked the River Terrace Inn. The Riverview Luxury Suite. He didn't want distractions.

He wanted peace. Privacy. Her. This wasn't about lust. This was about breathing again.

Together.

• • •

CHAPTER 22
The Getaway

No distractions. Just him, her, and the kind of love that lingers.

They both needed air. Needed escape. Not from God — from people. From the stares, the assumptions, the unrelenting weight of expectations.

So Nolen did what he rarely allowed himself to do.He took Novi away. A four-day weekend. A hidden resort tucked in Napa Valley — no ministry engagements, no rehearsals, no prying eyes. Just silence, soft sheets, and the sound of their breathing against each other's skin. He booked the room under a pseudonym. Paid in cash. Told the team he was staying with family. Novi claimed exhaustion and disappeared without explaining a thing.

Night One: The Reveal

They landed from their flight, and from the moment they stepped off the plane, Nolen took the reins. He arranged everything from the uber to grabbing dinner on the way. And the scenery was breathtaking. The wine, he'd ordered in

• • •

advance. A custom-crafted bottle that reminded him of her — intricate, soft, and unforgettable.

She didn't have to think. She didn't have to carry.

Their first night in Napa didn't begin with lust — it began with presence. The moment they stepped into the suite at River Terrace Inn, the world outside ceased to matter.

Golden-hour light poured through tall, paned glass doors that opened to a private balcony, framing the lush trees of Napa Valley like a living painting. Everything inside was warm, modern, and sensual. Soft wood floors ran beneath their feet, grounded by a rich, textured area rug. A velvet bench sat at the foot of a California king bed dressed in crisp ivory linen, its headboard tufted in storm-gray fabric that whispered understated luxury. Behind it, a striking mural of painted eucalyptus trees stretched up the wall, echoing the real ones just beyond the balcony.

In the center of the room stood a dual-sided gas fireplace — glowing, flickering — separating the bedroom from a cozy sitting area with a pair of mid-century chairs, a sleek coffee table, and a bottle of wine already waiting on ice. Above them, a matte black pendant light hung low, casting a golden glow that matched the heat radiating between them.

• • •

A small dining nook nestled beside the doors, with a hand-written welcome card on the table and a chilled glass of white already half-full, catching the light.

To the right, the bathroom was a sanctuary of its own. A freestanding soaking tub rested beneath a sunflower painting — open to the bedroom when the dark wooden shutters were drawn. A rainfall shower stood nearby, encased in glass. Twin square sinks were set in a minimalist vanity, flanked by rolled towels, sleek black fixtures, and a single bloom in a silver vase. The room didn't shout luxury — it whispered it. Every detail was intentional, curated. Just like his plans for her.

After they checked in, Nolen disappeared into the bathroom. When he returned, he had on one of the plush white robes provided by the resort. The collar draped open at his chest, and he moved toward her with a quiet confidence, cinching the belt as he walked. The robe suited him — elegant, casual, masculine.

He had a plan.

Nolen wanted to explore her slowly, deliberately, as if discovering her all over again. He didn't want to conquer her body. He wasn't looking to seduce her — not yet. He wanted

• • •

to understand her rhythm. To find out what made her open up. What made her sing without music.

He stood in front of her and pulled her into him, letting his fingers drift up her spine. Then he whispered into her ear, low and reverent.

"Undress… I want to memorize you."

She looked up at him — not startled, not shy. She nodded. She did what he asked, because she trusted him completely. And as the robe fell from her shoulders, pooling around her ankles, he stared.

He admired her body — perfect in his eyes, even with the stretch marks from childbirth. She was a living, breathing masterpiece. He ached to memorize her — nude, open, and his.

She stood by the balcony, moonlight softening the outline of her silhouette, the eucalyptus trees of Napa Valley stretching like a painted canvas behind her. She was art, framed by nature and desire. He came up behind her, ran his hands down her back, and pressed his lips to the warm crook of her neck. He breathed her in like devotion.

And the night — their night — truly began.

● ● ●

She'd always felt like time with him slipped through her fingers — never enough, always borrowed. But now... she had it all. Hours stretched before them, uninterrupted and hers. And she knew exactly what she wanted to do.

What she had longed to do.

She took the lead without hesitation, surprising him.

He stood there in the white hotel robe — soft, plush, barely holding to his frame — and she moved toward him with intention. In the amber glow of the suite's warm light, she dropped to her knees before him, her eyes locked on his as her hands traced a slow, teasing path down his hips.

No words. Just the quiet thunder of surrender.

"What are you doing? This is about you tonight," he murmured, voice thick with surprise.

She simply shook her head. "No."

Then, slowly, reverently — she kissed his belly. Then lower to his thigh. He sprang forth, hard and heavy — almost hitting her face. She chuckled. He apologized.

● ● ●

She leaned lower, her tongue trailing beneath his testicles as she held him, already erect. He wasn't used to this. Her passion. Her intensity.

She licked him slowly, then rubbed him with one hand, guided him into her mouth with the other.

It was almost too much.

She licked underneath his shaft, feeling the veins pulse with heat and hunger. Then the other side. He grew harder, thicker. He was in disbelief.

For one quick, inappropriate second, he thought — no wonder her worship to God is so powerful. She gives and serves completely to the one she loves.

And now, she gave herself to him.

She tilted her head back, mouth open, and took him in with sensual reverence. He was always careful with oral because of his size — usually, it was too much. But she held his thighs, guiding him deeper. A little at first... then more... then all.

He shuddered, his hand finding the back of her head, stroking her gently as she moved.

● ● ●

She took him even deeper, eyes still on his. Tears welled from the pressure she welcomed.

He tried to pull her up. She resisted.

She wanted him in her mouth — *needed* him. She wanted to taste this man who loved her, challenged her, provided for her, saw her. She wasn't doing it for show. She was offering her worship. Her trust. Her love... to him.

She wanted to give him what only she could give him, her way. He groaned loudly. Birds scattered from nearby trees.

"Novi... baby, I'm about to come... move back," he panted. She didn't move. She gripped his thighs tighter.

"Babe..." he groaned again, louder now. "Shit..."

He gave in. Grabbed her head. Drove deep.

Deep gulping and moaning sounds ensued. Pulsing, surrendering, and whispering her name like a vow.

"Nov..."

Then — with a sharp, guttural sound — he grunted deeply holding her head as he released in her mouth. He had came hard. Novi held him there, making sure he emptied

• • •

everything. He stared down at her. Stunned. Undone. No woman had ever succeeded — not like that. Not with that kind of love. He felt overwhelmed. This was love and intimacy. This was vulnerability.

She always had a way of making him feel like a man.

Novi didn't just accept him. She adored him and there was no shame — only satisfaction. He bent, lifted her gently, and kissed her mouth like she was made of breath and heaven. And he wasn't finished.

He laid her on the bed and made love to her — slow at first. Then sacred. He kissed her thighs. Breathed her in. That scent *her* scent... it drove him mad. He entered her slowly, filling her until her body arched. Each time she climaxed, he went down to taste her again, worshiping her with his mouth, like she was the cure to every ache.

She was his.

And he would serve her. Again and again. She cried out, her voice catching in her throat. "Please... I need a minute," she whispered, breathless, trembling beneath him.

• • •

He looked down at her, eyes full of adoration, lips curving into a soft smile then a small chuckle.

"You need a minute?"

She nodded. He smiled. "Not yet, beautiful."

Then he leaned in, kissed her deeply, and eased himself back inside her — slow, reverent, like a man savoring the only thing that's ever truly felt like home.

Each orgasm came harder than the one before — until the bed shook beneath them like it couldn't hold the weight of what they were creating.

She was gasping now, trembling, body spent... but he wasn't finished.

Later, when her legs stopped shaking enough to stand, he took her into the shower.

Steam curled around them, rising from the heat of their bodies and the water pouring down. Her hair slipped into long, wet waves. She turned her back to the shower, head tilted forward, and the water slid down the line of her spine, over her waist, over the curve of her hips. He watched, breath caught.

• • •

"Damn, girl... " he muttered, voice thick with need. She looked back at him, lips parted, chest rising with each breath — and that was it.

He moved behind her. Grabbed her hair gently. Pressed against her slick skin. Her head turned to the side, he kissed her. Their mouths merged together, all hunger and need. Wet. Desperate.

He lifted her leg, and held it effortlessly with his arm, and slid inside her from behind in one deep, claiming thrust. Fast. Full. Complete. She cried out — loud and unfiltered — as she came instantly, again, flooding around him like the water itself had been waiting to burst from her.

She held him close. Her arms locked around his head, her face buried upward into his neck. Like if she let go, she'd unravel. This wasn't just sex. It was surrender. Sanctuary. This was home. This was love — raw, real, and consuming.

They didn't sleep. Couldn't.

Every hour was a new wave.

Every glance, a green light.

Every moan, a promise.

• • •

By morning, when the sun spilled over their private balcony, they were still tangled in each other — damp, flushed, aching, satisfied. He lay beside her, watching her sleep, his fingers gliding down her spine slowly — as if learning her body by heart, one line at a time. Then, silently, he ran her a bath — careful, thoughtful. She'd given him everything. And he... was undone.

He was in love.

And there was no turning back.

Day Two: Ease
He catered to her. Room service. Bouquets of wildflowers that she loved. Local wine — the kind that opens you up from the inside out. He watched her sleep again, this time with no heaviness in her breath. No weight on her chest. Just softness. Stillness. Peace. He didn't want to be anywhere else. Being with her — being near her — was more than enough.

They stayed in robes until nearly 2 p.m., sharing breakfast on the balcony. He made her laugh so hard she doubled over when he brought up something his middle son, Dewaun, once told an older man at church:

• • •

"Sir, I think you need to go to the River Jordan so you can get washed clean. Then he asked him to ask Bishop Byrd if the church bus could take the man there."

"Kids are a mess!" she laughed so hard. They talked about their upbringing. She told him about her childhood, the guilt she carried, and the secret dreams she never spoke aloud. He shared what it felt like growing up without a real father and how lucky he was to have strong father figures like his grandfather, William Hamilton Jahlil, who'd held the Senate seat for decades before his mother ran and won it herself in Baltimore. She told him how awkward she always felt as a teenager.

He leaned back, grinned. "You wanna know a secret?"

She nodded, playful. "Yeah?"

"Babe... you're still a little awkward."

She smirked and he busted out laughing dodging a grape she threw at him that he caught in his mouth and chewed dramatically. He spoke of lessons learned... and admitted that sometimes he only visited his mentor, Associate Pastor Ernest Sandiford, because his wife Sheila made the best sweet potato pie and had full dinners any day of the week.

● ● ●

"Babe, I can't wait for you to meet them one day outside of church." he said softly. "I wanna shout to the world how I feel about you."

She blushed. And her heart filled with love, love for him. Then she slid into his lap on the patio. He slipped his hand between her legs. She was wet already. He lifted his fingers, tasted her, and his eyes grew with hunger.

"Look what you did to me," he said, voice low, serious. She smiled, knowing what was coming next was divine.

"I just wanted to spend time with you without sex, and you keep doing this to me."

"Well," she shrugged, "I apologize... well, I'll let 'her' apologize. I'm innocent in this."

They made love on the couch. Then on the floor. Then again in the shower. She rode him slow, her forehead pressed to his, whispering, "I need you, Nol. I don't want to *ever* be without you. I love so much." Novi said with so much longing and conviction that she felt immediately overwhelmed by it all. His hands gripped her hips, angling her just right — pressing deeper, harder, hitting her G-spot over and over.

• • •

He held her face with one of his hands and the other on her hip. He locked eyes with hers.

"Impossible," he whispered. I'm not going nowhere, because I love you more." Just then she erupted in an orgasm — neither one of them wanted to leave that embrace.

They held each other until they fell asleep.

Night Three: The Shift

That night, they curled in front of the fireplace. She was on her cycle. Frustrated. A little self-conscious. But Nolen didn't care. Not one bit. He ordered her a heating pad, a pile of her favorite candy bars, and tucked her into the softest throw blanket on the floor, right in front of the flickering fire. He rubbed her feet gently, then her lower belly. He kissed her bare shoulder as she lay back against his chest.

"This feels like home," she whispered, eyes half-closed, voice wrapped in exhaustion and peace.

He nodded slowly, his lips close to her ear. "It's what home should be." They didn't talk after that. They didn't have to.

• • •

Her breathing slowed. Her body settled. She fell asleep in his arms. But he stayed awake. Watched her. Studied the curve of her body, the fullness of her lips, the serenity that had finally landed across her face like a blessing. He wasn't used to this kind of peace. Not with any woman. Not even in silence. And yet — even now — he was aroused. Not by lust, but by proximity.

The sheer closeness of her. The warmth of her body. The way she made him feel just by existing near him. He pressed a kiss to her neck. Soft. Intentional.

She didn't stop him.

He kissed her breasts — slow, reverent. Sucked gently on one while his fingers moved to the other, stroking in slow circles, patient and careful. She sighed, moaned lightly, her body shifting into him even as she felt the dull ache of cramps. But somehow, his touch dulled the pain.

And then... she trembled. She came. Without penetration. Just from the way he touched her, held her, saw her. It caught her off guard — not from pleasure alone, but from the tenderness of it. From the overwhelming sensation of being loved this way... held this way. Cherished. And finally, fully seen.

● ● ●

Afterward, he kissed her forehead. Rubbed his fingers through her hair. And when she drifted off again, it was with a peace she hadn't known in years.

She woke up sometime later, still wrapped in blankets. The fire had dimmed to embers. Nolen was sitting beside her, watching the last sparks fade. She turned toward him, her voice low.

"What happens now? When we leave?" He looked at her. Not through her. At her. Held her gaze like it meant something. Because it did.

"We fight for this," he said. "That's what happens." She nodded slowly, a breath catching in her chest — not out of fear, but out of the slow, blooming realization that maybe… just maybe… she wasn't in this alone anymore. Hope curled in her belly like warmth. She believed him. She was acknowledged. Wanted. Chosen. And for the first time…

She let herself believe she deserved it.

Day Four: The Return

The sun rose differently that morning.

● ● ●

It filtered through gauzy white curtains, casting soft light over tangled sheets and bare skin. Their bodies lay wrapped around each other, spent, silent, full. The kind of silence that didn't demand words. Just breath. Just presence.

Nolen stirred first. He didn't want to move — not yet. Not when her arm draped so effortlessly across his chest. Not when her leg rested over his. Not when she was breathing like peace against his shoulder. But the clock ticked louder than it had all weekend.

They had to go back.

He kissed her forehead gently, then moved from the bed as quietly as possible. He didn't want to wake her — not yet. She needed rest. He needed time.

He stepped onto the balcony. The view was unchanged — sweeping vines, tall trees, the hush of Napa still holding them like a secret. But inside, the weight had started creeping back in. Not guilt. Not shame. Just... gravity. The knowing. He closed his eyes. Replayed her laugh. Her voice. Her surrender. Her body. Her heart. He had never felt more alive. And now, he didn't know how to survive going back to a world where she wasn't his in the light.

● ● ●

Inside, Novi woke slowly, reaching for him before her eyes even opened. But the bed was empty. She sat up, robe slipping down her shoulder. The ache between her thighs was familiar now. A reminder. Not of sex — but of love. Of being taken care of. Known. Chosen.

She searched across the room and saw him standing on the balcony, hands on the rail, eyes on the trees. He leaned against the frame.

"You always get this quiet when it's time to go back," she said softly. He looked over his shoulder, a small smile breaking through.

"I hate that we *have* to go back."

"I know," she said. "Me *too*."

They didn't rush to get dressed. Everything moved in slow, reluctant motion — folding clothes, packing bags, brushing teeth. Each movement was intimate. Familiar. A rhythm they had fallen into so easily it scared them both.

As she zipped up her suitcase, Novi paused. "Nol…" He looked up. "What if we didn't go back the same way?" she asked.

• • •

"What if we didn't lie to ourselves anymore?" He crossed the room to her, placed a hand at her jaw, his thumb brushing her cheek.

"I don't want to lie," he said. "I want to be real. With you. In front of everybody."

She nodded slowly, heart pounding. "I'm ready."

The ride to the airport was mostly quiet — not heavy, just thoughtful. She held his hand the whole way, their fingers laced between them. He kissed the back of her hand once. She leaned her head on his shoulder.

By the time the plane touched down at BWI, the sky had shifted — a gray tint now, a pre-storm kind of silence. Nolen walked her to the car that was waiting to take her home. He opened the door, helped her inside. Their eyes met before he closed it. "You good?" he asked.

"No," she whispered. "But I will be." He leaned in, kissed her lips slow, steady. The kind of kiss that says I see you. I'm still with you. And then... the door shut. Novi watched him walk away. Watched him disappear into the other side of the city, where things were waiting to fall apart. And she turned to face hers.

• • •

CHAPTER 22: PART II
The Getaway –
Look on the Outside

Not every disappearance is innocent — and not every whisper is wrong

---

The Nights of the getaway
when Nolen and Novi were still gone.

Teanir sat in her mother's house, quietly spiraling.

Elisse moved between anger with her daughter and anger *for* her daughter. She had once loved Nolen — he was a good-looking young man from a great family. Polished. Promising. A Jahlil. Elisse had encouraged Teanir to hold on to him no matter what, especially once she got pregnant. She wanted her daughter to have the picture-perfect life — a husband on her arm, a child on her hip. It was the dream *she* never got to live, and she wanted her daughter to have that fairytale ending. And let's be honest, the Jahlils weren't just a family — they were a brand. Prestige. Power. Legacy. Money. Being tied to them meant something.

• • •

But Teanir was tired of her mother's involvement. Tired of the pressure. Tired of pretending. She needed space to think. To vent. To throw her frustration at someone who wasn't so tangled in it all. Because no way in hell was she about to give her perfect mother-in-law, Senator Babette Jahlil, another reason to whisper her name with disgust — to call her ghetto trash under her breath like she'd done before.

She could've called a friend, but the truth was, she didn't have many. She never really trusted women — not because they weren't trustworthy, but because she never truly believed she had her husband's love. And when you don't feel loved, every beautiful, successful, smart woman starts to feel like a threat. So, she kept her distance. Pushed people away. It made for a lonely life.

She always had her mother, though. Elisse was ride-or-die and didn't flinch when things got ugly.

And sure, Teanir had two friends from back in the hood who would've gladly pulled up and whipped Novi's ass — no questions asked. If they had too much to drink, maybe worse. Novi might've ended up in the hospital. Or the morgue. But Teanir wasn't about to hand Nolen the sympathy card of standing beside that woman's hospital bed or, worse,

• • •

mourning at her damn funeral. She'd already had to watch him grieve Tanika — the woman who was always "*the one that got away*," the ghost of what "*should've been*." One ghost was more than enough. And Teanir wasn't about to let Nolen blame her for losing another.

Because everything in her soul still said the same thing: Nolen was her husband. This was just a detour. A test. And she wasn't going to let her marriage die without a fight.

Not after everything she'd already survived.

And when she didn't know who else to call, Teanir reached out to the one woman she knew would understand: First Lady Jacquiline Byrd.

There had always been whispers around the church about Bishop Byrd's wandering eye — quiet rumors passed between pews and parking lots. Teanir had even witnessed it firsthand — women approaching him boldly, sometimes in front of his wife. And yet, Jacquiline always handled it with grace. Dignified. Untouchable. She never flinched, never snapped. And somehow, she still commanded respect.

Lady Byrd had an army of church mothers who watched her blind spots — a spiritual security team that

• • •

reported what she didn't see. But the truth was, Bishop Byrd *did* love his wife. That part was undeniable. Even when he stumbled, his devotion to her was evident.

That's what made Teanir's situation different.

Nolen didn't love her. Not really. Not in the way that mattered to a woman. He cared, sure — maybe even loved her like a friend. Because to Nolen, friendship was sacred. Almost as sacred as intimacy. So even when the intimacy faded, at least she had his friendship.

But now, she didn't even have that.

She needed a strategy — not just prayer, but wisdom. Tactics. A plan of action from someone who knew what it was like to guard a marriage when the wolves circled close.

The conversation wasn't loud. It didn't need to be. Jacquiline 's voice, as always, was measured — soft, steady, and strong. She listened carefully, hands folded in her lap, her eyes deep wells of compassion. She felt for this young woman sitting before her, falling apart.

She had heard enough over the years — from behind closed doors, from murmured conversations between her husband and Associate Pastor Ernest Sandiford. She knew

• • •

Nolen had struggled. He was a good man, caught in a complicated situation, doing the right thing even when it didn't feel right to him. He had tried to make that marriage work — day by day, but Jacquiline also understood this: sometimes, love wasn't enough. Sometimes, the story had to be rewritten — not erased, but reexamined.

But one truth stood firm: God still had the final say.

She reached across the table and gently took Teanir's hands in hers. "God allowed you to marry him," Jacquiline said. "And God is a covenant-keeping God."

Then, softer but firmer still: "She's *not* his covenant, baby. You are." She spoke with such empathy and compassion that Teanir blinked back tears. Her throat tightened.

"But I don't even know how to get him back," she whispered. "I've prayed. I've waited. What am I supposed to do when he chooses someone else?"

Jacquiline's gaze didn't flinch. It was the kind of look only a woman who's bled quietly for decades could give — steady, maternal, laced with fire and peace at the same time. "A woman doesn't stay because she's weak," she said calmly. "She stays because she sees something worth preserving. That

• • •

doesn't mean you let yourself be walked on. You are nobody's doormat. But it means you fight — strategically. With dignity. You don't fall apart. You stand. And if you do fall, it better be on your knees in prayer."

Teanir swallowed hard. Her shoulders dropped slightly — not in defeat, but in release. For the first time in days, she felt seen. Not judged. Not pitied. Understood.

"I don't want to lose him," she said quietly.

"Then don't," Jacquiline replied, simple and direct. "But fight from a place of purpose, baby — not pain. Pain can eat you up from the inside, make you bitter, make you blind. And all the while, the people who hurt you... they go on sleeping just fine at night."

That was the turning point. The moment when Teanir decided she wasn't going to let this end her. She was going to fight — not for appearances. Not for image. But for her marriage. Even if it meant she had to humiliate herself. Even if it meant she had to do what others wouldn't. Because all was fair in love and war.

And right now — this was war.

Later that day, Teanir drove to Nolen's mother's house. She was ready. Ready to talk. To listen. To fix it. She just wanted her husband back. But when she pulled into the long circular driveway, something felt off. The house was quiet — too quiet. It looked like no one was home.

His truck was parked out back, exactly where it always was — untouched, unmoved. As she peeked through the glass window on the garage — the BMW — the one Babette kept tucked away in the garage like a prized antique — was gone. She told herself not to overreact. Maybe he'd just stepped out. Maybe he went for a drive. Maybe he was clearing his head.

She waited.
And waited.

Tried not to overthink the silence. She couldn't call. She was certain he had her blocked. Her messages had stopped going through two days ago. Her calls — straight to voicemail. But the truth arrived before he did. The sun started slipping behind the trees, and....

Nolen still hadn't returned.

• • •

Thursday Night – Devotion Heights Praise Team Rehearsal

Ellisse strode into the hallways of Devotion Heights with a manila folder clutched in her hand and a mission on her heart. She was going to help her daughter get her husband back — one way or another.

The plan was simple: expose Novi.

She intended to walk in, grab a mic during rehearsal, and call her out for exactly what she was — a homewrecker. She would embarrass her in front of the whole team, let them see the so-called "set apart and anointed" woman for who she *really* was. But to her surprise, Venus met her at the door with a whisper of news that momentarily derailed her fury.

"Novi's not here," she said, blinking with practiced innocence. "A few folks are out actually... including Nolen."

The words sank like a stone in Ellisse's stomach.

Venus's gaze lingered on the folder in her hand — thick, sealed, intentional. "Is that something I should pass on to Cassia?" she asked carefully. Ellisse felt the heat rise in her chest. The thought of Novi and Nolen being off together — while her daughter cried on the porch of her mother-in-law's house — sent her spiraling into a deeper rage.

• • •

"No," she said sharply. "We're not passing anything. We're meeting." She motioned toward the hallway. "Get Cassia and Janet. And whoever else needs to see this. Find us a room. This concerns the ministry here at Devotion Heights."

A few minutes later, a small side room was filled with Venus, Janet, Cassia, and Jeff. They sat quietly, expectantly — unaware of the storm Ellisse was about to unleash.

She didn't waste time.

She opened the folder and slid out the contents like they were court evidence. Photograph after photograph — graphic, undeniable, damning.

Novi.
Nolen.

Tangled in sin and sweat.

Her "son-in-law" being ridden by the very woman the church had just voted in as a Worship Leader.

Venus gasped. Cassia blinked and covered her mouth. Jeff looked away. Janet simply stared — eyes wide, unblinking.

Ellisse pointed a manicured finger at the images.

• • •

"This is what's been going on. While *my* daughter prays, fasts, and cries herself to sleep — this is what that girl has been doing."

Silence settled like ash in the room.

Venus cleared her throat. "This… this needs to go to Bishop Byrd."

Ellisse snapped the folder shut. "Oh, it will."

She stood, heels clicking against the tile like war drums. Her face was tight with fury; jaw clenched so hard her temples pulsed.

Without another word, she turned and left the room, huffing and puffing, her footsteps echoing down the hallway so fiercely that curious heads began to peek out of doorways.

She didn't care.
Let them see her.
Let them whisper.

Let the entire ministry know — war had just been declared.
She stepped outside, pulled out her phone, and called the one person who deserved to know every detail.

• • •

Her daughter.

Who was still sitting outside Babette Jahlil's house —

waiting on a husband who wasn't coming back.

Teanir was sitting on the steps of her mother-in-law's house. She could've easily sat in the back of her house on the sofa or on one of the lounging chairs, but she didn't want to miss the opportunity for when Nolen would pull up in the driveway. Then came the call from her mother — casual at first, but with an undertone of concern.

"Did you hear neither Nolen nor Novi are at rehearsal tonight?"

That's when the flip switched.

All the prayer, the tears, the long nights spent begging God to heal what felt broken — all of it burned into a single realization:

She wasn't going to just sit around and look stupid. Yes, she was a Christian.

Yes, she believed in forgiveness, faith, and favor. But she wasn't about to keep playing the respectful wife while

● ● ●

another woman lived in her husband's arms. She needed to move. And not out of rage — but out of strategy. Teanir reached out to the one person she knew would feel it just as deep.

Zayven.

She sent the text. Told him to meet her at the Starbucks in Harbor East Friday morning. She didn't need the usual weekend chaos — end of the week was better. The café was nearly empty, a few laptops open, a barista humming along to a mellow playlist, and she was sitting by the window, holding onto a manila folder and a blonde roast like they were the only things keeping her grounded.

Teanir couldn't even sip it. She stared at the cup but couldn't bring herself to lift it. Her stomach churned. All she could think bout was where her husband's lips were. What he was drinking. If he was drinking with *her*.

Zayven finally arrived.

He looked tired. Confused. Annoyed.
Probably thought it was going to be another conversation about prayer and faith and staying strong. Instead, Teanir slid the photos across the table.

• • •

One motion. One moment.

Proof.
Novi.
Nolen.
Entangled.
Exposed.

Zayven sat back like he'd been sucker-punched. His eyes scanned each frame, his breath catching. He looked wrecked — speechless, angry, and ashamed.

"How…? Why would she…?" he whispered.

Teanir didn't respond. She didn't need to. The truth was already sitting between them, thick in the air. They both knew what this was. They had both dropped the ball in their marriages. And now — this was the fallout.

Teanir had always suspected Zayven wasn't really working the way he claimed. He always seemed available. Always posting like a man with money yet struggling to make a car note.

And Zayven?

He'd heard the stories.

• • •

The backdoor conversations from men at the church — especially Pastor Ernest Sandiford — about Nolen being a stand-up guy. The kind of man who'd married Teanir out of obligation after the pregnancy and tried to do the right thing.

But at what cost? Now Zayven sat across from her, jaw clenched, eyes rimmed red. His wife... was gone. Gone and making love to someone else. Gone, building memories that might not be undone. He pulled out his phone. Tried to call Novi. Straight to voicemail.

"You're not going to reach her, Zay," Teanir said softly, matter-of-fact. "She's with him. I'm sure of it." He mustered up a slow nod with a look of disgust on his face. Said nothing for a moment.

The silence was heavy. He looked like he wanted to cry but couldn't. Like he wanted to ask a hundred questions but knew the answers might kill him. He finally looked at her. "Can I... keep these?"

Teanir shook her head.

"No," she said plainly. "I still have to live with him after this. If he comes back. If we make it. I can't have another reason for him to walk away."

• • •

She gathered the photos. Secured the folder. Zayven stood slowly, thanked her for her time. He didn't look angry anymore. Just... broken.

And so was she. But broken women still plot comebacks. Because she had to be smart now. Play every card close to her chest. Because when this blows up — and she knew it would — it won't be quiet.

It will be explosive.

Public.

And irreversible.

She was going to win — no matter what.

• • •

CHAPTER 23
The Dam Breaking

They returned to still waters — but nothing stayed calm for long.

Novi stepped out of the Uber that Saturday evening from being with Nolen in Napa, and stood still for a second. Her carry-on was light, but her chest was heavy — still full of the kind of peace only Nolen gave her. The sun was soft against the sidewalk, dipping slowly behind the row of modest townhomes on their quiet street.

She walked to the front door expecting chaos. At this hour, the house should've been echoing with cartoons and screaming laughter, little feet stomping and toy boxes being dumped over. Saturdays were noisy in the Jaxson household.

But today... silence.

That was her first warning.

She pushed the door open. And there he was — Zayven — sitting on the couch like he'd been dropped there. His body was slack, hoodie wrinkled, eyes red-rimmed and swollen. A quiet, dangerous stillness filled the room.

• • •

Her breath caught. "Where are the kids?" she asked carefully.

He didn't move. "At your mother's." His voice was so flat it scraped.

Novi took a small step forward, her heart already thudding against her ribs. She tried to read him — how much did he know? Zayven didn't give her a chance to pretend.

"You weren't in L.A.," he said. "You weren't with your sister. So tell me... where the hell were you really?"

She opened her mouth, but the lie wouldn't come.

"Don't," he warned, holding up his hand. "Please... don't lie to me. Not again."

Her shoulders dropped. She let the silence hold the truth between them. He stood, and for a moment, he just looked at her like she was a stranger.

"You've been with him," he said. Not a question. "Nolen Jahlil."

Tears welled in her eyes. "Zayven..."

• • •

"Don't." He shook his head, voice cracking. "I've been calling you for *days*. You didn't even check on your kids. Your phone's been off since Wednesday. You were gone almost four days."

"I needed — "

"Needed what?!" he exploded, pointing at her. "Needed to sneak off and screw somebody else's husband?! You made me think something happened to you. You disappeared!"

"I wasn't trying to disappear — "

"You did disappear, Novi!"

His voice broke. His hands trembled. And then he sank back into the couch, his shoulders collapsing under everything he'd been holding.

"I found out Friday. Pictures. Teanir showed me. At a damn Starbucks."

Novi's stomach flipped. Pictures? Nolen never said anything. Does *he* even know?

She closed her eyes, a tear slipping down her cheek. He looked up at her again. "How long has it been going on?"

• • •

She hesitated.

"How long?!"

She finally answered, "A little while."

He flinched.

"You in love with him?" he asked, already knowing.

"Yes."

Her voice didn't waver.

He nodded slowly — like her words were knives he'd been expecting, but they still cut just as deep.

"You know I've been trying," he said quietly. "I've been trying to make things right. I've been thinking of a plan for us, Novi. I got a call to preach in Philly — Mount Hope Fellowship. They said they might even consider me for a position. And if they hire me, we might get housing. There might even be a salary. I was going to surprise you."

She looked away, her heart breaking all over again. "You always have plans, Zay. But they're only yours. You never ask what I need. You just assume I'll go along like I always have." She walked toward the home office and returned with

● ● ●

a stack of envelopes. Slammed them down on the table. "Let's be honest," she said. "This position? It's another dream you're chasing. One that isn't even real yet. Just like all the others." She picked up one envelope, then another.

"NOTICE: Foreclosure. That's our home, Zay." "ATTENTION: Past Due. That's our vehicle, the one you got repossessed." Her voice rose. Her hands shook.

"And when I went to pay the past-due balance, you had drained our entire savings account! We. Have. Nothing. Left!" She screamed so loudly it shocked even herself. Years of bottled-up anger broke loose in seconds. Years of covering. Of pretending. Of shrinking. Of surviving.

"Everything I've done... I did to hold this family together. I paid the bills. I raised the kids. I carried the weight while you chased 'brand partnerships' and ministry 'opportunities' that never came. You bought new clothes and sneakers every month while I sacrificed — hoping, begging — for partnership. But you refused. Time and time again."

His voice dropped, barely a whisper. "You gave up on us."

• • •

"No," she said, softer now. "I just finally realized... it's time to give up on you."

He looked stunned.

"You giving up on me? What about for better or worse?"

She scoffed bitterly. "It's only ever been worse, Zay. When was better gonna happening?"

His chest rose and fell with quick, shallow breaths. And then — a loud boom — his fist went through the wall. And in a second he started to cry. A loud heart-wrenching cry that even now she couldn't tell if it was real or performance.

"SO WHAT NOW!?" he shouted. "YOU DONE? YOU LEAVING ME!?"

"I don't know what the next step is," she admitted. "But I know my heart doesn't live *here* anymore. And I won't keep pretending it does."

He stared at her, empty now.

"Is there even *anything* left to fight for?"

She paused. Then, in a whisper: "I'm tired."

• • •

"TIRED OF WHAT?!?" he screamed at her.

"OF FIGHTING!!," she screamed back at him. "Fighting for a marriage that's all about you! Fighting to keep the bills paid. Fighting to be both parents to our kids. Fighting to keep up appearances for church folks. Fighting to remember who I even am when I look in the mirror."

She started to cry. Not for him. Not for the marriage. But for herself — for finally letting the truth out. For finally saying the thing that had been choking her for years. The freedom in it washed over her like a wave.

Zayven nodded slowly. He didn't cry again.

He turned his head toward the window, watching dusk settle in while the woman he once loved stood quietly by the door, suitcase still in hand.

Neither of them spoke after that.

Because the truth was already loud enough.

On that same Saturday evening, by the time Nolen pulled into his mother's driveway, the sky was already dissolving into

* * *

twilight — amber bleeding into deep blue. He'd taken the long way back on purpose. Novi had left earlier in an Uber, and he wanted to give her space. Time to walk into whatever storm might be waiting. He wasn't naïve. What they'd done, what they'd shared — it carried gravity. And consequences.

His mind replayed their last night in Napa — the way she'd melted into him without fear or hesitation, the way she whispered his name like both prayer and surrender. He could still smell her perfume on his shirt. But now, here — back home — it was time to face the life he'd been trying to leave behind.

He walked around to the garage where his black BMW had been safely stored, slid it inside, and gently pulled the cover over it. Babette hadn't returned from her CODEL trip yet, but even if she had, she wouldn't have asked questions. Not yet. His truck sat in its usual spot out back — dusty, slightly crooked in the gravel. He climbed in, the weight of reality pressing down the moment the door slammed shut.

This was the part he hated.

The returning.

• • •

By the time he arrived at the house he shared with Teanir, it was nearly 9:15 PM. The lights were on. Porch light flickering slightly. Everything looked quiet — too quiet.

He parked in the driveway, cut the engine, and sat for a moment, hands gripping the wheel like it could anchor him.

This wasn't Napa.

This was the other life. The one with sharp edges and buried resentments. The one that waited like a scorned woman, arms folded.

He stepped out, boots crunching softly on the gravel, and walked to the door. He didn't knock. It was still his house. His name on the deed. His toothbrush still by the sink.

But the moment he stepped inside, he knew she was waiting. Teanir was seated on the edge of the couch, dressed in a t-shirt, leggings and slippers. Legs crossed. Eyes fixed.

The television was off. No music. No movement.

Just silence thick enough to bite.

"You're late," she said flatly.

• • •

Nolen didn't respond. He dropped his keys into the ceramic bowl on the side table and kept his voice even. "You eating tonight?"

"Don't do that," she snapped, standing slowly. "Don't walk in here like you just came from Bible study. Where have you been?"

He sighed. "I needed time."

"Time?" Her laugh was short, sharp. "Is that what they call it now? Time?"

"I'm not here to argue."

"No," she said, stepping closer. "You're not here to talk either. But you're gonna listen."

She walked to the coffee table, picked up the now slightly bent manila envelope that had made its way around Devotion Heights, and slapped it against his chest.

"You still need to explain THAT."

Nolen didn't flinch. He looked down at the envelope but didn't reach for it. He already knew what was inside. Photos. Proof. The cost of four days of peace.

• • •

"I showed it to Zayven yesterday," Teanir continued. "At Starbucks. After I was sitting outside your mother's house waiting for you. You know how embarrassing that is, Nolen? For your wife to be sitting like a damn fool while her husband is out playing house with another woman?"

He finally looked at her. "I didn't lie to you, Tea."

She laughed again, more venom in her voice now. "Oh, right — you just didn't tell me. Difference?"

He sighed deeply and finally said it.

"I'm in love with her."

Silence.

She froze. The truth slid across the room like broken glass. Teanir's mouth parted slightly. She struggled to catch her breath before she could speak.

"You said that so easily."

"It wasn't easy," he said, voice low. "But it's real."

She sat back down, knees weak. "So that's it? You just... come home to deliver the final blow? You don't even fight for

• • •

what we built? Fight for our marriage — for the sake of our boys?"

"What did we build, Tea?" His voice was calm but sharp. "This marriage... it wasn't love. It was obligation. You know that."

Her eyes blazed. "No. I made it love. I worked for this. I carried your sons — all of them. I gave you my best years."

"I never asked for that," he said, quieter. "We made a choice, and I stayed. I tried to make it right. But we were never right. You and I both know that."

Her eyes welled with tears. "So what now, Nolen? You gonna run off and be with her? Just... live happily ever after and run off into the sunset while I sit here raising your sons?"

"No," he said gently. "We can co-parent. I'm going to be there for them. And I'm going to do it with respect — for you, for them, and for me."

She stood again. Angry. Desperate.

"YOU DON'T GET TO WALK OUT CLEAN, NIGGA! You don't get to play the noble while YOU out here fucking THAT BITCH — who is SOMBODY ELSE'S WIFE

• • •

— While CHEATING ON YOUR OWN!" She clapped angrily in between those words.

"I *didn't* walk out clean," he said, raising his voice for the first time since walking in the house. "I walked out bleeding."

He took a breath, then added softer, "And for the first time in years...I could breathe."

They stood there, facing each other. Years of resentment piled between them like wreckage.

"I love you," she got out, her voice gasping for air between sobs.

"I know."

"And you, you never really loved me." Now the tears were flowing so freely they hit the floor like raindrops.

"Tea, I tried," he answered honestly. "But you deserved more than trying."

That broke her. Just a little. She turned away, arms folded tightly across her chest. Her voice trembled when she spoke again.

• • •

"I'm going to make sure — with everything in my body — that YOU regret this."

He nodded slowly. "You probably will."

Then, without another word, he grabbed a bag he'd left in the coat closet, walked back out the door, and into the night.

He didn't slam it.

He didn't look back.

And as he stepped into his truck and drove off, he didn't feel like he won.

But he felt free.

But freedom... always comes at a cost.

• • •

CHAPTER 24
Eyes Forward

She walked over broken glass like it didn't cut, bleeding all the while.

Teanir sat in her usual spot on the front row of the sanctuary — spine straight, heels crossed at the ankle, Bible on her lap. Her lipstick was a little bolder today. Hair straighter than usual. She smiled when greeted, nodded politely, and kept her eyes forward.

But the whispers were getting harder to ignore. And she was just about sick of hearing them.

"They say he ain't been home in days…" or "I feel so sorry for her…."

"I heard she's been begging Bishop to intervene…"

"That's what happens when you trap a man, now she out here looking crazy…"

"I heard Novi got that snatch, no man leaves his wife is she got that good-good…"

Or the worst one of all which was, "She better than me, why stay with a man that don't want you…"

• • •

"Shame on her Mama for embarrassing that girl like that... that's not how you keep a man..."

None of them said it to her face — not yet. But the looks, the pity... it was louder than words.

She wasn't stupid. She had known about Nolen cheating for months.

Everyone thought she was blind — too busy with the kids, too focused on appearances, too shallow to see what was right in front of her. But they were wrong. Teanir had a sixth sense for humiliation. She could smell it in the room before it ever had a name.

She'd grown up in it. Bathed in it.

Her mother made sure of that — reminding her from a young age that a woman's worth was often tied to how well she could endure being disappointed in private while still smiling in public. Teanir had watched her mother suffer through betrayal after betrayal, silently scrubbing dinner plates and fixing her lipstick while the world called her "strong." And when it was Teanir's turn to become a woman, she inherited that same lesson: don't ask too many questions.

• • •

Don't react too loudly. If you're humiliated, wear it like perfume — light, sweet, and undetectable.

So when Nolen started acting differently — pulling away just slightly, responding slower, avoiding her eyes in bed — she noticed. When he started smelling like cologne she didn't buy, started getting dressed with intention even when he said he was just "running errands," she clocked it. When his silences got heavier and his kindness felt rehearsed, she felt it in her gut.

No, Teanir wasn't blind.

She just wasn't ready to blow it all up.

Not yet.

Because if she learned anything from her mother, it was this: sometimes a woman knows... but she waits. Not because she's weak, but because she needs the right moment to reclaim her dignity on her own terms.

And now — she was ready.

The first time she asked Nolen about it, he shrugged. A gaze she noticed lasting too long in Novi's direction and him not looking away.

"You trippin'," he said flatly. "We're on the same praise team. That's it."

The second time, he didn't answer at all. Ignored her and acted like she didn't ask it.

She saw the way he looked at Novi. Even when no one else seemed to notice, Teanir did. The quiet hunger in his eyes. The subtle lean of his body whenever Novi walked into the room. The way his voice softened, just slightly, when he said her name. It wasn't obvious to most, but Teanir had learned to read between the silences. She knew what desire looked like, even when it was dressed in restraint. And most of all she knew her husband.

What struck her more was how Novi didn't respond to it — at least not right away. She kept her distance. Stayed focused. Professional. Godly. But over time, something shifted. Novi began to linger a little longer after rehearsals. Her smile came easier. And Nolen, being Nolen — charming, magnetic, the kind of man who could win a woman over with just one look and with Novi, he leaned in even more.

Teanir understood the allure. Her husband was a walking temptation.

• • •

Tall.

Handsome.

Well-spoken. The type of man who could pray you into worship and touch you into ruin. She knew what it was like to fall for him. She knew how hard it was to ignore him when he wanted to be seen.

But Novi should've been stronger.

That's what hurt most.

She wasn't just any other woman. This wasn't some random Instagram follower sliding into his DMs or a thirsty congregant hoping to be noticed. This was Novi — the anointed one. The intercessor. The appointed. The woman who called fire from heaven during worship and carried the oil like it was stitched into her bones.

If anyone should've been able to say no, it was her.

Teanir wasn't naïve. She didn't put the full weight of blame on her. Nolen was the one who took vows. He was the one who promised forever — regardless of the road it took to bring them both there. And her disappointment in Novi ran deeper than betrayal — it felt like spiritual betrayal. Because people in leadership are called to a higher standard. They're

● ● ●

supposed to have the strength to resist what others indulge in. They're supposed to carry more oil, more discernment, more self-control.

Instead, this woman who had once stood in front of them all, eyes closed, hands lifted, drenched in the Spirit, became the very thing she hated to see every Sunday morning.

A taker.
A destroyer.
A homewrecker.
A willing participant in someone else's pain.

And for that, Teanir didn't just feel betrayed. She felt ridiculed. By both of them.

But now, Teanir sat with her head held high, face unreadable. Her mother had told her to stay put. Smile. Be graceful.

Let them talk. But she felt it — that fire in her gut.

The rage. The ache. The shame.

Because now, everyone knew. Her mother told her she had asked the prayer ministry to pray for her daughter because her husband was cheating on her with the Worship Leader.

• • •

And yet — she was still here.

Still pretending. Still keeping up appearances. Smiling through rehearsals waiting on her husband. Sitting through service. Watching this woman — month after month — connect with her husband in ways she never could. Ways she stopped trying to.

She had to pretend she wasn't angry at her mother, though she was.

Deeply.

That she wasn't angry at her husband, though she was.

Her core family had failed her... and somehow, she was expected to keep functioning.

Still dying, silently — in public.

With eyes forward.

This Sunday, she kept her face neutral — no cracks, no slips, no signs of the storm behind her ribs, keeping her eyes

● ● ●

forward. That look that told the pews her marriage, her family, her life was steady. Whole.

But from her seat in the second pew, she was forced to watch Novi take the microphone, with full knowledge that this woman who had been leading worship… and slipping into her husband's arms and into his bed after the fanfare was over.

And this morning, the sanctuary was alive with expectation. Devotion Heights' signature worship service — colored lights, banners raised high, the Winds of Glory in the aisles preparing to go into praise or warfare at any moment. It all looked perfect, pressed, and polished with its usual pageantry. The expectation of worship buzzed through the room like electricity.

And yet… something was off.

The praise team assembled as usual, taking their places. Novi adjusted her mic pack and stepped toward center stage, as she'd done countless Sundays before. She wore her best smile — polished, poised. But she felt unease in her spirit. Last night with Zayven had shaken her more than she let on. The silence, the confrontation, the pain — it had left a residue.

• • •

Still, she came. Ready to lead.

Only… she never got the chance.

As she stepped toward the lead microphone, Jeff Casen was already there. He turned slightly, leaned close to her ear, and said quietly, "I'll be leading this morning. I'd appreciate your support singing background."

Novi froze for a second. Her face didn't crack, but her soul flinched.

She nodded slowly, stepping back. Confused.

No explanation. No warning. Just… replaced.

She slid into the background line next to Venus, who looked like she'd just unwrapped a secret and couldn't wait to watch it unravel. A smirk that turned into something colder — something calculated. Novi's chest tightened.

She turned slightly and caught Janet's eyes. Janet shook her head slowly — disapprovingly. Novi felt the disappointment, the judgment.

Her pulse quickened.

Does everyone know? she thought.

● ● ●

She glanced toward Cassia at the keyboard — normally warm, usually kind — but this morning, she wouldn't even look at her. Eyes fixed on the keys. Avoidant.

Something was wrong.

Novi's breath shallowed. Her throat felt tight. The worship had barely started, but already she could feel the undercurrent — the weight of whispers. The shame.

She turned her head toward Nolen. He felt it too.

He was at his usual post behind the drums, but even from a distance, she could see it on his face. Tension. Discomfort. Awareness.

Nolen glanced toward Teanir, seated in her usual spot — but this time, more put-together than usual. Her hair done in a style she rarely wore. Her makeup flawless. Her dress intentional. Not loud, not trying — but deliberate. Presentable. Beautiful even, though not in a way that stirred him.

Just enough to remind him she was still watching.

Still performing.

And maybe — just maybe — planning something.

• • •

He turned back to the drums. Focused. Played as he always had.

But the Spirit didn't fall like it normally did.

Worship was... stale.

The songs felt hollow. The air, rehearsed. And when the final worship song ended, the room — which was usually blanketed in a holy hush — sat in thick, weighted silence instead.

The flow shifted — there was even time for announcements.

That never happened.

Novi stood there, still smiling outwardly, but discouraged. Her hands trembled slightly. Her throat dry. She looked down at her shoes, then back up at the congregation she had led so many times before.

She could feel the judgment like humidity in the room, sticking to her skin — making it hard to breathe.

Nolen caught her eyes again. She looked at him, and he saw it — the unraveling. But he couldn't do anything. Not here. Not now.

• • •

The worship set ended with polite claps. Nothing more.

Then Bishop Byrd stepped forward, Bible in hand, voice warm and clear as he greeted the congregation.

"Turn with me," he said, "to James Chapter 1, verse 14…"

Novi blinked.

She already knew what was coming.

The sermon title flashed across the screen behind him, bold and deliberate:

"When Temptation Causes You to Fall."

The sanctuary grew still.

And as Bishop Byrd began to speak, the weight of the title settled over the room like a cloud. For the first time since stepping into the church that morning — Novi's legs threatened to give way beneath her.

And somewhere, across the sanctuary…

Teanir smiled.

* * *

CHAPTER 24: II
The Aftermath

Not all conviction thunders; some of it comes as a whisper.

The service had ended.

People were moving about in the usual after church daze — hugs, small talk, shallow smiles. But no one spoke to Novi. No one except Odessa, who offered a soft pat on the back and a look filled with sympathy.

Nolen packed up his gear quickly, head down, barely making eye contact with anyone. Teanir watched him from a few pews over, her eyes pleading for acknowledgment. She stood, adjusted her dress, and tried to walk beside him as he exited — but he quickened his pace and walked right past her. Her attempt to keep stride with him failed. It wasn't subtle. And people noticed — especially her mother, Jeff, and Venus.

Outside, Novi sat in her car. She hadn't even turned the engine on. Her hands rested on the steering wheel, motionless. She checked her phone — no texts. No calls. Nothing from Nolen.

• • •

She dialed.

Straight to voicemail.

Then a text came through:

Buzz.

NOLEN:
I'll hit you when I get in the truck.

She stared at the message, lips pursed. Her body was still humming with anxiety, her heart stuck somewhere between disappointment and rage. She sat like that, stewing in silence, until she finally drove home.

When she arrived, Zayven was still there. Like a squatter clinging to a narrative that no longer existed.

"I want to work this out," he said as soon as she stepped inside. "We can still fix this. We can make this our testimony. It could be huge — go viral, even. 'How God restored our marriage after infidelity.' Baby, think about the impact. Think about the branding. The ministry. The money. We'd be unstoppable. A real power couple."

Novi felt like she might throw up.

• • •

He wasn't talking about love. He was talking about optics. About followers. About damage control. Not family. Not healing. Not her.

"No," she said flatly. "Call your boys. Pack your stuff. You're not staying here."

She called her parents to pick up the kids. Zayven didn't argue. He just sat there for a long time,

frozen in disbelief that *his* spin had failed.

In the side parking lot after church, Nolen was loading his drums into the back of his truck when Jeff Casen approached. "Hey man, just wanted to say — I appreciate you playing today, especially with everything going on."

Nolen didn't respond. Just kept loading the kit.

Jeff continued, assuming a brotherly tone. "Since I joined DHC, I've always felt like you and I had a cool vibe, you know? And listen, don't stress about Novi. We're taking care of it. Me and my wife — we've been praying for you and Teanir since we heard about... *everything*."

• • •

Nolen's phone buzzed again. Novi.

He couldn't take the call, not with Jeff standing so close. He declined the call again. Steam started rising inside him. How the hell did Jeff know?

They had only been home for one day. Teanir wasn't one to gossip — he knew that about her. She hated people in her business. Always had. And despite everything, that was something he still respected about her.

So who talked?

He wanted to ask Jeff, but he wasn't about to give him that much access to his personal life.

"All good, man. Appreciate it," Nolen said tightly.

He slammed the trunk harder than necessary, climbed into his truck, and peeled out of the church parking lot, leaving faint tire marks behind.

His head was spinning.

Later... on the road home his phone rang again. It was Jamahl.

• • •

"Nol, what it do?"

"Man... It blew up. Even at church."

"What you mean?"

"Tea found out about me and Novi. Photos. Audio clips."

"Damn man... when?"

"Last week," Nolen said, still in disbelief. "She threw the pics at me — asked if that was me. If it was Novi."

"Dawg... I told you to be careful. I bet you and Novi, with y'all freaky asses, were out there in the woods, grinding on leaves like wildlife and shit."

Nolen let out a small laugh. Jay had a way of making a mess feel bearable.

"Nah, man. In my truck. I don't even know how it got recorded. But the pictures... yeah, I saw them."

"You gon' keep a few? Hang 'em in the office?" Jay cracked.

"Man, you stupid," Nolen chuckled back.

● ● ●

Then he got serious.

He told Jay about Jeff's comments. The stares. Novi getting sidelined during worship. Jeff taking the lead. How the room felt dry. And how the sermon — of all things — was titled When Temptation Causes You to Fall.

Jay listened. He always did.

"You good though bruh?" Jay asked finally.

"Man… I don't know."

They talked the entire drive back to Nolen's house. So long, in fact, that Nolen forgot to call Novi back. Not out of spite. Not on purpose.

Just… overwhelmed.

But one thing sat in his chest like a rock: How did Jeff know?

And the only person who knew… was *Teanir*.

There was a quiet hum this Sunday after church in Elisse's kitchen today, she was downright giddy! One Sunday down.

• • •

Novi in the background. The plan was working. But that wasn't enough. She wanted her destroyed.

Permanently.

Meanwhile, Teanir and the boys arrived at her mother's house. As soon as they walked in, she told them to wash their hands because she had laid out food for everyone. A plate of baked chicken, cabbage, and cornbread was set in front of them — and especially for her *only* daughter, a spread of comfort food she loved.

"You held your head high, baby," her mother said proudly. "You looked forward and did what you needed to do."

But Teanir didn't feel proud. She felt hollow. Because she was still losing him. The man she loved. The father of her children. Gone. She broke down at the kitchen table, face in her hands. Her mother rushed to her, arms wrapping around her tightly.

"What do you need, baby? What can I do?"

"I want my family back, Mama. I want my husband."

"You sure?"

● ● ●

"Yes. I'll do whatever it takes."

Elisse didn't blink. "Then we don't destroy the man. We go after the woman. Her reputation. Her influence. That's where we strike." Teanir hesitated. She didn't want revenge — she wanted repair.

But still… she listened.

In the shadows of the storm, the group chat lit up.

Buzz.

VENUS:
Elisse, we're here for you.
The integrity of this church matters.
Let us know how we can help.

JEFF:

JANET:

Cassia said nothing.

Elisse stepped away from her daughter, read the message, and responded:

• • •

ELISSE:
Thank you. We're hurting.
As a mother, I hurt for my baby girl and my grandsons.
Just so you all are aware, I've requested a meeting with
Bishop Byrd this week.

JANET:
Would you like us to join you?

ELISSE:
No, I'll speak with him alone.
I'll keep you posted if anything changes.

Then she slipped her phone into a drawer and headed back to the kitchen, a smile forming at the corners of her lips.

The plan was already in motion.

And it was falling into place perfectly.

CHAPTER 25
Weight of the Platform

They weren't just missing. They were missed — out loud.

Elisse sat with her legs crossed at the ankle, hands folded neatly over the manila folder in her lap — the same one that had already circled too many hands. The air in Bishop Byrd's office was warm, the blinds tilted just enough to let morning light stripe across the leather chairs and polished oak desk.

Sheila Sandiford, the church secretary, sat in the corner with a yellow legal pad and a gel pen that clicked once, then again. She wasn't just there to take notes. She was a signal. A reminder that the church had structure. Procedure. Order.

Elisse didn't like that she was in the room. She knew how close the Sandifords were to Nolen. She also knew they represented what every church marriage was supposed to — longevity, forgiveness, spiritual weight. But she swallowed that and pressed on, her tone as controlled as her posture.

"There's a crisis on the altar, Bishop," Elisse began, smooth but urgent. "This isn't just about my daughter. It's

• • •

about the integrity of leadership. We're presenting a message to the world through worship. What message are we sending when one of our worship leaders is openly involved in an affair with a married man? What does that say about our church — about you?"

Sheila raised an eyebrow, then looked over at the Bishop.

Elisse didn't flinch. "We're in a spiritual war, Bishop. And the enemy is using this woman to discredit everything Devotion Heights has worked for. That's Legacy. Your legacy. I'm asking — formally — that you remove her and sit her down indefinitely."

Sheila didn't speak. She lowered her eyes to her notepad and began writing.

Bishop Byrd leaned back slowly in his chair. His fingers drummed against the armrest. He'd heard whispers. But hearing it laid out like this — with evidence — brought it too close to the pulpit. Too close to his own past.

He knew Novi's gift. He'd seen her usher in the presence of God when no one else could break through. He also knew how fragile the church's image could be. One crack, and the whole thing unraveled.

• • •

"I'll need to pray on it," he said finally, voice even.

Elisse didn't smile. She simply nodded and rose to her feet, placing the folder carefully on the edge of his desk.

"For the sake of the people, Bishop... don't wait too long."

He walked her to the door and asked Sheila if she'd be so kind as to see her out. Once the door closed behind them, he turned back to the desk and opened the folder. Tucked between the photos was a sticky note with a message — one only he would understand. One that shook him to his core.

Moments later, Sheila returned to his office.

"Is there anything else you need, Bishop?"

He snatched the note quickly, crumpling it in his fist and slipping it into his pocket before she could catch a glimpse.

She noticed his sudden shift — his face pale, his posture uneasy.

"You okay, Bishop? You don't look well. Like you just seen a ghost."

He cleared his throat. "It's been a long day...and those photos were not something I ever wished to see — especially not of the young people in this church."

• • •

Sheila nodded solemnly. "Bishop, if I may... I feel like Elisse is up to no good."

But he didn't respond. His mind had drifted elsewhere. Lost in the weight of what he'd just seen, and even more so — what that note meant.

After a long pause, he finally spoke.

"We all make mistakes," he murmured, eyes distant. "But there are consequences to the actions we take — especially when others get caught in the crossfire."

He walked to the door, hand resting on the knob, and added, "I'll be in prayer about how to move forward."

Then he turned to Sheila.

"Cancel the rest of my day. I need time alone."

And with that, the door quietly shut behind her.

Across the hall, Cassia sat in her office, the hum of the A/C rattling through the vent above her. She stared at the closed door, the faint sounds of the meeting barely audible — but the tension was thick enough to taste.

She knew this wasn't just about ministry. This was about power. Control. Image. And watching Elisse maneuver made something sink in her gut.

• • •

This wasn't about healing her daughter's marriage.

This was about punishment.

About reclaiming dignity — by taking someone else's.

Cassia closed her laptop and leaned back in her chair, her fingers resting on the edge of the keyboard, eyes unfocused.

God, how did we get here?

Meanwhile, at the Sandiford's house

Sheila slipped her shoes off the moment she stepped through the door. It had been a long day — longer than most. Her hands ached from typing, and her spirit ached from what she'd witnessed in that office with Bishop Byrd and Elisse.

She poured herself a glass of water, sat at the edge of the bed, and called her husband.

Ernest answered on the third ring, breath short.

"Honeybear"

"Baby you got a minute?"

• • •

"Yeah, go 'head. I'm out here at Carey's. Truck is giving me a little trouble. Can't get it started. I think I done left the key fob somewhere. I told you I wasn't ready for all this futuristic mess."

She smiled despite herself. "Well, when you get back in the truck — after you calm down — I need to tell you something."

He could hear the weight in her voice. "What happened?"

"Elisse. She came in today. Met with Bishop. Sat in his office with that folder everyone's been talking about — pictures, audio, all of it. She asked for Novi to be removed. Called it a threat to the purity of the platform."

Ernest was quiet. The kind of quiet that meant the anger was building behind his chest like pressure behind a dam.

"She really went that far?" he finally asked. "I'm not surprised... but that don't make it right."

"She's not thinking straight, Ernie. She's not thinking kingdom. She's thinking revenge."

• • •

He exhaled through his nose and looked down at his truck, sitting stubborn and silent in the Carey Hardware parking lot. The sun was beating down. His shirt stuck to his back. The heat was thick, and now his blood pressure was trying to match it.

He pulled out his phone. "I'm calling Nolen. I need him to come help me get this truck going. Might as well talk to the boy while I got him."

Carey Hardware was one of Ernest's favorite places in town. It reminded him of when stores knew your name, when cashiers smiled with their eyes and not just their mouths. The staff was always the same — dependable and kind. They carried the tools he liked, and if they didn't, they'd order it without complaint.

Today, though, he wasn't browsing. He was pacing the parking lot, sweating in his button-down and slacks, slapping the side of a truck that wouldn't start.

The keys — or rather, the electronic fob — had vanished. First time buying a keyless vehicle, and now he couldn't even get it home. He leaned against the hood, grumbling to himself. He called Nolen. Nolen's voice came through clear when he picked up the call.

● ● ●

"Praise the Lord, Mr. Ernest, everything good?"

"Nope. This new truck won't start. I'm out here lookin' like a fool. You nearby?"

"Yes I am, I'm headed your way now."

"Alright. Appreciate it, son."

They hung up.

And as Ernest stood in the sun, handkerchief dabbing sweat from his brow, he muttered under his breath, "I swear these cars too smart for their own good."

But what really had him burning... wasn't the truck.

It was Elisse.

It was the church.

And it was the slow, ugly unraveling of a ministry that was supposed to be about grace.

Ernest wasn't just planning to get his truck running. He was planning to tell the boy the truth — about what had been said, what had been shown, and what might be coming next. Because some messes don't just blow over.

Sometimes, you need a man to step in and clean it up.

After Nolen got off the phone with Ernest, he called Novi.

It had been a whirlwind — chaotic, tense, exposed — and all he wanted was to make sure his girl, the true love of his life, was okay.

They spoke briefly. The call was quiet, but thick with emotion.

She told him she'd kicked Zayven out. Her parents had taken the kids for the weekend.

He sighed, pressing his fingers to the bridge of his nose. "You need to go to The Spot," he said softly. "Just breathe, baby. Clear your head. You know it's safe there."

The Spot.

Once his safe haven, now their private space. A place no one asked questions, no one watched, no one whispered. A space where their love wasn't hidden — it just was.

He closed his eyes for a second, remembering the last time they'd been there. The way her body curved into his. The way she let go — completely, unapologetically. He wished they could go back again, even just for a night. Make love. Fall asleep tangled together like the rest of the world didn't exist.

• • •

On the other end of the line, she cried. Not loudly. Not dramatically. Just... *tears*. Slow, aching tears that made his chest feel tight.

"Baby... *please* don't cry," he whispered. "I promise I'm gonna fix this."

She cried again — not just for the love she always wanted and had, but for the ministry she was watching slip through her fingers. Because everything was falling apart. The exposure. The shame. The music. The people, and now... the weight of what it might cost her — her ministry, her position, and her calling.

She hadn't really considered the fallout. Until now.

"I just... I didn't think," she said through quiet sobs. "I didn't think it would blow up like this."

"I know," he said gently. "I wish I could hold you right now," he admitted. "Just...lay there with you. Block out everything else."

She smiled behind the phone and closed her eyes for a moment.

"I love you," he told her. His voice didn't shake. "That hasn't changed. Not because of this."

● ● ●

She exhaled. Shaky, but honest. "I know, Nolen. I love you too."

And for a moment, that was enough.

They hung up, both still weighted...

But slightly less alone.

Nolen pulled into the parking lot of Carey's Hardware and spotted Ernest standing beside his truck, waving a frustrated hand at the hood like it had personally betrayed him. It was moments like this that reminded Nolen — despite Ernest's sharpness and wisdom — he really was getting older.

He chuckled to himself and pulled up beside him.

"Nice ride, old man," Nolen said, stepping out with a grin.

"Yeah, I thought so too, son, until I came out with all this stuff and can't even get it started," Ernest huffed, shaking his head. "And it's hot out here."

He wiped his glistening forehead with a neatly folded handkerchief.

"You check your bags?"

• • •

Ernest gave him a sharp look — the kind that said, Of course I did.

"Lottie asked me the same thing when she called asking for money again. Grown woman, still begging her mama and me 'til Friday. Yes, I checked my bags, son."

Nolen held his hands up in retreat. "Alright, alright. Let's go check inside — maybe you left it in the store."

They walked back through the automatic doors. Ernest let out a quiet sigh of relief as the cool air wrapped around him. The woman at the counter looked up and smiled.

"Oh, back already?"

Ernest replied, "I never left. Can't find my keys."

Nolen had an idea. "Hey, would y'all mind checking the security cameras? Maybe we can see where he set them down?"

The woman nodded. "For Mr. Ernest? Of course. He's family." They were led into the back — a rare courtesy. Ernest had been a loyal customer since the store opened. As they watched the playback, they saw him walk over to the electrical supplies section and, distracted by what he was comparing, casually set his keys on top of a light fixture.

● ● ●

"There they go," Nolen said, pointing. "Let's see if they're still there." They made their way back to the aisle, and sure enough, the keys were exactly where he'd left them.

"Here you go," Nolen said, handing them over.

Ernest let out a deep, relieved breath. "That's what happens when you get older, son. You forget you do things like that." He laughed — soft and self-aware.

"Why don't you follow me back to the house, help me unload this stuff from the truck… and have a slice of pie?"

Nolen hesitated for only a second. He needed comfort. Not just the meal, but the man. The stability.

He had thought briefly about heading to The Spot — to see Novi, to hold her, to let the heat of her body and presence ground him again. But something about Ernest's voice, his steadiness….

Was what Nolen needed more.

Ernest Sandiford was legacy without ego.

He was the father Nolen never had. The spiritual covering Novi quietly respected. The invisible backbone of

Devotion Heights Church. In a world where titles shouted and platforms seduced, Pastor Ernest was a man chosen by character, not charisma. He was the steadying hand when others fell. The voice of reason when storms rose. And a reminder that not all power is loud.

They arrived at the Sandifords', and Nolen helped Ernest carry his purchases into the garage.

"Honey, is that you?" Sheila's voice called from inside.

"Yeah, Honeybear. Nolen came to help me. Couldn't get the truck started, but we're good now."

She appeared in the doorway, smiling, and waved them in.

"You staying for dinner, baby?"

"I'd love to," Nolen replied.

Ernest motioned for him to follow downstairs into his man cave. It was a sacred space — leather couches, jazz records, an old humidifier, and the scent of pipe tobacco that lingered in the wood.

They sat down. Nolen didn't even need prompting. He started talking. Ernest listened, really listened, the way only men who'd lived full lives knew how.

• • •

Ernest ran a hand over his close shaved silver hair, then took a sip of his sweet tea. His earth-toned skin, weathered hands, and deep laugh lines made him look every bit the wise patriarch he was — today dressed down in overalls and a T-shirt instead of one of his usual crisp suits.

"Son," he said finally, "I've been married to Sheila for over forty years. And we've had hard times. She stayed. And I loved her for it. I wasn't perfect, neither was she. But we worked through it."

Nolen leaned in, listening. There was no judgment in Ernest's tone. Only experience.

"You remember what we talked about before? Doing things the right way. Teanir's a good woman. She's the mother of your children. I know it's been hard. And I can't say I know exactly how you feel, because when I met Sheila, I was head-over-heels in love. Followed her around the schoolyard like a lost puppy." He chuckled. "Brought her flowers every day until she said yes to a date. Then I met her at the soda shop, had a burger, and I knew right then I wanted to spend the rest of my life with her."

Nolen smiled. Stories like this reminded him of what alignment could look like. Legacy. Partnership.

• • •

"I know that ain't your story with Teanir. And that's okay. But that don't excuse you from showing up. From being there."

"I have been there," Nolen said. "I've provided, I've shown up for my boys. I haven't left."

Ernest leaned forward, voice firm but kind. "That's not what I'm saying. I'm not talking about money. I'm talking about presence. Protection. Respect. You don't have to live with her to honor what she is to your sons. When Lottie divorced Sean, she thought her world was ending. But Sean still shows up for her and their daughter. That's what real men do."

Nolen folded his hands together, quiet. He could feel the weight of Ernest's words. He thought briefly about what life would look like not being married to Teanir anymore. What that meant for his boys. And what life could be — with Novi.

Ernest placed a hand on his shoulder. "I'm praying for you, son. Not for the easy choice, but the right one. And no matter what Elisse is stirring up, just know — me and Sheila, we got you."

Nolen looked up, caught off guard.

● ● ●

"What do you mean — Elisse?"

Sheila appeared again with two fresh glasses of tea and a plate of her peach cobbler — her telltale dish for heavy conversations. Sweet potato pie was for peace. But peach cobbler meant storms were coming.

"Here you go, baby," she said, setting the plate down and giving Nolen a kiss on the forehead. "Y'all need anything else?"

"No, honeybear," Ernest replied.

She went back upstairs, and Ernest waited a beat before continuing.

"Sheila sat in on a meeting today. Elisse brought Bishop Byrd a folder — photos, recordings. Made a formal complaint."

Nolen's jaw tightened. Appetite gone. Fury rising.

"Sat down with the Bishop...and asked for Novi to be removed from the platform. Indefinitely."

His breath caught in his chest. He clenched his jaw, every muscle tight.

Had Teanir known about this?

● ● ●

Is this why it felt like the entire church knew about his affair with Novi?

Nolen had more questions than he could process — more than he had answers for. His thoughts swirled, one louder than the next. Ernest saw the heat rising in him, the tightness in his jaw, the storm behind his eyes.

"Son," Ernest said gently but firmly, "be careful how you handle things from here on out. I'll never leave you in the dark. If I know something, you'll know something."

He paused, then added, "Take care of Novi in this, son. We watched that girl grow into a woman. A mother. A powerful worship leader."

Just hearing her name calmed something in Nolen. Even in the middle of his rage, she was the anchor.

All he wanted was to take care of her — the woman who had given him more love, more pleasure, more tenderness than he'd ever known in his life.

Ernest looked at him solemnly. "The devil is after both of y'all. And if you're not careful, this could impact your lives in a way you may never recover from."

• • •

Nolen wanted to speak, but the words got caught in his throat. He was too angry — too full. All he could manage was a quiet, "I need to go."

He politely declined dinner. Even the peach cobbler didn't tempt him. Sheila, reading his spirit, didn't push. She simply said, "I'll make you a plate, baby. You can come get it later."

Nolen drove straight home.

But the house was empty. No Teanir. No boys. Just silence.

He pulled out his phone and called her.

She answered on the second ring, a flicker of hope in her voice.

"Hello?"

"Where you at?"

Something in his tone made her stomach drop. Not the sorrow of a crumbling marriage — this was different. Deeper. A holy warning in her gut, the kind only the Spirit gives when danger's near.

"Where's Elisse?" he asked, tightly.

• • •

Teanir hesitated. She didn't want to lie, but she didn't want to expose her mother either. "She's... in the other room. I'm at her house."

"What's wrong? What happened?"

Nolen's voice cracked, and the pain came through.

"Did you know your mother was going around the church showing those pictures and playing that recording!? Did you give them to her? Why would you do that?"

Teanir's heart stopped. She hadn't given her mother anything. She'd never even told Nolen that Elisse was the one who hired the PI. He'd just assumed Teanir had done it all herself.

"I didn't do that," she said quickly. "You know me. You know I wouldn't. That's embarrassing."

And she meant it. She knew how her mother moved — quiet, deadly. Elisse was surgical when she wanted revenge. She didn't just go for the wound — she went for the artery.

"Where is she, Tea?" Nolen asked again.

Teanir hesitated. Part of her wanted to protect him from himself. Another part didn't want to be pulled deeper into whatever storm he was preparing to unleash.

• • •

"She stepped out. I'm just here at the house. You want me and the boys to come home?"

"Nah... " Nolen exhaled sharply. "I'm going to my mama's. This ain't right, Tea. You *say* you want to work on our marriage, and you out here doing this kind of BS with your mama."

"I'm not," she whispered. Her voice, normally sharp and accusatory, was soft — almost pleading. She didn't want to enrage him. For the first time in their entire relationship... she was afraid. Not of him. But of what he might do.

They hung up.

Teanir sat still for a moment, then stood and walked to the living room. Elisse sat on the couch, flipping through channels like it was any other Sunday afternoon.

"Mama," she said, her voice low. "What did you *do?*"

Elisse looked up, wide-eyed but composed. "Nothing, baby. What's wrong?"

"I just talked to Nolen. He said you've been showing people those pictures and playing the audio. Did you do that?"

Elisse didn't flinch. She sat up straighter, eyes narrowing, jaw tightening.

• • •

"You want me to sugarcoat it for you, or you want the truth?"

Teanir didn't respond. She didn't have the strength to.

Her mother leaned forward, voice rising with every word. "Because baby, we're in a war. And wars ain't fought fair. So what you wanna hear? That I didn't do it? Because YES — I DID. I showed them what that nasty heifer was doing with my son-in-law."

Her voice sharpened to steel.

"I'm fighting for the legacy of my daughter and my grandsons. I'm not about to let some half-anointed side piece ruin your marriage. What you wanna hear, Teanir? You know me. You know how I get down."

And suddenly, the rage returned.

Teanir felt it boil up inside her — hot and thick. Not just at Nolen anymore. But now, at her own mother. It had already been humiliating enough, asking the prayer team to cover her crumbling marriage.

But this?

This was something else entirely.

● ● ●

Her mother had paraded her shame — passed it around like communion in the church halls.

Shame. Rage. Grief.

Even with her deep complexion, her anger showed on her face this time. It radiated through her bones.

She wanted to scream. To cry. To disappear.

She never imagined it would come to this — her own mother weaponizing her humiliation, waving images of her husband making love to another woman like a flag.

And the woman?
Beautiful.
Anointed.
Called by God.

Everything Teanir used to dream of being as a wife in her marriage. Everything the church celebrated while pitying her — the wife who stayed with a man who never truly loved her.

She sat down in silence. For the first time in her life, she didn't know who to be mad at first.

Nolen.

• • •

Elisse.

Herself.

She felt betrayed by the two people who should've protected her the most. And now... she didn't know how she could *ever* show her face in that church again.

● ● ●

CHAPTER 26
Canceled Culture

They didn't throw stones —they posted them.

Novi's Point of View

The silence was the first thing Novi noticed.

No calls. No texts. Not even a single DM.

The group chat for the praise team — the one she had poured her heart, gift, and Saturdays into — was gone. Removed. Just like that. No warning. No explanation. One moment she was in; the next, she didn't exist.

Even in her daily errands, the judgment was thick. At a local store, she ran into one of her so-called "praise team sisters," who glanced her way and offered a tightly wound smile before saying, "We're praying for you, sis. God still forgives."

It was laced with something — pity? Condescension? Disgust?

Novi didn't respond. Couldn't. Her throat tightened. Her face didn't change, but inside, she crumbled. She dropped

• • •

everything she had in her cart and walked out — eyes forward, back straight — until she hit the safety of her car.

There, with the door shut and the engine off, she exhaled... and unraveled.

How did this happen?

One moment. One moment she had spent years trying to avoid. One choice that felt so inevitable — it was as if her body had made it for her. Being in Nolen's arms had felt like salvation. His embrace? The sweetest song ever sung.

Now, she was an outcast.

She leaned her head against the steering wheel and closed her eyes. The only thing that brought a whisper of comfort was The Spot — the private sanctuary Nolen had shown her. Their place. Not even his wife or his closest friends knew about it. That meant something. She had been chosen. Even in that.

But tears welled up again. How could something that felt so divine... cause this much destruction? She tried to understand. She did understand. He was married. She was married.

But just like that, the Holy Spirit whispered:

• • •

"Consequences."

Novi went silent in her spirit and drove home in a daze, letting the stillness speak for her.

Later that evening, her phone buzzed. Odessa.

"Hey girl. You alright?"

Novi hesitated. "I'm dealing with it... as best I can. I just feel... ostracized. Like my gift, my calling — it's been tarnished. I don't even know how to get it back."

Odessa exhaled on the other end. "Girl, I can't even imagine. If it were me, I'd probably leave the church and move in with my man."

That pulled a small laugh from Novi. The first in days.

"You're funny, Odessa. Thanks for the laugh."

"You know I got you. But girl, everyone is talking about it — and the pictures of y'all doing the nasty in his truck?"

Novi froze.

Pictures?

• • •

She knew Teanir had shown Nolen. And she knew Teanir had met with Zayven. But who else? Who else had seen them?

She felt exposed. Violated. Shamed.

"Odessa… who showed them?"

"I mean, it's not just you in them, they exposing Nolen too. I think it's Elisse. She's mad at him for cheating on her daughter."

"Elisse? She's showing the pictures!? How did she even get them?"

"Teanir probably gave them to her. I know if it were me, I'd run straight to my mama and show her everything."

Novi went quiet. She understood that. If she'd been betrayed… she might've done the same. But she had always been overly private. Even when dating Zayven, no one knew until the wedding invitations went out. She barely knew Teanir, honestly. Their only real interaction had been at a women's conference, eating dinner with a group of wives, talking about parenting and being spirit-filled. Teanir barely spoke then. Novi figured she was just quiet. Maybe it was an only child thing.

• • •

"What are you gonna do?" Odessa asked.

"I don't know. My parents have the kids for the rest of the week. My mom… she was disappointed. But she held me. Prayed for me. My dad hugged me and told me I was forgiven. That God still had a mighty work for me to do. But I just feel… sad. Disgraced. Alone. Hurt."

"Well, you know they from Park Heights," Odessa said bluntly. "She might find a way to get you beat up — or worse — messin' with her husband like that."

Odessa had a way of being on your side and against you at the same time. Like she enjoyed the rollercoaster. Hope, then despair. Lift, then drop.

"And you know," she continued, "when they were in college, Nolen was a hoe anyway. Cheated on his girlfriend back then with Teanir."

"Wow…"

Novi already knew. Nolen had told her everything — his past, his mistakes. She didn't excuse it, but he had been young. Stupid. Human.

"So Teanir don't need to be coming for you like she all innocent — even if she is the wife."

• • •

"How's Don?" Novi asked, shifting the conversation.

"Girl, I don't know. I'm not talking to him right now."

"What happened?"

"Well, he ain't married like Nolen, so I don't have that problem — but women stay throwin' themselves at him. Last week I went by his place 'cause he wasn't answering, and saw Sister Turner laying on his bed through the basement window. I screamed, cried. He ain't even come out."

Novi winced. "I'm sorry. So y'all broke up?"

"We together," Odessa snapped. "He not getting off that easy. But I ain't talkin' to him right now."

Novi ended the call by saying she had another call coming in. She didn't. She just couldn't take any more of Odessa's chaos.

She needed quiet. She needed to feel her own ache.

Buzz.

CASSIA:
Hey baby, are you busy today?

● ● ●

Novi blinked. Her thumb hovered. Cassia? After everything? She hadn't even made eye contact with her on Sunday.

Truth was — she didn't have an appetite.

Not for food.

Lately, it felt like God and Devotion Heights were feeding her a steady diet of despair, and the shame tasted bitter in her mouth.

She pulled up to the restaurant. The glow of the red neon sign reflected off the water like fire on the bay. From across the harbor, it looked peaceful. Inviting. She wasn't sure she deserved either.

Inside, Cassia was already seated near the panoramic window, the skyline of Baltimore lighting up the harbor like a Christmas tree.

● ● ●

Novi clutched her purse tighter as she walked toward the table, bracing herself for whatever was about to come.

Cassia stood, opened her arms, and said softly, "Let's pray first."

Novi didn't expect that. They held hands. Prayed. And as soon as she closed her eyes, her own heart betrayed her. She didn't even know what to pray. She just hoped God was still listening.

Cassia spoke first.

"Baby, I asked you here because I've been wrestling in my spirit about you and Nolen for a while now."

Novi took a sip of water, wishing it were something stronger. She stared at the menu. On any other day, before everything blew up, she would've ordered the Lady Baltimore. But now even the thought of it felt suffocating — eighteen layers of cake pressing down on her like eighteen layers of despair, catching in her throat, making it hard to breathe.

"It was brought to my attention a while back," Cassia continued. "But I never came to you. Nolen is a grown man — it was his responsibility not to pursue this. And don't take this wrong, but women… we're just different. We hold on. We feel

• • •

too deep. We stay too long. Men can walk away without a word. But we? We hold everything."

Novi nodded.

When the waitress came, she declined to order. Her emotions were too loud for her stomach to work. The water helped her keep from crying.

"Can I ask... who told you?"

Cassia didn't flinch. "Venus. And Janet."

Of course. It didn't even surprise her.

"I brought you here to love on you. To pray for you. To warn you. Because this isn't just about what you did — it's about what they're doing." Novi swallowed hard. The tears she'd been holding burst out all at once. Heads turned. Forks paused. Conversations hushed.

"Excuse me," she whispered.

She ran to the restroom, pressed cold water on her face, and stared at her reflection. If Nolen were here... his presence alone would've calmed her.

She returned, still fragile.

"You okay, baby?" Cassia asked gently.

• • •

"I'm okay."

Cassia leaned in. "Something's off. I've been asked to 'distance' myself — or lose my position. They're planning something. They want you gone. Not just from the team… but from the church."

Novi's mouth dropped open. "From the church?"

Cassia nodded. "They're coming for you. Not Nolen. Just you."

"But why me? We were both in this. Why just me?"

Cassia looked away for a second, then back.

"This ain't about the affair anymore. This is about power."

Novi blinked hard.

Cassia softened. "But God is sovereign. He's still God, even in scandal. Guilt will eat you alive, but grace… grace reminds you that even broken people are still used by Him."

Novi looked down at her hands. At the table. At nothing. She felt guilty — not for loving Nolen, not even for making love to him. But for what it cost. Still, Cassia didn't judge. Didn't take sides. She showed up. She listened. She paid for dinner. And in that small act, Novi felt — just for a

• • •

moment — less alone. They hugged goodbye in the parking
lot.

It wasn't redemption. But it was mercy.

CHAPTER 27
Between the Sheets & Truth

Loving her was truth — and he knew it would cost him.

Nolen's Point of View

The entire whirlwind of their romance played in his head. He thought back to the first time he saw her — before any attraction, before any real connection — and remembered thinking, Wow, she's really beautiful.

But he'd seen beautiful women before. Many, in fact. Beauty alone had never been the only thing that drew him to a woman — not even back in college.

When he met Tanika, she was beautiful in an understated way. There was a mystery about her. She knew a lot of things, held deep conversations, and, as a bonus, her family checked every box that would make her an easy merge into his own. His parents loathed anything even close to ghetto, and Tanika was safe. Palatable. Proper. The kind of woman his Roland Park-raised, suburban family could accept.

Even with Teanir — before he ever approached her that day; she had been waiting outside school — he had already

• • •

done his research. Full-ride scholarship. Math major. Beautiful and smart. That combination always turned him on. Teanir had a striking presence too — those piercing blue-gray eyes against her deep brown skin made her unforgettable. Physically, he was intrigued. Tanika had femininity; Teanir had edge. But it was all surface. Beauty, intellect, and opportunity.

With Novi... it was different. Completely different. They connected spiritually first. That had never happened before.

With Tanika and Teanir, it was physical. Curves. Skin. Scent. The softness of their hands, the shape of their hips, the perfume that lingered after a hug. He had always noticed the feminine things. But with Novi, he had connected with her *before* any of that. Spirit to spirit. Soul to soul. If he believed in past lives, he might've said she was his wife in another one.

It was that deep. That compellingly familiar. It gave him chills just thinking about it.

He connected with her spiritually. And as a musician, spiritual connection was sacred. Connecting musically with singers was easy — he did that his whole life. You learn their

● ● ●

flow, where they're going in a service, and you follow. But with Novi, he knew her flow before she even opened her mouth. Before they were even in the same room. He felt her. Understood her direction like they shared the same soul. It wasn't normal.

And when they finally connected physically?

It was an explosion.

Not just at The Spot, where he had devoured her like a man starved. But in every buildup — the tension, the longing, the energy between them. Their bodies became a physical expression of what had already happened in their spirit.

Novi wasn't just a soulmate. She was the embodiment of every unspoken wish. Every half-prayer he'd ever whispered in the dark. She was the living answer to a love he didn't believe existed. She saw him — truly saw him — and didn't try to mold him into something more digestible. She accepted him. Loved him. Filled every gap he had without trying to fix him.

And he hoped he was doing the same for her.

He started having flashbacks — intimate, raw, emotionally vulnerable moments. The times he dominated

• • •

her with no restraint, and she matched his energy —
completely open, fully surrendered, never withholding. The
few times their lovemaking turned so spiritual, so vulnerable,
that he actually teared up during the act. Quietly. Holding her
close while he moved inside of her so she wouldn't see.

But she *always* knew.

He chuckled, remembering when she asked, "Are you
crying?" and he buried his face into the bed, still inside her,
trying to hide the tears. No other woman had ever made him
tear up.

Not one. He closed his eyes.

Despite all the chaos swirling around them, he found
peace in the truth — he was in love. The kind of love that
makes you stop giving a damn about what others think. The
kind that burns so true, people's opinions fade into
irrelevance.

He thought about Napa. About how every moment
had been effortless. No awkward silences, no forced
conversations. Just chemistry. Sensuality. Presence. The way
she took him in her mouth felt... worshipful. Almost wrong in
how divine it was — like worship that belonged only to God.
But she gave it freely, fully, without shame. She let him release

• • •

into her, drink from him — there was no judgment, no disgust.

Just reception. Intimacy.

Most women treated it like the dirty ending to a favor. He could still hear the past reactions: "Don't get that on me." But Novi?

She wanted him.

All of him.

It humbled him.

She made love to him in a way that made him feel undeserving. And all he wanted was to return that, in every way he could. No matter the cost.

She knew him. Understood him. Understood his mind, his needs, his silences.

But if he was being honest with himself, he had to ask the hard question: Was it love he was after? Or an escape? Was Novi *his* out from a marriage he never wanted in the first place?

Teanir was beautiful. In fact, the only dark-skinned woman he'd ever been attracted to — because, truthfully, he

● ● ●

had a type: light-skinned, long hair, average height, banging body, pretty feet.

Always.

So why now? Why this connection?

Was it because he was ready to be done?

Was this divine... or just convenient?

He thought about his sons — Brandon, Dewaun, and Jordan. Would his choices destroy them? Would it scar them? But how long should he live without love?

He thought about Novi as a mother — nurturing, strong, protective. She handled business. Emotionally and financially present for her children. She cooked, too. Real meals. Meals that made you feel seen, loved, and full. Not like the bland leftovers or takeout bags he was used to.

Teanir didn't enjoy cooking — and when she did, it showed.

He imagined what their blended family could look like. Him. Novi. The boys. Maybe even a child together. But he also knew — if it came to it, he'd fight for custody. No other man was going to raise his sons.

• • •

Novi wanted to contribute.

Teanir just wanted to be a wife. No dreams. No goals. No plans. He hated that. Tired of being trapped in his own head, he grabbed his phone and called his boy Jamahl.

"Yo, you home?"

"Yessir," Jay said. "Roll through."

Nolen needed to talk. Needed to process everything, his marriage, Novi, and the church fallout. Later, after hours of decompressing on Jay's leather lounger, his phone buzzed.

Notification: Photos shared anonymously in a Facebook church group.

What the hell?

He stared at the screen, stunned. There they were — screenshots of him and Novi. Intimate. Tangled up in his truck. It wasn't the worst angle, but it didn't need to be. The implication was enough. The comments were already piling up. Every scroll was another dagger — scripture thrown like stones, gossip dressed as prayer requests, pity twisted into judgment. By the time he hit the bottom of the thread, it wasn't just a post anymore. He couldn't tell who was behind it.

• • •

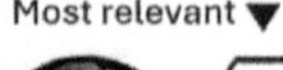

Anonymous post. No name. No source. Just the damage left behind like glass shattered on the sanctuary floor.

He felt his throat tighten. Anger, shame, protectiveness, they all hit at once. He didn't care what they thought about him. But Novi? Seeing her dragged like this? That was a different kind of rage.

Buzz.

CASSIA:
Bishop wants to see you in his office.
Then rehearsal. Call him to set up a time.

Of course he did.

● ● ●

Nolen put the phone down, ran both hands down his face, and exhaled. The fallout had officially begun.

Time to face it.

• • •

CHAPTER 28
Righteous Manipulation

It looked like righteousness. It moved like politics.

It was Thursday, another rehearsal day, and right after Nolen received a text from Cassia, his phone lit up again. This time it was Bishop Byrd, asking to meet with him a few hours before praise team rehearsal. Nolen was reluctant. He didn't want to go, not after everything, not with those pictures circulating online. But Devotion Heights Church was Byrd's church. And the man was one of the signatures on his paycheck. How could he say no?

"Yeah, that's cool, Bishop,"

Nolen replied evenly. His tone didn't reveal the irritation rising inside him.

"Alright then. I'll see you in a few."

Strangely, the air outside felt refreshing. Maybe it was the pre-storm breeze, the kind that wrapped around you with purpose, the kind that comforted even when nothing else could. He smiled to himself for a second. That was something Novi would've noticed. And just like that, he felt her. She was

• • •

probably feeling the same breeze, maybe even the same calm. They always connected like that, even from a distance. Usually, one of them would say it first, shoot a text, or whisper something about it when they were together.

So, in true fashion, he pulled out his phone to confirm.

NOLEN:
Hey babe, what you doing? Where you at?

NOVI:
Just sitting outside in my backyard... feeling the air.
It's comforting. This breeze is so crisp.
I thought about grabbing my jacket but I love
how it's flowing around everything.
Kind of peaceful. What about you?
You going to rehearsal tonight?

He sighed, deep and heavy. He didn't want to go, but this was his job. The praise team leaders had salaries, but musicians? They only got paid when they showed up. Cassia put that system in place, probably to avoid lazy no-shows. The money was good, so he was going. And he wasn't about to give anybody another reason to whisper about him and Novi skipping rehearsals together.

NOLEN:
Yeah, I'll be there. Bishop wants to meet
with me before rehearsal. We'll see how that goes.

• • •

The moment he hit send; he got irritated again. He didn't want to talk about this anymore. Not right now. So, he shut it down.

NOLEN:
Baby, I'll hit you afterwards when I'm on my
way over. I've got some errands to knock out first.

NOVI:
Okay, I love you.

NOLEN:
I love you more.

Later – 4:00 p.m. | Devotion Heights Church

Bishop Byrd was already in the building, giving last-minute instructions to Sheila, the church secretary and wife of Pastor Sandiford. He asked her to prepare the office with bottled water and a soda — just a small gesture before his meeting with Nolen.

Sheila followed her usual routine, but this time, she added her own touch. She anointed her hands with oil and quietly prayed over everything in the office — the desk, the chairs, the doorknobs. She didn't know what was going to unfold, but her spirit told her it wasn't going to be clean.

• • •

"Alright, Sister Sandiford, you can go ahead and leave for the evening," Bishop said. "Tell your husband I'll be calling him about those minutes from last month. We need to get those filed."

She blinked. Protocol dictated that someone always be present during office meetings, especially when women — or controversial situations — were involved. Why was she being dismissed?

Still, she complied.

"Alright, Bishop. I'll grab my things. See you tomorrow."

As she exited, she passed Nolen walking into the church. Without hesitation, she embraced him in a hug that said, We got you. God's got you.

"Thank you, Sista Sheila," he said softly.

"You don't have to thank me, baby. Stop by anytime, you hear?"

He nodded and kept moving, walking straight into Byrd's office.

The bishop stood at the door, gestured toward a chair. Nolen sat, unsure what to expect. This entire mess was

* * *

draining, and knowing Elisse was the source made his blood boil. He remembered what his mother had said about her just days ago...

She called Elisse ratchet gutter trash. Bottom of the barrel. Said she never liked Teanir, thought she was a gold-digger from the jump. The pregnancy, the marriage — none of it changed her mind. She didn't care how smart Teanir was. In fact, she hated that her son had to compromise his potential by being tied to a woman she viewed as beneath the Jahlil name.

She didn't know Novi well — other than the fact that thousands flocked to Devotion Heights Church because of the oil on her and that Praise Team. Oil Novi had helped cultivate there. She liked that Novi was classy, even elegant, and would've made the perfect daughter-in-law if she had married her son instead.

Novi was always gracious at church, and everyone liked her. She would've made an ideal politician's wife — gregarious, quick to smile, and a good mother. All the things Teanir would never be.

She hated that she felt her son could never reach the goals she had envisioned for him, held back by what she

• • •

considered old fashioned gutter trash — and Elisse had raised that kind of a woman. No better herself, Elisse had the nerve to parade around with pornographic pictures of her son in a compromising position.

How would that look for his political run if those ever got out?

And she knew Elisse well enough to know that she would do anything for a quick result. She'd heard the rumors — how Elisse secured her restaurant by sabotaging the other chef and played dirty. So dirty, in fact, that the woman had to drop out of the competition, leaving Elisse the default winner.

She was gutter - and all things that flowed to the bottom of it.

Back in the office, Bishop finally sat behind the desk. He rested his hands over the large Bible, pressing his fingers together.

"Son... This isn't an easy conversation. But let's pray first."

Nolen bowed his head. The prayer was short, more obligatory than sincere. When they finished, Bishop leaned back and started talking.

• • •

"I'm not here to blame you," he began. "Your marriage with Teanir… this situation with Novi… you're not the first man to deal with something like this. You won't be the last."

Nolen's eyebrow twitched. Situation? That's what he called Novi?

The Bishop went on. "Temptation is a stubborn mule. It doesn't go away easy. We're men — we want to feel needed, seen. And when you've been married a while… things get stale. I get it."

He leaned forward.

"Novi is a beautiful woman. No denying that. But marriage is a covenant. I want to help you work on yours."

So we're doing this, Nolen thought. The whole "go back to your wife and act like this never happened" speech.

He listened as Bishop talked, but his spirit was growing more and more agitated. He thought he was here to be heard, to be counseled. But this was about performance. Appearances. Control.

"By the time First Lady is done with Teanir," Bishop added with a smile, "she'll be the woman you've always needed."

• • •

Nolen just sat there. His silence was louder than any protest.

"I'm taking you under my wing," Bishop continued. "As my spiritual son. I'll guide you in your marriage, your ministry, and your career. But you've got to follow my lead. If not, nothing you do will prosper."

Nolen nodded. Not in agreement. Just acknowledgment.

Bishop picked up the phone and called First Lady. Told her to call Teanir. Said they were going to "rebuild their covenant." Told Nolen the meeting went well.

Nolen couldn't get out of there fast enough.

What disturbed him most wasn't just Bishop's warped view of Novi — it was the dismissiveness. The way he reduced everything they'd built together into a "situation." It didn't sit right. And then there was the Facebook post — the photos. He thought about mentioning it. But what if it was Bishop who leaked it?

Better to keep that card close for now.

• • •

As Nolen walked into the sanctuary, he could feel the eyes on him. Venus. Janet. Kara. All of them looked at him like he was fresh prey. Sympathy, pity, lust — it was hard to tell the difference sometimes.

He already knew Venus wanted him. She once "accidentally" took his check home and invited him over to retrieve it. Cougar energy on full display.

Janet? He always thought she might've been a lesbian, even though she was married to Chris, the bassist. She never wore dresses. Always in pantsuits. Strong jawline. Hard stare.

And Kara? A clinger. Always nearby, always touching. Looking for her opening.

But it was Novi he wanted. She should've been here, leading. Instead, they had Jeff Casen, whose only real motive for joining DHC was overheard in the hallway: "This place is a goldmine."

Nolen sat at the drums, trying to focus. But he played with frustration — and it showed.

• • •

Cassia pulled him aside and made sure the sanctuary was clear of anyone else.

"Hey baby, how you holding up?"

"Not good," he said bluntly.

"I can see that. I met with Novi this week. We had dinner." He blinked. That shocked him. She wasn't against her?

"I wanted to make sure you're good," Cassia continued. "I don't agree with what's happened, but I want you to know — Ronnie and I are here for you."

"Thank you," he said, but the gratitude felt heavy. Cautious.

"Novi's in trouble, baby. Real trouble. They're trying to erase her from Devotion Heights. Not just from the praise team. From the church. I've been threatened and told to 'distance' myself or lose my job."

"What? Why? Are they trying to kick us both out?"

She shook her head.

• • •

"No, just her. Elisse has power in this church you don't understand. And Bishop… Bishop ain't who you think he is. He's changed a lot from those early days when Devotion Heights was just Glenn Dale Missionary Baptist Church. He's driven by power, greed, and image."

Nolen was floored. He could hardly breathe. This explained how he didn't hear him in that meeting at all. He didn't care about him, he has another agenda – one that it seems he wants to use to make him work it out with Teanir.

This was never about sin or discipline. This was about power. Politics. Control.

He needed air. He needed his boys. He needed Novi.

"I love you, Cass. Be safe."

They hugged. He walked out into the night. What once was a house of God now felt like a den of snakes. A place of oil and deliverance now soaked in ego and envy.

He was loading his drums into the car when a voice came from behind him.

It was Zayven.

• • •

CHAPTER 29
When Men Fight

It's rarely about what is said — and always about what they lost

Zayven's Point of View

The courtyard behind Devotion Heights Church was usually quiet after service — reserved for handshakes, polite hellos, or the occasional family photo. But tonight, he waited there, watching the door, waiting for Nolen to come out from rehearsal.

He had tried pleading with his wife for another chance. Begged her to see it from his view. He loved her — in his own way. Maybe not the way she wanted to be loved, but it was love. His version of it. And that should've been enough.

He thought about all this independent women nonsense society raised women on. Back in his mother's day — back when women in his family held real values — things were traditional. Like they should be. Women didn't have voices unless they were speaking about recipes, cleaning the house, or raising children. Now that women worked, it felt like a slap in the face to everything men had tried to build.

• • •

He thought about Novi. When he met her — twelve years younger than him — he knew he had found a wife he could mold. A woman who feared God. A woman who understood that submitting to her husband meant obeying him. Period.

She was determined to be all that God called her to be. Back then, she raved about the job she loved. He was working at the time too, but she made more money than him — and that cut him deep. He had two degrees and still couldn't out earn this young woman. He resented her for that. Thought, "Y'all want equality so bad? Then go out and work. Pay the bills." And he quit his job. Made it her responsibility. She was too prideful to ask anyone for help, so no one ever knew.

Manipulation, he figured, might've been his spiritual gift. It always got him what he wanted.

Eventually, he got the life he wanted. He'd watched Novi grow up in that church. Waited. And once she was legal, he made his move. She was green. Pure. He was her first. She wanted to wait until marriage — but he knew if he could get her good in bed, she'd never leave. He'd use that guilt, twist it, weaponize it. Make her feel obligated.

And he did.

• • •

With two decades of experience, he trained her in everything sexually. He thought she'd eventually learn to love him. He twisted scripture to fit his desires. Told her what they'd done was sinful — but he'd marry her, so she wouldn't look like a hypocrite. So that she could still sing in God's house. He knew the anointing meant everything to her. Especially once he found out she was adopted. Family mattered to her and he was determined to make one with her.

He never wanted a partner. He wanted ownership.

And when she started pulling away, he got strategic. Never pulled out during sex. Wanted her barefoot and pregnant. Said it all the time. He knew children tied her to him. That was more secure than any paycheck could ever be.

Now, look at him.

Sitting in a church courtyard, waiting on the man threatening to take all of that away from him. He'd worked too hard. He wasn't about to let go of what was his. He'd knock this young nigga out cold if he had to.

The air was different tonight.

Heavy.

Electric.

• • •

Zayven paced, fists clenched, jaw locked. He wasn't even on the preaching schedule. No one had asked him. And that fact alone made this rage burn even deeper.

Thought in his mind from what everyone was saying. They were talking. About him. About her.

About them.

He watched from the shadows as Nolen walked to his truck, loading up his drum kit and yelled loud enough for him to hear him.

"You think you slick," he said, voice angry. "I guess you think that makes you a man? Sleeping with someone else's wife while yours is home raising your kids?"

Nolen turned slowly, telling himself to remain calm but he had an edge to him that didn't feel like doing this tonight, not here. "You don't want to do this here."

"Why the hell not? Everything else happened here," Zay spat. "The flirting. The rehearsals. The late-night texting. Hell, even the lies. All of it — right here. In *my* church."

Nolen let out a chuckle — low, dismissive. To him, Zay's claim was nothing but illusion.

• • •

"This ain't your church."

"You can't deny it. You fuckin' my wife." He stepped closer. "You punk-ass bitch nigga."

Nolen laughed out loud. This wannabe preacher out here cursing like a street kid. Mr. Perpetrating Holy Man just said that.

"I won't deny it. But I never let my woman raise a family alone while I chased a pulpit I didn't earn."

Zayven froze. That hit. Hard. That's what folks were saying behind his back — and now Nolen said it to his face.

"You don't know what the hell you talkin' about."

"Don't I? Novi's working two jobs, my nigga, while you're out here dressed in thousand-dollar suits and preaching from IG Lives like that's gonna keep the lights on."

Zayven snapped hard, his words sharp and burned with fury. The sting of dismissal — of being disrespected by someone he considered beneath him — was too much. "I'm a man of God! I answered the call. Which, young brotha, you know nothing about."

● ● ●

"Nah, bruh. You ignored the *call* to be a husband. You wanted a platform. Not a family. You left her empty. I just showed up in the silence... my *brotha*."

Zayven stepped forward until they were face to face. He wanted to knock him out, but he held back. "You think she's yours now? That make you better than me?"

Nolen stepped back, shook his head, lips pressed tight — the pause stretched long enough to make Zay feel the warning. "I don't have to think. I felt it. Every time she looked at me. Every time she cried in my arms. I've touched parts of her soul you'll *never* see, man. You lost her long before I ever touched her body."

Zayven's nostrils flared. His chest rose. His rage was boiling.

Then Nolen quietly stepped closer. "You think you a victim?" He looked Zayven right in the eyes matching his dare and provocation for something physical if needed. "You ain't been a husband since the day you put that ring on her finger."

"You don't know nothing about what I do!"

"Nigga, I know you ain't held a *job* longer than six months in your entire marriage. I know she's been raising

• • •

your kids, paying your bills, and carrying your wannabe ministry."

Zayven's jaw locked. His heart pounded. The anger was palpable. He felt heat rising in his chest and in his hands.

"I know she cries in the car before leading worship while you check your suit and tie in the mirror, Nigga."

Zayven had enough. He swung — rage behind it. Nolen dodged, caught him, slammed him hard against the side of the truck. So hard that the sound of the metal rang out.

Zayven struggled, but Nolen held him there, locked tight with his forearm up under his neck. Nolen got close enough to his ear and said in a growling voice filled with anger.

"She stayed out of loyalty. But loyalty don't pay the bills. Loyalty don't stock the fridge. Loyalty don't raise two kids while you play preacher in a borrowed collar."

He pushed against his neck again and said to Zayven, "And if you *ever* put your hands on me again, I'll make you regret it in ways prayer can't fix."

Zayven's breath came ragged.

Defeated.

● ● ●

Cornered.

Nolen stepped back. Zayven slid slightly down the truck, wind knocked out of him, physically and emotionally.

"Gone home man. Be a father. Try being a man before you play one."

Zayven slid lower, breathing hard. He got up and started to walk away… but paused.

Zayven feeling defeated but knew he still was Novi's husband and that meant something that not even Nolen could grapple with. "She still wears my ring, nigga." Feeling immediately validated in his words.

But then Nolen walked around to his truck and not even not turning around hit back, "For now."

• • •

CHAPTER 30
The Removal Preparation

Truth was brought to the altar... but not for healing.

The conference room on the second floor of Devotion Heights Church adjacent to Bishop Byrd's office. the one usually reserved for budget talks and holiday planning. Now as of late it has been reserved for high level staff discussions and confidential matters. Today, the roster held the weight of betrayal, and the scent of gossip dressed up as concern.

A thick manila folder sat unopened in the center of a long mahogany table, polished high to shine. Inside: timestamped photos, audio transcripts, and printed text messages — damning evidence of the affair between Nolen and Novi.

Venus sat poised, draped in navy silk and righteousness, her eyes gleaming with vindication barely veiled behind faux concern.

Beside her, Janet crossed her arms smugly, her lips pursed like a woman finally delivering a long - overdue "I told you so."

•••

Across from them, Cassia sat stiff, hands folded in her lap. Her brows were furrowed. Torn. Silent.

Jeff Casen entered last, corporate and polished as ever, sipping from a Devotion Heights coffee tumbler. "Sorry," he said casually. "Traffic."

Bishop Byrd sat at the head of the table, eyes closed, hands steepled beneath his chin. When he finally looked up, it was with the weight of a man who had already made a decision.

"Let's get to it."

Venus leaned forward, grabbed the evidence and opened the folder turning it towards Bishop Byrd.

"Photos from outside the hotel. Audio phone calls from inside of Nolen's truck. Timestamped. Labeled. Verified." She passed copies to the Bishop. "And this was not a one-time lapse, Bishop. This was a pattern. Over several months."

Bishop studied the photos as if he was looking for an answer, and also like it was his first time seeing them.

Venus cleared her throat, She reached into her oversized leather bag and pulled out another thick envelope.

● ● ●

"Bishop," she began, sliding it across the table. "More documentation. I spoke with Elisse and she had additional information. These… these are not just isolated moments of weakness."

Bishop opened the envelope and thumbed through the photos — intimate angles taken from afar, grainy yet damning. Novi and Nolen. Hands held in parking lots. A kiss exchanged inside a vehicle. The timestamped images stretched over months. Different locations. Different times. Same story.

Cassia's stomach dropped. These weren't just from the previous set Elisse had presented. These were deeper cuts — surveillance-level precision. The kind of pictures that said: this was not a mistake. This was a lifestyle.

Venus continued. "Bishop, I told Elisse I would keep her updated. She's willing to provide more if needed. I also know, from a few of the praise team members, that some of these have already leaked."

Bishop's eyes narrowed. "Leaked? To who?"

Janet, silent until now, finally spoke. "A few have been uploaded anonymously to the 'Women of Worth' Facebook group. And they're spreading. I saw a post with over 250

• • •

comments — mostly from women from other churches across the DMV. It's... bad."

Jeff, arms folded, sat back in his chair and exhaled. "A private church Facebook group should never be the courtroom for this kind of mess. We all know what the Internet does with scandal — it multiplies it."

"Agreed, and no one said it was fair," Venus responded, her voice like ice. "But it's happening. The world is watching."

Cassia's eyes barely looked at the photos. She shook her head and looked down with her arms folded. Her chest tightened and her jaw clenched. "This is disgusting," she whispered.

Venus nodded, misinterpreting her. "I know. It's heartbreaking. But we must protect the body."

"No." Cassia interjected. "That's not what I am saying, I'm saying they both made this mistake."

Venus scoffed softly. "A mistake is a moment Cass. This was an affair. Ongoing. Brazen. And most importantly — a threat to the integrity of this ministry, and the integrity of Devotion Heights Church."

• • •

Jeff cleared his throat. "While I personally hold no ill will, I support whatever decision aligns with the spiritual and public image of this house."

Cassia glanced at him, eyebrows raised. "You support Venus?"

Jeff offered a shrug, noncommittal. "I support order. I stand behind whatever the executive team recommends. I trust your discernment, Bishop."

Cassia turned to him, eyes narrowing. "Really, Jeff? You were just saying how you believed God was using their ministry."

Jeff blinked slowly. "I support what's best for the ministry... as a whole."

Cassia thought about the scripture of a double-minded man is unstable in all of his ways. Jeff had no allegiance to anyone outside of himself. He was the epitome of this scripture. If you spoke with him about an issue, he'll say he agrees with you. And if the other person spoke of the issue he'll say he agrees with them.

"Order with bias isn't order," Cassia snapped.

• • •

Venus leaned forward. "Cass, I know you love Novi. We all do, really. But love can't excuse sin. And we must protect Teanir and her children from further harm. What message would it send to do nothing?"

Cassia sat back. Quiet now. Not agreeing — but outnumbered.

Bishop's face tightened. He turned slowly to look out the window even though the blinds were only partially open. "We've been in talks about launching satellite campuses. Streaming services across the country. Elevation-level moves. This kind of noise... this will destroy the credibility of everything we've built."

Janet leaned forward. "Which is why she must go. And frankly, Bishop, I believe it's time to promote someone who's proven herself faithful and above reproach."

Bishop raised an eyebrow. "And who do you suggest?"

"Me," Janet replied calmly. "I've been here. Serving. Consistent. I don't bring drama or distraction to the platform. I lead with order. It's time."

Venus chimed in like a seconding motion. "She's right Bishop. Janet should also lead the single. It's already charting. Why not ride that momentum with a clean vessel, one that's not tainted?"

Cassia flinched at the word vessel — as if Novi had suddenly become contaminated. Disposable.

Bishop didn't hesitate. "Alright. We'll have Sheila to schedule the removal meeting with Novi. I want Venus, Jeff, Cassia, and Lady Byrd present."

Cassia pushed back from the table slightly; her hands folded in her lap. "I won't be part of that meeting."

Everyone turned towards her. Venus, disgusted by her stance. Janet looks at Venus and Jeff looks at Cassia.

"What?" Venus asked.

Cassia's voice was clear, her tone even, but there was an unmistakable fire in her eyes. "I won't sit in any room where we're pretending this is justice. This is politics. You're removing one person from a two-person affair — and for what? Optics?"

"Cass" Bishop began.

"No," she interrupted, standing. "You'll have to answer to God for this. Because this ain't righteousness. This is retribution. And it's lopsided."

● ● ●

The silence was sudden. No one moved. Not even Jeff.

Cassia turned to leave, but Bishop called after her.

"Cassia, please wait."

She paused near the door but didn't turn around. Bishop stood, walking to her with slow, deliberate steps. He placed a hand on her shoulder.

"What's going on with you?" he asked quietly. "I thought you trusted me. After all these years, you can't follow me on this?"

Cassia finally turned, eyes filled with emotion.

"I follow God. Not agendas." Her voice was softer now, but each word landed with weight. "Isaiah 10:1 — 'Woe to those who make unjust laws, to those who issue oppressive decrees.' You're making decrees, Bishop. And you know in your heart that it's wrong."

For the first time in a long while, something cracked in Bishop Byrd's expression. Not shame. Not guilt. But recognition. A flicker of a man who once stood for something more than PR and platforms.

He wanted to change. Cassia saw it. But he wouldn't. He couldn't. Too much was at stake.

• • •

"She has to go," he whispered.

Cassia said "she deserved better than this. Bobby."

A nickname that she called him when he was first called into the ministry. Robert, he used to say, was his father's name. But since being promoted in ministry she respected the title he earned as Bishop. But now, she needed her words to land on her friend and for him to acknowledge what he was doing wasn't right.

Bishop looked at Cassia with a determined look on his face. "Then let us pray she finds it."

Cassia walked away without another word.

Bishop Byrd returned to the meeting and closed the folder. His voice was heavy.

"I will speak with Novi personally. Until then… She is to be removed from all ministry functions No worship. No Bible study. No public presence on behalf of this church until we meet with her."

He looked at Venus. "A time for her restoration will be considered at this meeting. I want you to pray about how long you feel that time should be. Venus, I'm leaving it up to you and Jeff to decide."

• • •

Janet smirked. Venus nodded slowly, satisfaction hidden behind solemnity.

The meeting ended. The folder remained.

Back in the conference room, Venus leaned over to Bishop.

"I also think it's time for Janet to lead worship starting this Sunday."

Bishop noticed that not only did Janet have another agenda but that Venus was lock-step with it as well. He didn't have another female worship leader and it was something about the female voice singing praises to God. He thought about it and hoped he was making the right decision. He nodded.

On his way out, Bishop spoke to Venus "Do make sure to call Sheila to set that removal meeting first thing tomorrow. I don't know how full my calendar is, but I'd like to set something up for at least 2 hours, just in case we need the extra time."

Jeff sighed and rubbed the back of his neck. "This... ain't gonna blow over easy."

• • •

Venus smiled thinly. "It's not meant to. It's meant to clean house."

CHAPTER 31
The Clarion Call

The Bishop answered — not to God, but to leverage.

After the meeting concluded and Venus boldly declared, *"It's time to clean house,"* everyone left the room one by one. Bishop Byrd sat still for a moment, the echo of her words lingering. His thoughts drifted back to the post-it note in the folder Elisse had left behind — *that* note. The one he quickly crumpled and shoved into his pocket before Sheila could see it. Even now, it unnerved him.

He questioned how Elisse could have possibly known what she did. The contents of that note weren't just invasive — they were intimate. Dangerous. The kind of knowledge that could only come from surveillance... or betrayal. It had been keeping him up at night.

As he stepped into his car, his phone rang. Startled, he glanced at the screen.

Elisse.

He had been planning to call her himself, but the fact that she rang first sent a chill through his body. It didn't feel

• • •

like divine timing — it felt like a summons from something far darker. He answered with a tired voice. "Praise the Lord."

"Praise the Lord, Bishop. This is Sister Elisse."

"Yes, how can I help you, Sister Scandri?"

"I just got off the phone with Venus. She told me about the meeting... and that you're finally going to take care of Novi once and for all."

He winced slightly at the eagerness in her tone. This should have been a matter of spiritual discernment, handled through prayer and council — not a crusade led by a mother with a vendetta.

"Well, Sister Scandri, that meeting was confidential. However... we did receive your additional photographs and audio files. You were quite thorough."

"I make it my business to be," she replied. "You never know when being thorough will come in handy."

He paused, the silence between them loaded.

"Well, Bishop," she continued. "I wanted to confirm you received my post-it."

"... Yes. Yes, I did."

● ● ●

"So we have an understanding, then?"

"What sort of understanding are you referring to, Sister Scandri?"

She cleared her throat and exhaled sharply.

"The kind that says if you *don't* get rid of Novi — and if you *don't* make Nolen go home and fix things with my daughter — then everyone will find out what kind of man you really are. The church. Your family. The board. Your neighbors. *All of them.* And not just that. Channel 8, NBC, CBS, ABC, FOX Baltimore... and the *Baltimore Sun.*"

He froze. A traffic light ahead of him turned green, but he didn't move. A car behind him honked. He waved an apology and pulled into a nearby empty lot, heart pounding in his chest.

"I don't understand how you came by this information," he said finally.

"It doesn't matter *how.* Just know I have it," she replied. "And if you care anything about your church, your marriage, your *name* — you'll do what needs to be done."

She let that hang before adding, "Teanir is my only child, Bishop. And I will *not* let her lose everything while you

• • •

sit on your hands. Now, it's your turn to make sure she gets what she deserves."

His body grew heavy, chest tight with panic. He wanted to ask for another meeting. He needed to know more — how deep this went, how much she had on him. But before he could say anything, his phone beeped with another incoming call.

It was his wife.

"I won't keep you, Bishop," Elisse said, hearing the beeping. "You better make this happen. Threaten Nolen — I don't care how. But by the end of this week, he better be back home with my daughter. You understand?"

He hesitated.

"All I know is this," she finished. "If you don't pull the trigger, *I* will. And believe me... you've got way more to lose than most."

Her voice softened mockingly. "Have a blessed evening, Bishop."

The line went dead.

He snatched the incoming call just before it went to voicemail.

• • •

"Hey love," his wife said warmly. "Can you pick up dinner on the way home? I took the chicken out too late."

"Yeah, of course," he replied, voice distant.

He drove the rest of the way home in silence, the weight of blackmail pressing hard on his chest. His mind spiraled — not about justice or integrity — but about survival.

He needed a plan.

Because damned if his life would be on display for the world to see... all because a young man couldn't keep his pants zipped.

• • •

CHAPTER 32
The Setup

In love... no — but obsessed to remove what was in the way.

The next morning, Venus woke up bright, early, and excited — like a child on Christmas morning, ready to tear into gifts from Santa. She slipped on her robe and barely acknowledged her husband Kendrick.

"Good morning, babe," he said warmly, moving in for a hug and kiss.

He had made dinner and theatre plans for that evening and was trying to confirm their outfits and schedule. But as he began asking about timing and attire, she cut him off abruptly.

"I don't know what you're wearing. That's something you should've figured out. I need to make sure I'm fully prepared for a call this morning — got to schedule the meeting with Sheila to finalize kicking Novi out of the church."

Kendrick blinked. "Wait... you're kicking Novi out of the church? Why? She's the most anointed one in the entire ministry. The way you said that didn't even sound right."

• • •

"It's what must be done. She's been whoring herself throughout the ministry."

"The entire ministry?" His eyes widened. "Wait — who else has she been sleeping with?"

"Nolen Jahlil."

"Jesus... who else?"

"It's just him," Venus said matter-of-factly, "but she's whoring herself to him — and that's enough. It's created a whoring spirit within the praise team. At this rate, she's turning the entire ministry into whores. And for that, she has to go."

Kendrick stared at her. "Babe, you just made that up. Why are you adding all this?"

"Ken," she said sharply, "I don't have time to go back and forth with you. She has to go. And I've been given the responsibility to make sure it happens. As administrator of this ministry, I have to ensure this kind of thing doesn't happen on my watch. And if it is happening — which it is — I'm going to take care of it."

"You're taking care of it," he said slowly. "It's amazing how personal you've made someone else's situation."

• • •

"Well, I'm needed. They need me. And poor Teanir — she doesn't have a clue how to keep her man happy. Nolen is a young man with needs she doesn't know how to meet. She needs training. I'm going to help her keep her husband."

Kendrick watched the excitement build on her face as she spoke about Nolen. He remembered the day she claimed the security cameras weren't working when she gave him his paycheck. Something about that had never sat right. He knew his wife. Before they were married, she'd made her rounds — always aligning herself with whoever held power or influence.

Now he wondered: Was she truly protecting Teanir, or trying to get closer to Nolen?

A look of disgust crossed his face. Without another word, he turned and went back to get dressed.

Venus grabbed her phone and called Sheila.

"Good morning, it's a great day at Devotion Heights Church in the DMV! We're praising the Lord and equipping the saints. This is Sheila — how can I bless you today?"

"Good morning, Sheila. This is Venus Johnson."

"Well good morning, honey. How can I help?"

• • •

"Bishop asked me to schedule a meeting with myself, Jeff, Bishop, Cassia, Novi, and Lady Byrd."

Sheila paused slightly, typing as she repeated, "Okay... you, Bishop, Jeff, Cassia, Novi, and Lady Byrd?"

"Oh, no — Cassia said she can't make it. So, take her off the list."

Sheila's eyebrow lifted slightly. The combination of people... the exclusion of Cassia... and Novi? Her gut told her something wasn't right. She took a moment, intentionally stalling.

"What date are you looking at? How much time should I block?"

"Whatever the first available is — I'll need two hours."

Today was Tuesday. Sheila thought to herself, Let me push this as far out as possible. Something's not sitting right.

"I have an opening next week, Wednesday evening."

"That's too far. This is urgent. Maybe we can do something before church?"

"Bishop doesn't take meetings on Sundays," Sheila said with a hint of satisfaction.

• • •

Venus exhaled. "Okay... what about Friday evening?"

"I've got a 7 to 9 p.m. slot this Friday."

Sheila silently hoped it would fall apart — Fridays were unpredictable.

"That's perfect. I'll let everyone know," Venus replied.

"What's the title of the meeting?" Sheila asked, part secretary... part watchdog.

Venus paused, then smiled to herself. She knew exactly what Sheila was doing. "Just call it Future Ministry Forecasting."

Sheila made note of it and hung up.

But her heart was heavy.

At her parents' house, Novi received a text from the Office of the Pastor:

MEETING: Future Ministry Forecasting
Friday, 7pm – 9pm
Location: Bishop's Office
Attendees: Bishop Byrd, Venus Johnson, Jeff Casen, Lady Byrd

• • •

Novi read it twice. She hadn't heard anything about a forecasting meeting. And Cassia wasn't listed. A tight, uneasy feeling formed in the pit of her stomach.

She tapped "Accept" and added it to her calendar.

Then she stared at the screen.

She needed Nolen more than ever — his touch, his scent, his voice. Just the thought of him usually gave her enough strength to push through.

But not this time.

This time... she felt the beginning of something unraveling.

• • •

CHAPTER 33
Uninterrupted

The world pulling them apart, but he carved out something still.

Nolen sat at The Spot. He'd been staying at his mother's house in Roland Park, turning over everything in his mind — what he truly wanted, how he and Novi would move forward, what their future could look like now that their relationship had been dragged into the open.

It was all a mess — thanks to his vindictive mother-in-law and his soon-to-be ex-wife, Teanir.

But none of that mattered in this moment . He needed Novi. Needed to hear her voice, feel her skin, anchor himself in the woman who was already home to him. She was going to be part of his family, his new beginning. She was the woman he deserved, the life he deserved, the love he had always longed for.

He smiled at the thought, then sent her a text:

NOLEN:
Sunshine, what you doing?

• • •

NOVI:
Nothing. I'm at my parents' house,
spending time with them and picking up the kids.
They're trying to get me to let them stay another night.
My mom wants to take them to the zoo tomorrow lol.
What about you? You miss me?

NOLEN:
Does a fish miss water when he not in it?

Novi laughed out loud. He had a way of taking the simplest phrases — things that might sound corny coming from anyone else and turning them into something that made her heart smile every time.

NOVI:
Yes he does lol!

NOLEN:
Let your parents keep the kids another day. I need to see you.

Her heart skipped. It had been weeks since he touched her — weeks of chaos and whispers, weeks of aching for his embrace, his scent, his presence.

NOVI:
Okay, that sounds good.
I want to see you too.
Where should I meet you? The Spot?

• • •

NOLEN:
Nah. I'm getting us a hotel.
I need to stretch out with you.
Meet me at the Baltimore Marriott Waterfront.
I'll leave a key for you at the desk.
See you soon. ☺

Her pulse quickened as she read his message. A hotel. Not just a quick meeting at The Spot, but a place where they could exhale — stretch out, linger, and exist without interruption.

She slipped her phone into her purse, trying to hide the smile tugging at her lips.

The kids were happily settled at her parents' house, and for once, she didn't have to worry about racing back or sneaking glances over her shoulder. Tonight, she could simply be his.

For the first time since the storm began, she felt something she hadn't dared in weeks: Excitement. Hope. Being with the love of her life — with no questions, no gossip, no stares — just them. That alone gave her something to cling to.

She had love. She had Nolen. And she was ready.

• • •

She told her mom the kids could stay for the zoo trip but to call when they were back. Her parents adored their grandchildren — if she let them, they'd keep them all summer and return them two days before school started.

At home, Novi packed a small bag. She fussed with her hair in the mirror, knowing it would be ruined soon enough anyway. Then she thought of the way he'd looked at her the last time — the way his touch stripped away the noise, the drama, the opinions of everyone else. With him, it was always just them. No judgment. No guilt. Only the raw truth of what they felt and this love that God himself allowed to grow.

By the time she stepped into the hotel lobby, a flicker of dread caught her. What if someone from Devotion Heights saw her? She wished they'd gone farther, outside Baltimore — but it was too late now. She retrieved the key from the front desk and made her way upstairs.

When she opened the door, Nolen was waiting. He pulled her in immediately, kissing her with an urgency that literally took her breath away. She dropped her bag, his hands cradling her face as he walked her backward toward the bed. He kissed her like a man reunited with the love of his life after war.

• • •

And in a way, they had been at war.
A war with judgmental church folk.
A war with failing marriages.
A war to be seen. To be loved. To keep love.

She melted into his arms — those same arms that had carried her through laughter and heartbreak. She loved him. This was exactly where she wanted to be, and at last, the war paused.

"I missed you… can you tell?" he smirked, flashing that grin that always disarmed her.

She smiled back. "I missed you more… can you tell?"

He chuckled. "Nope. Can't tell. You still got all these clothes on…"

She grinned, already unbuttoning her blouse — half-open anyway — and slipping out of her slacks, revealing black lace underwear.

"What's this?" he asked, his brow raised. He had a rule — dresses or skirts, no underwear.

"This is just what I had on today. I'm sorry. How can I make it up to you?"

"I thought you'd never ask… Take them off."

• • •

She obeyed. He lifted the underwear to his nose, inhaling deeply — his body already overcome with need.

"Damn, girl."

Then he kissed her again, deeper this time, urgency flaring between them. He led her to the bed, raised her legs onto his shoulders, and gripped her thighs as he went down on her — hungrily, like a man starved after battle, devouring her cries, her moans, her surrender.

She cried out, shaking beneath him as he feasted on her completely, not stopping until she came hard in his mouth and he drank every drop.

"I want you to come so much that there's nothing else to think about but us," he whispered, eyes locked on hers, licking between each sentence. "Novi..." lick "I want you..." suck, flick "...like this."

She came again, convulsing in his grip, and he held her steady like a shield.

He knew her body. Knew every tremor. Every swell. Every surrender. He kissed her through it, and then his words cut through the night.

"Be my wife."

• • •

One last flick, one last pull, and she gushed into his mouth again, crying out his name.

He rose and pulled her higher onto the bed. He needed to be inside her — the only fortress where judgment couldn't reach, where gossip couldn't poison, where love reigned uninterrupted.

He slid into her with purpose. His face showed the ache of missing her too much, and he filled her fully. She gasped at the pressure — the ache of his passion — but welcomed it. It was pain wrapped in pleasure, rebellion wrapped in release — and she came hard. Again. And again.

Every thrust was defiance. Every gasp, every moan was a cry of protest against the world that wanted to keep them apart.

He flipped her over, kissed her neck, and entered her from the side, one leg raised on his shoulder. He groaned her name again and again — a name once whispered in restraint, now shouted like victory, as if every syllable broke another chain.

"Face me, baby. Look at me," he said softly, love and fire in his eyes.

• • •

He cupped her breasts, rolled her nipples between his fingers, pressing her past every limit until her body shook and collapsed beneath him. He chuckled at the sight of surrender written on her body — it kept him hungry, kept him alive.

She couldn't even stand. He teased, "Can you please go and grab me a towel?"

She tried, but the moment she got to all fours, he was behind her again, sliding in slow — just to feel her ripen and release one more time. The bed was soaked. Neither cared.

She begged for a break, breathless.

"Okay, baby, you want a small break?"

She nodded.

He stood. She slid off the bed, thinking the break was real. But he dropped to his knees, spread her thighs, and kissed her there again. Her legs convulsed violently, her cries like battle drums, his name falling from her lips with every lick.

"Nolen!"

"Call my name," he commanded.

And she did — over and over, his name falling like surrender and victory in the same breath.

● ● ●

When it was over, they collapsed together — sweat and tears, laughter and silence. They lay there, spent, safe, wrapped in each other.

Their bodies had spoken everything their mouths didn't need to.

Longing.

Need.

Ache.

Love.

Pain.

Truth.

They understood each other in a way no one else could. This was war. And this was love. Uninterrupted. And tonight — they had won.

• • •

CHAPTER 34
Tomorrow Can Wait

The world would wait. Tonight, they chose each other.

Nolen woke and felt her absence immediately. The space beside him was cold.

On the balcony, silhouetted against the city lights, stood Novi. The hotel robe draped softly around her, the wind teasing her curls — loose when he had taken her to bed, now tightly coiled and dancing in the breeze. She looked like poetry in motion.

He rose and joined her. The moment she felt his presence; she closed her eyes. Nothing felt better — except having him inside her. She reached back, took hold of his arms, and smiled.

"I thought you were sleeping," she whispered, kissing his hands.

"I was," he said, voice low. "But I didn't feel you next to me. Hard to stay asleep without you. Come back to bed."

• • •

She turned into his chest, holding him close. He felt it instantly — something heavier pressed between her heartbeat and his.

"What's wrong?" he asked.

She looked up, startled. "How did you know?"

He gave her a look. "I know you babe, and not just like this..." His hand traced down her arm... but in my spirit. I can feel it when something's off. And right now, I feel it... what's got you afraid and anxious."

She sighed heavily, tears filling her eyes.

"I thought I drew all that out of you when you walked through that door," he said quietly. "Guess I didn't do a good enough job."

She looked up, unsure if he was joking. Her face *always* betrayed her, and he could see the flicker of irritation, the confusion — the sting of him falling back on the way men often did, assuming sex could fix everything.

Then he reached for her hand, a soft smile curving his lips. The warmth of it disarmed her. Novi exhaled, smiling back, relief washing through her chest as she softened.

"You did," she said quietly. "I was just looking at my

• • •

phone. Sheila sent me a message… Bishop wants to meet with me."

"What's it about?"

"Future Ministry Forecasting." She shrugged, though her eyes betrayed her.

He kissed her forehead. "Well, there you go. Nothing to stress over, baby."

But even as he held her, his gut told him otherwise.

"I don't know… something doesn't feel right. Venus, Jeff, Bishop, and Lady Byrd will be there. But Cassia's not on the invite. If this were really about ministry forecasting, wouldn't she be there too?"

He paused, jaw tightening as Jeff's words from the parking lot replayed in his mind. The unease pressed heavy against his chest.

"Babe, what is it? Why are you so angry all of a sudden?" Just as he could feel her, she could feel him. Their connection was unlike anything either of them had ever known — soul to soul, spirit to spirit.

He swallowed back the truth. Tonight wasn't the night for shadows. She deserved her joy, the glow that made her eyes

• • •

shine, the soft, unguarded music of her laughter. Tomorrow could carry the weight of schemes and whispers.

Tonight was theirs — warm, breathless, wrapped in skin and closeness.

Their bond was unlike anything he had known, a closeness so deep it felt as if they breathed each other's emotions. He forced his mind away from the storm, let himself think of Napa, and smiled.

"I'm good, baby," he murmured, pulling her close. "It's getting chilly out here. Let's go back inside... and maybe I can go back inside too."

Her laughter rang soft against the night air, and together they slipped back inside.

He held her, and for now, that was enough. Though his body ached to claim her, tonight her nearness was the greater gift. Her scent lingered on his skin — familiar, intoxicating. Home. She drifted into sleep in his arms, while he lay awake, watching her. Protecting her.

He knew they were plotting against her. If it came to it, he had the means to take her far away. To hide her where no one could touch what they had. But those thoughts were for another day.

● ● ●

Tonight, all that mattered was her peace, her warmth against him, the sweetness of her love. He thanked God for her — this woman who had undone him, and loving Novi didn't feel like sin or something that should've been forbidden.

Novi was perfect. Even her body — especially her body. There was a flawless symmetry to her curves, the kind that felt effortless and deliberate, as if crafted with intention. She was the kind of beautiful that made him pause, the kind that lingered in his mind long after he looked away. He'd seen many women, but none who left him restless just by existing. He closed his eyes and let those thoughts lull him to sleep.

"Tomorrow will take care of itself," he whispered as he drifted off.

The next morning, Nolen had arranged a couple's massage and breakfast on the balcony.

"Good morning, sunshine," he said, pulling her close. "Get showered. We've got massages coming."

When Novi saw the spread — and when he told her the therapists were on their way up — she smiled. No, she beamed. And that smile reached somewhere deep inside him, satisfying a hunger no meal ever could.

• • •

He stood next to her, kissing her forehead. She exhaled and said "Don't you think I've already been massaged enough?" she teased, laughing.

"Nope. I think you need a lot more." He started the shower, stepped in — glancing back at her. "You ready, gorgeous?"

"Uh, no. If I get in there with you, we're not getting any massages today."

He chuckled softly. She was right.

Just the sound of the shower made him think of her body... and just like that, he was hard. Again. He tried to calm himself, tried to think of anything else — baseball game... third man out... safe on first...

He glanced down, hoping the distraction would work, then chuckled. Nope. Not a chance.

He called out to her, half-apologizing — but the truth was simple: he needed her again.

She playfully complained there wouldn't be enough time.

"They'll wait," he said. "I can't help it when you're near me."

• • •

He came up behind her at the bathroom mirror, kissed her neck, and gently lifted her leg, holding it steady in his hand. Slowly, deliberately, he slid inside her from behind, his eyes never leaving her reflection in the mirror.

He searched for that look — the one she'd given him at The Spot the first time, and again that night in Room 318. That unguarded, look of this woman…undone.

And then he saw it. And it undid him.

Her leg trembled and he caught her just as she started to lose balance, held her steady beneath her breasts, and kissed her shoulder as she came hard, pleasure spilling down her thighs.

But he didn't stop. He kept moving until her back-to-back orgasms left her breathless, her chest heaving, her body weak beneath his. He drove deeper, grunting low against her neck as he emptied himself inside her completely.

They showered quickly.

By the time they emerged, the massage therapists had already been waiting 45 minutes. Nolen apologized at the door, his tone calm and steady, as if even this disruption could be handled with grace. Novi, on the other hand, embarrassed

• • •

easily. The thought that they might have heard everything made her stomach turn.

But then he looked at her — that quiet, grounding gaze that always steadied her — and the heat of embarrassment melted away.

They walked to the massage tables and stretched out side by side. As she exhaled into the silence, he reached across the gap and laced his fingers with hers. The gesture said more than words could: *I'm here. You're safe with me.* His hand locking with hers made her feel safe, covered, and secure.

Room service arrived with lunch just as they finished.

That's when his phone lit up. Bishop Byrd. Nolen's brows furrowed. Why now?

"Who is it?" Novi asked softly.

He didn't want to lie, but he didn't want to fracture their peace either.

"No name came up — so no one important," he said casually.

Technically true. He'd never saved Bishop Byrd's number, and now he was glad of it.

● ● ●

There was no way he was letting anything — or anyone — interrupt this. Not her. Not today.

They ended the day wrapped in each other's arms, watching the harbor, feeling the wind.

For the first time in a long time, it felt like old times.

It felt like home.

• • •

CHAPTER 35
A Man in Love

He chose her — not in secret, but in the face of power.

The afternoon sun filtered gently through the stained-glass windows of Devotion Heights Church. Bishop Byrd sat behind his desk, fingers steepled in quiet contemplation, waiting for Nolen to arrive. The energy in the room was still — deceptively calm. There was no judgment in the Bishop's heart today — at least, that's what he told himself.

Only concern.

Love.

A desire to restore order.

And also — though it made him uneasy — a desire to protect himself. Not just himself, he told himself again, but the people who would hurt the most if his own dirty laundry were dumped out for the world to see: his congregation, his reputation, his community, and most importantly, his wife and children. He wanted to approach it from a place of wisdom — wisdom that should make sense to any reasonable man.

The door opened.

• • •

Nolen stepped inside, his walk steady but cautious.

"Bishop," he said with a respectful nod.

"Son," Bishop replied, gesturing toward the chair across from him. "Sit down, please."

There was a pause. Not awkward — but heavy.

"I appreciate you making time to meet with me," the Bishop began, his voice warm but lined with paternal concern. "I asked you here because... I care about you. And I'd be lying if I said I didn't also care deeply about Teanir and your boys."

Nolen sighed. His sons — always the topic. As if they didn't mean the world to him. As if he wasn't thinking about their wellbeing with every decision he made — including choosing Novi. He wanted to tune out right then, but he decided to hear the Bishop out.

Bishop leaned back, his tone heavy but deliberate. "I care about your trajectory here, in this ministry. It's no secret the political weight your family holds in this city and state. But aside from that—I respect and admire the Jahlil family. I've known you since you were a boy, Nolen. I've seen the man you've become.

Talented.

• • •

Smart.

Determined.

Called.

"But now, you're standing at a crossroads son." Bishop Byrd had a way of making you feel like you were the best thing God ever put on this earth — layering on warmth and compliments like a father figure. But beneath it all was a setup. The hammer always came next. It was his gift. It was also his weapon. Manipulative — because he made it sound like care.

Nolen nodded slowly, eyes locked on him, listening — guarded.

"Now, I won't pretend this hasn't gotten messy," Bishop continued. "But the Bible is clear: a man leaves his father and mother and cleaves to his wife. That covenant is sacred, son. It's an oath you made — before God, your family, and your wife. Marriage isn't easy, even with the finest of women, But it's holy. And what's holy must be protected."

He leaned forward, lowering his voice—the way he always did when he wanted people leaning closer, hanging on his words.

• • •

"You've got boys, Nolen. Sons who look up to you. Sons who will learn what manhood looks like by watching you. What do you want them to see? That when things get complicated, you leave? Or that you stayed, prayed, persevered, and fought for your family?"

The words cut deep. Nolen felt the familiar sting of guilt press against his chest. He pictured his boys — his little men — watching, copying, and learning manhood in ways that words could never teach. But he also remembered the silence in that house, the weight of a loveless marriage, the ache of pretending. Was that the manhood Bishop wanted him to pass down?

Nolen shifted in his seat, jaw tightening. He wasn't sure if the Bishop was challenging him or cornering him. Either way, he refused to let guilt decide his future.

Nolen exhaled, his shoulders already tight from the weight of the conversation.

"I understand what you're saying, Bishop. And I respect you, you know that. But with all due respect—you don't know what that house felt like. You don't know what I carried from day one. I sacrificed every single day in a marriage that wasn't built on love—just obligation. The only

• • •

reason I stayed as long as I did was for my sons. But I can't go back to Teanir. There's nothing there for me anymore. Nothing to hold on to. We never had love—not real love. And I'm tired of pretending. For real, it's wearing me thin."

The Bishop looked down, lips pressed flat.

"I know reconciliation can feel impossible," he said softly. "But God is still in the business of healing what's broken. You think I've been married to First Lady Jacquiline all these years without trials? You think we haven't had seasons of silence, of grief, of distance—her more than me, I'll admit."

He rose and came around the desk, leaning against the front with his hands folded, his posture calm but deliberate. "I'm not asking you to pretend nothing happened. I'm asking you to believe God can still work—that He can redeem what the enemy tried to destroy. Go back home, son. To Teanir. To your boys. Don't let a moment of passion rob you of the ministry of being a husband and a father."

Nolen looked up, jaw clenched, anger simmering beneath the surface. He thought about how widespread this had become... everybody weighing in, everybody with an opinion on how he should move forward with his life. Where

● ● ●

were all these concerns when he was reckless in college and Teanir kept getting pregnant?

He hated people in his business — especially church people. Especially Bishop Byrd, who had been like a father to him once.

"I've made my peace with it. I don't believe God would want me to stay in something He never called me to. Teanir and I were never meant to be. We both know that."

Bishop Byrd's tone shifted—colder now, sharper. The pastoral father talk wasn't working. He had to press harder. Not just for Nolen's sake, but for his own. He hated the feeling of someone holding something over him, hated having to push this far. Normally, he would've prayed, offered counsel, and trusted God to do the rest. But not this time. This time, he needed the seed planted, watered, and forced to grow—one way or another.

"So you just throw it all away? Your witness? Your role? Your future in this church? All those plans your mama's made for you in politics—for what, son?"

Nolen didn't flinch.

"I'm not throwing anything away. I'm choosing joy. Peace. Love — Bishop, *real* love. And it's sad you don't seem

• • •

to know the difference. And you bringing up politics like that? That's not gonna move me. My mother can't stand Teanir. She's the one who said being with her was holding me back. You don't know what you're talking about. And even if that were the case, I'd still give it all up for the love and support I know I have with Novi."

The Bishop's voice exploded, shaking the room. Sheila, outside the office, rushed to shut the second door.

"This is not an option! You will NOT walk away from your wife, your kids, or continue to jeopardize this ministry!"

Nolen's confusion burned into fire, but Bishop pressed on, stepping closer, his tone sharp with authority.

"Man to man... if you think you can disobey the leadership in this house—without consequence—think again."

For the first time, Nolen saw him differently. Not as a spiritual father to admire, but as a man exposed. Desperate. Threatened.

And he thought of Novi.

If this is how he's coming at me, how will they come at her? He stood.

• • •

"Where you think you going, boy? I ain't done talking to you."

Nolen turned, fire in his chest. "But I'm done listening."

Bishop stepped forward, voice low, biting. "Don't think that this church, this community — even your name — will survive this unscathed. There will be repercussions. Repercussions that will make you wish you had made a different choice."

Nolen had his hand on the door.

"I hear you. And if God tells me to go back—I'll go. But until then, I'm not moving because of threats or guilt. I'm moving based on what's real. And this—this love—is real."

Bishop exhaled, realizing he had gone too far. Still, he couldn't back down. He had to protect himself.

"You sure this ain't just lust, son?"

Nolen met his eyes, steady, though heat surged in his chest. Insulted. Wounded. How dare he reduce what he and Novi had into something cheap, something carnal.

"I know what lust is, Bishop. This ain't that. She sees me. We connect — deep. I've never had that with anyone. As

• • •

a man, I raise my boys. I've been present and will continue to do so. And contrary to what you believe, Novi wants that too. She believes in me, and I believe in us. This is love, not lust."

He paused, then said it plainly.

"Bishop. I've given up so much already, and I'm not losing Novi or my happiness for anybody."

The Bishop straightened, fighting to hold authority. His hands lifted in a helpless gesture.

"Then you leave me no choice. Consequences will come — spiritually, professionally, personally. A storm is coming, and you're not ready for it. Don't say I didn't warn you when it knocks you to your knees."

Nolen's voice was low but unshaken. "This whole fiasco about us is a storm already," he said. "And guess what? I'm still standing." He looked at Bishop Byrd with a look of disgust and disappointment. He turned and walked out. Without speaking another word.

Leaving Bishop Byrd alone — fuming, rattled, and calculating.

Threatened in a way he hadn't felt in years.

Later in the day, Nolen made the call to his attorney.

"I'm ready to start the divorce proceedings," he said, voice steady. "I've waited long enough."

The attorney didn't need much explanation. He'd heard stories like this before — but never one this tangled in spiritual warfare and public scrutiny. He agreed to begin immediately. But the news traveled fast. Within 24 hours, Elisse had caught wind of the attorney's involvement. She wasn't surprised. She was activated.

"Time to make that move," she said out loud.

But before she dealt with Nolen, she had one more thing to ensure:

That Bishop Byrd made good on his end of their deal.

That Novi Jaxson — his precious worship leader — would be removed.

Erased.

Silenced.

Once that was done, she'd turn her full attention to Nolen.

• • •

And she'd get him back under her thumb.

By any means necessary.

Because political family or not —

There's nothing stronger than a mother's love for her child.

And Elisse was ten toes down for Teanir. Always.

• • •

CHAPTER 36
The Removal

If restoration is like crucifixion – she'd carried the shame alone

Elisse was ready to take Novi down — and today was the day.

She'd been in close communication with Venus, who had now become her unofficial informant for all things Devotion Heights. Funny, Elisse had never realized how much of a busybody Venus truly was until all of this came to light with her son-in-law. But Elisse was from the hood — she knew an opportunist when she saw one. And baby, Venus Johnson was one through and through.

Still, that was good for her. You use tools for what they're purposed for. And Venus Johnson was purposed and poised to help get that home-wrecking wench away from her son-in-law, out of the church, and out of sight. Her daughter and grandchildren shouldn't have to sit through another Sunday looking at that lying-ass face.

It should've been Bishop doing more. But she hadn't had time to speak with him yet about how the meeting with Nolen went — or if he was going back to Teanir. She couldn't

• • •

focus on that yet, especially after hearing from a church member who worked at City Hall. The message was clear: Nolen had filed for divorce.

Whatever Bishop did clearly wasn't enough. If anything, it may have pushed him further away. Bishop Byrd was about to learn a hard lesson:

Don't play with Elisse.

Back at her restaurant, Elisse fanned herself in the hot kitchen It was warmer than usual, with four large catering orders going out — and one of them was for the church. A post-meeting "celebration" that would follow Novi's removal.

Bishop and the leadership would be surprised, but Elisse was going to be there in person — to see the wreckage for herself and get firsthand information instead of just relying on Venus, who had a habit of exaggerating. Balanced information always matters, and what better way to get it than while serving up her famous fried chicken, cornbread, cabbage, mostaccioli, butter pecan pie, and homemade ice cream?

Her cell phone rang. It was Teanir.

• • •

"Mama — " her voice broke almost instantly.

"What is it, baby? What's wrong?"

"You know Catrice? Sister Mabry's daughter that works at City Hall?"

Elisse already knew where this was going. She wanted to tell her daughter not to worry, that everything was being handled — but Teanir, even with her Park Heights upbringing, had a soft heart. Empathy even for someone like Novi. She couldn't tell her just yet.

"Yeah, I know that girl ain't never liked you. Her own mama told me she had to check her for running her mouth. You can't trust people like that. What's she lying about now?"

Teanir paused. She remembered how Catrice used to taunt her — jealousy, blue-gray eyes, her hair, everything. Still, she wasn't quick on her feet like Nolen and hated that she was even thinking about him now.

"She said Nolen filed for divorce." Her voice broke once again. Tears followed.

"Girl, you know that girl got it out for you. Don't believe a thing unless you've been served. Did Nolen say he was filing?"

• • •

Teanir thought about it. No — he hadn't said it. But everything since the affair came to light said otherwise. Still, she convinced herself that no woman could have sex that good — not good enough to make a man abandon his entire life. She believed it was a trick of the enemy. And that if she prayed harder, fasted longer, and waited on God, He would show up.

"You right, Mama. I'm trusting God to save my marriage and my family. You know there are two things I don't play about — my money and my family."

"Good girl. You know your mama's proud of you. I gotta finish these orders before I head out. I love you, Tea. Kiss the boys for me."

Elisse hung up and immediately texted Venus.

ELISSE:
What's going on? Y'all in the meeting yet?

VENUS:
Hey. Not yet. Bishop's finishing a call.
We're all just waiting in the lobby.
Novi's not here yet. I hope she shows up.

ELISSE:
Let me know when she gets there. And when it's over.
I want to bring y'all some food.
I know it's been a long day.

• • •

VENUS:
Girl, yes! And can you bring Ken some of
your Butter Pecan Pie?
He loves it.
I'll Zelle you the money.

ELISSE:
Don't even worry about it.
I'll bring him an extra pie — on me.
It's the least I can do after all
you've done for my family.
I appreciate you.

VENUS:
Sheila's calling us in now.
I'll text you when she gets here.

ELISSE:
Ok.

Elisse exhaled deeply, a long-overdue breath. The plan was in motion. One piece of the puzzle nearly complete. She thanked God and hummed to herself as she packed up the last of the food.

By the time Novi arrived, the sun was already low — casting long golden streaks across the polished floor of Devotion

• • •

Heights. The admin desk buzzed like always. The same floral arrangements stood at the front vestibule.

But the air?

It had shifted.

Something cold.

Something wrong.

She passed Jeff Casen in the hallway. He nodded — small, polite. Nothing else.

Not a smile.

Not a word. Not even an ounce of friendly banter as he always had with her.

Inside the office, Venus sat to the left of Bishop Byrd, looking like she was about to officiate a memorial. Lady Byrd sat to the right; concern stitched into her brow.

Cassia wasn't there.

Novi sat down, heart pounding.

Bishop's face was stone. "Novi," he began. "We've been made aware of some very serious and troubling developments."

● ● ●

Venus folded her hands like she was at a funeral. A grieving widow. Her tone was drenched in faux concern – and had the nerve to look solemn as if she was losing something.

"There has been undeniable evidence presented," she said with fake gravity. "Photographs. Audio recordings. Confirmations of behavior unbecoming of your position — both in your house and in this one."

Novi's throat tightened. Her vision blurred with tears. She tried to speak — but all that came out was one broken word.

"I — "

Bishop didn't even blink.

"This isn't about guilt or innocence anymore," he said. "This is about stewardship. About protecting the integrity of this church."

Her ears rang. All she could hold onto were the words "not about guilt"—as if the decision had already been made. They weren't here to listen.

"You are extremely gifted, Novi. You have a presence, an ache for God that no one can deny. The members here love

• • •

you—we love you." There it was again…that fatherly, manipulative tone.

"We've entrusted you with leading worship, with being an example for others to aspire to," Bishop continued. "And as the Bible says, to whom much is given, much is required. You failed to uphold that responsibility. And now, because of what you've done, the blood of many is on your hands—your marriage, and Nolen's."

"Nolen… " she whispered, barely audible, choking on her own heartbreak.

She wanted to say: I love him.

But she knew: they didn't care.

She had no one. No Nolen. No Cassia. And in this moment, not even God felt present.

"I have given my all to this music ministry, to the call" she finally managed. "I've sacrificed. Prayed. Fasted — "

Venus stood up slightly in her seat, gesturing wildly now by shaking her head so that her shoulder length hair whipped on either side, her voice speaking with indignation.

• • •

"To the call?" Venus repeated, her voice high-pitched with disbelief as she jerked her head back like she'd been slapped.

She blinked rapidly, then looked around the room — slow and deliberately pausing on each face like she was scanning for witnesses to the blasphemy she just heard.

She didn't wait for an answer.

She leaned forward, eyes wide, her voice with more purpose with each word. "What was the call? The call to destroy a family? To seduce a married man? Was that the call of God, Novi — or was that the call of your flesh?"

Lady Byrd, noticing the tension in the room — and not fully agreeing with the way Venus was going in on Novi — cleared her throat and spoke.

"Well, let's settle down now and get some order," she said calmly, her voice carrying just enough weight to silence the room. "We are not here to further accuse you, Novi, or beat a dead horse. The fact of the matter is this: because of the situation you now find yourself in, it is in the best interest of the ministry—and of Devotion Heights Church—that you take some time to reflect on your actions. Think about how you can return to God... even in this."

● ● ●

Bishop Byrd sat back in his chair, silently pleased. This was exactly what he needed. His wife didn't speak often, but when she did, people listened. Her words carried authority and the air of wisdom, always striking the right chord between compassion and correction. He loved that about her.

And now that she had softened the edge, it was his turn to drive the point home—to put the nail in the coffin.

"We are a ministry of order," he said smoothly, his tone warm but sharpened by finality. "And just so you're aware, Novi, we had a leadership meeting prior to this one to discuss how we would move forward and what the consequences of your actions should be. This is not something we're taking lightly. Much thought and prayer have gone into this."

The calmness of his delivery only made the words heavier. It wasn't just correction, it was judgment, cloaked in prayer.

Novi's face burned. Shame spread through her chest, thick and suffocating. And then came the whisper of doubt. What if they were right? What if her gift had been tainted, her choices a stumbling block for people who once looked up to her?

● ● ●

She stared at her hands in her lap, too heavy to lift her gaze. She could still feel Nolen's love like a pulse in her veins, but here, under their scrutiny, it felt smaller, fragile. For the first time, she wondered if she had ruined not only herself—but him too.

Novi sat frozen, numb. Her mind drifted — not to herself, but to Nolen. She thought about what this meant for him. He loved playing the drums. Loved being an instrument to the praise and worship in this house. Everyone knew he didn't need to serve at Devotion Heights — his family was wealthy and connected. There were dozens of larger, flashier churches he could have chosen. But he stayed here. He chose this house. This ministry. Because of the oil. Because of the music.

She couldn't bear the thought of him being removed too.

"If I may," she said, her voice trembling, "please pray about and reconsider if you're thinking of removing Nolen from the ministry. This ministry is his life." Her words fell almost in a whisper, as she fought the tears and the lump rising in her throat, threatening to betray her at any moment. "He really loves it—as much as he loves his sons. If you take that away, it will crush him. Please... don't."

● ● ●

Bishop looked at her, visibly thrown.

His first thought? She was deeply, unmistakably in love with Nolen. He knew that kind of love — the kind where you'd give up your own heartbeat if it meant the one you loved could live.

His second thought unsettled him more: how long had this been going on? For feelings to run this deep, to sound this entangled? This wasn't lust. This was love's devotion. This was the kind of love that rivaled vows, that pulled at the soul.

And then another question surfaced, sharp and cold: why was she pleading for him? Why focus on Nolen's future when her own was hanging in the balance? Most people would cling to self-preservation. Was she really that selfless… or just blinded by love?

Either way, she must not have realized — Nolen was never part of this meeting. He never was.

"Daughter," he said flatly, "I don't know what you're talking about. I've already spoken with Nolen and instructed him to return home to his wife. This meeting is about you. We are not removing Nolen—nor had we ever intended to remove him from ministry or from this house. He has a place here that cannot be replaced. But you? With your position—

• • •

we have many worship leaders. We don't have many drummers."

Bishop sat up straighter, locking eyes with her—his gaze sharp, final.

"Now, as I said, I've appointed leadership over the Praise Ministry. That leadership now falls to Jeff Casen and Venus Johnson. I've asked them both to determine an appropriate course of action for your deeds—your deeds alone."

He turned to them.

"You may speak."

Novi's stomach sank, shame burning through her like fire. She had begged for mercy on Nolen's behalf, only to learn he was never the one on trial. It was her. Only her. The room felt smaller, air thinning, their eyes pressing in from every side. Her voice, her gift, her calling—it all hung in the balance, and in this moment, she wondered if she had already lost it.

Venus leaned forward, ice in her voice and a heavy sigh as if it hurt her to say what she was going to say.

"We're recommending an indefinite removal from all ministry responsibilities, effective immediately," she said

• • •

smoothly. "That includes Sunday services, Bible study, prayer meetings, and any musical engagements — including the single you recorded. While we are aware that it's your voice on the track, Bishop has cleared it, and Janet will now be the official voice for all future worship engagements."

Her tone sharpened. "This is for your sake... and for theirs."

"For my sake... and theirs?" Novi whispered, her voice breaking as tears slid down her face. It felt like a weight had slammed down on her chest, pushing her into the floor, making it impossible to lift up her head and look them in the eye.

"For the body of Christ," Venus said coldly.

Novi swallowed hard. Her throat burned. Her chest tightened.

"Is that all?" she asked, slowly rising to her feet.

Bishop folded his hands, but the finality in his tone cut like a blade.

"No. It isn't. Marriage is something we honor in this house. We don't walk away when things get hard. We don't flee when it gets uncomfortable. When the Lord releases me to restore you, then we'll have a discussion. But until then, you are to step down and take some time away from Devotion Heights."

He paused. "Ask the Lord for direction. There are other churches and ministries that will welcome you with open arms."

Jeff nodded. "I agree with everything that's been said here today. I've been married for a long time, and I believe your departure from this church will give you the space to work on your marriage — outside of Devotion Heights. And at the same time, allow Nolen and Teanir to work on theirs... from within this house."

Lady Byrd's discomfort was written all over her face. This? This wasn't what they had discussed at home. Removing Novi from ministry — fine. But from the church itself? That wasn't part of the original conversation.

She opened her mouth, but before she could speak, she noticed Venus — her smile, the way she kept glancing down at her phone, texting.

Something felt off.

'That's when Novi spoke again, her voice quieter now, but laced with pain.

• • •

"Just so I'm clear… I'm being sat down indefinitely. I'm not allowed to worship in this house — the same house I've served in since I was a child. And during this time, I'm to seek another church while I work on my marriage… but Nolen and Teanir can remain here and work on theirs?"

She paused. "Why am I not being offered the same grace?"

Venus didn't hesitate.

"Because you're a distraction," she snapped. "As long as you're here, Nolen will never give his family — or his wife — the attention she deserves. This isn't just about you. It's about all of us."

Bishop jumped in, cutting the air.

"Novi. We've been clear. And now you're clear."

His eyes narrowed, voice stern.

"If you need a recommendation to another church, I'll make that call. But as of now, we do not want to see you return to Devotion Heights until everything — your marriage, your life, your walk with God — has been fully restored."

He raised a single brow as he delivered the final blow. A sentence of separation.

• • •

From her church.

From her community.

From her spiritual home — the one she'd grown up in, the one where she first met Jesus.

She was now spiritually homeless.

Hurt. Devastated. Hollowed out from the inside.

And no one in that room — not one person — cared enough to reach for her hand to offer prayer.

She walked out without saying another word. Her heels echoed across the marble floor, sharper with each step.

By the time she reached her car, she could barely breathe. She gripped the steering wheel and sobbed—not just from shame… but from betrayal. From silence.

For a long moment, she let the tears pour, chest heaving, body shaking. But beneath the ache, beneath the hollow wreck of what they had done to her, something else stirred.

They had stripped her of a title. They had tried to silence her voice. But they hadn't taken her song. They couldn't.

• • •

Novi wiped her face with trembling hands, the sting of humiliation still raw, but her jaw set tighter now. They might have cast her out of the building, but they would never cast her out of God's presence.

And in that moment—between grief and grit—she whispered through her tears:

"I still belong to You."

CHAPTER 37
Her Plans

She prayed with them. Then plotted without them

Elisse stood in the kitchen of her restaurant, still humming a gospel tune as she checked the text from Venus.

It's done – she's out!

She smiled so hard it nearly cracked her lip gloss. Victory was hers.

Grabbing the last of the catering trays, she packed up her famous fried chicken, cornbread, cabbage, mostaccioli, and of course — two full Butter Pecan pies. One for the church, and one specially wrapped for Kendrick. She told herself it was just food, just generosity. But deep down, she knew she was making a statement.

She arrived at Devotion Heights with practiced humility, telling Sheila at the front that she had all this food left over and didn't want it to go to waste. A gesture of kindness, of course.

Lady Byrd wasn't fooled for a second.

• • •

Still, she accepted a to-go plate with grace, nodding politely, offering a thank-you with just enough sincerity to keep the peace. She knew Elisse was posturing — but the woman could cook, and no one turned down her greens.

Bishop, however, didn't budge. He declined the food altogether — unusual for a man who never passed up a hot meal, especially not Elisse's. He said he didn't have much of an appetite. And in fact, he didn't. The meeting that ended with sitting Novi down—and sealing it with her removal from his church—quietly turned his stomach.

He felt nauseous.

Everything in him, as a man of God, questioned what he had just allowed to happen. Cassia's words echoed in his ears from their last meeting, when she challenged his integrity. And she was right. But he couldn't let his secret surface — and Elisse was both hood and devious enough to make sure it never stayed buried. Even the smell of her greens made him dizzy. He sat back down in his chair.

Lady Byrd clocked it instantly. She'd been married to him long enough to tell the difference between a full stomach and a heavy heart. Something was off. And she knew her

• • •

husband well enough to know when something wasn't right — this was one of those times.

But why hadn't he talked about it with her? They had always prided themselves on open communication; it was what saved their marriage time and again, even through his many infidelities. And thinking on that, a part of her wondered: why had he been so brutal toward Novi when he knew firsthand the weight of that kind of sin and indiscretion? And why wasn't Nolen part of the meeting?

She thought about his words and hated the gnawing sense that he had used her. She never would have agreed to banish Novi from the church if she'd known the full story. Remove her from ministry? Perhaps. But cast her out of her spiritual home? No. All have sinned and come short of the glory of God.

She glanced at her husband, the thought pressing deeper. Was it guilt? Regret? Maybe it was finally hitting him — what they'd just done.

She tucked that suspicion away quietly, locking it behind years of knowing how and when to ask the real questions.

• • •

As Bishop made his way toward the door, Elisse intercepted him with a firm grip on his hand. Her voice was syrupy, but her tone deliberate.

"You've done a wonderful thing for our family, Bishop," she said, staring him square in the eyes. "You have nothing to worry about from the enemy. God will do His good work — in your family, and in Devotion Heights Church. Again... thank you, Bishop."

Her words carried a double meaning. He'd failed with Nolen, yes—but removing Novi? That was step one. A big one. Good enough, for now.

Bishop said nothing, just nodded once and glanced down at his watch. Elisse's painted smile never faltered as she watched them walk out.

That hard-headed boy would come around she thought. One way or another.

Nolen Jahlil was going to do right by her daughter.

She had plans.

• • •

Novi called her best friend Velani and told her everything. By the time she pulled up to her house, the tears hadn't stopped.

She was heartbroken. This hurt more than anything she'd ever felt in her life. She didn't know how to breathe, how to move forward. For a fleeting moment, she even thought about calling Zay — telling him they could work it out — just so she could walk back into her home church. The place where she met God. The place where she met Nolen. The place where she learned what love and devotion looked like.

Velani was pissed.

"And they didn't even start or end that meeting with prayer!" she spat, pacing, already wound up. "That says it all right there bff."

Novi sat curled up on the couch, knees pulled tight to her chest, eyes swollen, voice trembling.

Velani stopped, hands on her hips, eyes blazing.

"I can't stand that hoe-ass, bitch-ass, old-ass, wanna-be hoe," she snapped. When Velani was mad, her mouth was pure fire. "Anybody that makes my best friend cry like this? Gonna have to deal with me. Period."

● ● ●

She turned back to Novi, arms flailing. "I got a mind RIGHT NOW to call that damn Bishop — that old ass bitch's husband and let them know she came at Nolen in that nasty-ass robe, trying to seduce him. And you KNOW I'll throw in too that she tried to suck him off too. Just because her hoe-ass would've done it if he was down to get down. She ain't slick. They need to sit her ass down too."

"No, Vee... I just want to be done being humiliated. I can't do it anymore," Novi whispered.

"And Teanir's mama is a hoe-ass bitch too. Who the hell humiliates their own child like that?! Passing around pictures and recordings like it's gossip hour. Now the whole damn church about to know her daughter got weak-ass snatch and couldn't keep her man. That's what she gone be known for now. And truth be told, she probably won't ever get another man, so she holding on to this one for dear life."

Novi wanted to collapse. Cry. Disappear. But Velani wouldn't let her.

"Now look," Velani said, grabbing her and wrapping her arms around her tight. "I know I wasn't the biggest fan of y'all in the beginning — 'cause his ass was married — but the way they did you, sis? That was BOGUS as hell."

• • •

She held Novi like a sister, tight and protective. The tears came heavier.

"We are NOT going to let this weak-ass church shit break you, you hear me?!"

Novi nodded through her sobs.

"This — this right here — is why people don't go to church no more. Because we see these phony-ass Christians a mile away. Fuck that church," Velani said with her whole chest, full of anger and disgust.

Novi sniffed. She had to speak — had to clarify what was still real for her.

"No, sis... it's not the Church. It's just that church. God always has His arms open — always. He loves us unconditionally. I made a mistake. I sinned. But God... *God* is always faithful."

Velani stopped pacing. Her jaw flexed.

"I hear you... but if this is the example of God and it's God's church – then where the hell were their open arms? Where was the love for you from *God's* church? Where is the redemption? The grace? They supposed to be like Christ, right? So where is Christ in any of that, Noelle?"

• • •

Velani only used her middle name when she wanted to get through to her gently. That made Novi stop. She couldn't argue with it. Velani had a wild way of putting things — but she was right.

Velani stepped away to get more tissues. When she came back, her tone softened.

"Have you talked to Nolen yet? What did he say?"

Novi shook her head. "No... I came straight here."

"Girl... he needs to come through for you. If he's the man you say he is? This is his moment. Right now."

Novi nodded slowly, but her mind was racing.

She remembered how Bishop said Nolen was told to go back home — and how clear he made it that Nolen was never going to be asked to leave the church. That stuck with her. It rang inside her like a warning bell.

She hadn't heard from him all day. He texted her every morning and evening without fail, but now it was already late — and still nothing.

Was this it?

Had that meeting been her answer all along?

• • •

Had Nolen already chosen to go back to Teanir? She burst into tears again, harder than before. She loved him more than anything. And now her heart felt like it had been shattered into a thousand tiny, breathless pieces. "I just want to sleep," she whispered. "Can I sleep here for a while?"

Velani didn't hesitate. "Of course, Bff. You rest. I got you."

And she did.

Always.

Elisse had such great news; she couldn't wait to share it with Teanir. She drove straight over to the house — this was the kind of news you delivered in person.

When Teanir opened the door, the smell hit her first — then the mess.

The house was a disaster.

Elisse frowned as she stepped inside, careful not to trip over the piles of laundry and her grandson's toys scattered across the floor. Teanir had never been the best housekeeper, but she usually kept things halfway presentable. After all, she had three rambunctious boys, and keeping a spotless home was nearly impossible.

But this… this wasn't just untidiness. This looked like depression.

"Baby… look at this house," she said softly, stepping over a toy and a trail of crumpled fast-food wrappers.

Teanir quickly bent down, scooping things up from the floor and the couch. "Hey, Mama — I didn't know you were coming over."

"Just clear me a little space to sit. I got some great news," Elisse said, eyes gleaming.

Teanir figured it had to be something about the restaurant. Her mother had been talking about opening another location for months. She welcomed the distraction — anything to pull her out of the pit she'd been sinking into.

"I just found out that Novi Noelle Jaxson has been removed from the praise team and from the church," Elisse said, beaming like a lottery winner.

Teanir froze. "What do you mean, Mama?"

• • •

"Exactly what I said, baby. That heifer is gone. She's no longer allowed in the church or on the ministry team. Bishop and the leadership met with her today. She's out."

Teanir stared at her in disbelief, and then — finally, she smiled. A real smile. Her first in months. She closed her eyes and let it wash over her: relief, hope, the possibility of reconciliation. Her mother leaned in and gave her a big hug.

"See, baby? I told you God was gonna work it out."

Elisse looked around again, disapproving.

"Now, Teanir, you gotta get this together. A man don't want to be living in a house that looks like this. You hear me? You need to get yourself together. Go shower. Do your hair. Clean up. Cook your man a meal for when he comes home."

Teanir hesitated. "Mama... Nolen ain't been here. He's been staying at Babette's. The boys are there with him half the week now. He's... he's not coming home."

Elisse didn't blink. Not once. She was locked into her plan — confident and calm.

"Don't you worry about that, baby. God is a prayer-answering God, and He's going to take care of you. Just like I

• • •

take care of you," she said, grabbing her purse. "Start with the house. One thing at a time."

Teanir walked her to the door. As she closed it, she stood there for a moment — quiet, thoughtful.

For the first time in a long time, she felt something close to peace.

Maybe God was working it out.

At least now, Nolen wouldn't be distracted — no more eyes drifting across the sanctuary to Novi, no more silent messages exchanged during the sermon instead of listening to the Word. No more temptation. No more seduction disguised as worship.

She'd have his attention again.

Well... outside of Venus Johnson making eyes at him. But Venus was older, and Teanir told herself that wasn't a real threat. She clung to that thought like a lifeline.

Teanir smiled, turned on some music, and started cleaning.

For the first time in months, she moved with lightness. Every sweep of the broom, every folded

• • •

shirt, felt like an act of faith. She believed — truly believed — that God was restoring her marriage.

But even as the hope swelled inside her, a sliver of doubt crept in. What if she was wrong? What if the door never opened, the footsteps never returned, the promise never came?

She pushed the thought away quickly, humming louder, gripping her belief as if letting go would break her in two. She had to trust that God was working it out. Because never in a million years had she imagined they would not only sit Novi down — Devotion Heights' most anointed worship leader—but actually kick her out of the church. That had to be the Lord moving on her behalf, clearing the path for her marriage.

So, if God was giving her this sign, she couldn't doubt Him now. Not now.

Not when restoration finally felt within reach.

Once Elisse was back in her car, she set her purse on the seat beside her and pulled up her savings account — the one she'd been stacking for years, officially "for the boys."

• • •

It was a solid number. More than some people's retirement. She stared at it for a long moment, lips pressed together, before giving a slow, decisive nod.

On paper, this money was for her grandsons' future. College tuition. Opportunity. Legacy. That's what she told herself. But deep down, she knew the truth. She would burn down a building for Teanir. If saving her daughter's marriage meant spending every dime, then that's exactly what she was going to do. The boys would be fine. They'd benefit in the long run anyway — through stability, through access, through the kind of protection only a mother could secure.

This wasn't charity. It was strategy.

She pulled into her garage, got out of the car, and walked into her townhome.

She needed an attorney.

Not just any attorney. Not a scripture-quoting, "let's-do-right" type. She needed sharp teeth and sharper paperwork. Someone who could slice through the Jahlil name, the money, the legacy — someone who could dismantle a man and make it look clean on paper.

Inside, Elisse dropped her keys, sank onto the couch, and out of habit reached for the Yellow Pages in the basket by

• • •

the door. She flipped a few pages, scoffed, and tossed it aside. Get with the times, Elisse.

She grabbed her phone, opened Google, and typed:

"Best cutthroat divorce attorney in Baltimore."

Click. Scroll. Click. That's when she saw it.

William Colbert. Divorce & Custody Law. Over 5,000 five-star reviews.

She tapped his profile photo. A white man, late fifties maybe. Salt-and-pepper hair. Clean-shaven. But it was the eyes that got her — cold, calculating. That slick little smirk said he knew every loophole in the book and had no problem exploiting all of them.

Elisse leaned back on her couch and smirked. That's him. That's the one.

Some might call it divine guidance. Others would call it her hood-rat instincts — the same instincts that helped her hustle plates out her mama's kitchen at twelve, or sidestep fights in the projects without catching a scratch. She preferred to call it discernment. Divine discernment, she told herself. A spiritual gift.

• • •

Whatever it was, she felt damn sure this man would go for the jugular. He would know how to protect Teanir's interests. And if Nolen ever got slick — if he ever really tried to divorce her daughter — this man would make sure he paid the price. A steep one.

His sons.

That was the one thing Nolen wasn't willing to lose. Elisse knew it. She would use it. She would weaponize it — for her daughter's marriage, for her daughter's name.

And when she told herself it was for the glory of God, for the sanctity of marriage — she almost believed it. Almost.

But deep down, it wasn't about God. It was about Teanir. Always had been.

She dialed the number and set up the first consultation.

This wasn't just a legal hire — it was an alliance. A quiet, backdoor war about to be waged on behalf of her daughter, her grandsons, and the life they were still going to have.

Even if it killed her to make it happen.

● ● ●

CHAPTER 38
The Threat

His future became a list of consequences — unless he obeyed.

Elisse showed up at Nolen's job unannounced, dressed in a T-shirt, jeans, and a fresh blowout—as if she'd just dropped by for lunch at his invitation. But her eyes told the truth. All business.

He was surprised to see her, but not shocked. Elisse was unpredictable like that. She didn't bother with small talk. His secretary gave him a wide-eyed look that said, I'm sorry, but she walked right in—what was I supposed to do?

Nolen raised a hand, signaling it was fine, and allowed Elisse into his office.

"Have a seat. What's up?"

"I have a friend at City Hall," she said, her voice syrupy-sweet but edged with venom. "And I know about the divorce filings."

Nolen froze. The muscles in his jaw tightened. Slowly, he stood, his eyes flicking toward the glass wall of his office before closing the door firmly.

● ● ●

He let out an exhausted sigh. Unbelievable. She had really brought this here. To his job.

If his mother knew, she'd probably scold him for not calling security to escort Elisse out. But that would've been worse — the optics, the gossip. Better for his coworkers to whisper about his bossy mother-in-law barging in than to watch her dragged out by force.

At least this way, he still had some control.

"I also know Teanir hasn't been served yet," she added with a raised eyebrow, letting the silence hang.

She leaned in closer. "I thought maybe we could get lunch—my restaurant, of course. It'd give us a chance to talk like adults. No lawyers, no drama. Just two people who love those boys of yours. It's important we do this the right way so nothing backfires and hurts them."

Nolen sighed, rolling his eyes, tilting his head back against the chair. What does she really want that she can't just say here? Why the theatrics? Why come to his office just to ask him to leave and eat at her restaurant? They could've hashed this out right here, where he could shut it down and get back to work.

• • •

Still, reluctantly, he agreed. Not because he trusted her — but because of his sons. She knew how close they were, how much they meant to him. Being a father was the best calling he'd ever had. It was the one thing he swore he would never fail at. He didn't care how Teanir took the split, but the boys? They mattered. He was already walking a fine line, and he needed to do everything possible to make the transition smooth for them.

"Great, let's drive over together. I'm parked out front," she said smoothly. A tactic, pure intimidation — something she'd learned years ago in spaces where control was survival. Little foxes, she thought... wear him down slowly. He was young; she had experience on her side.

"I'll meet you there," Nolen countered, his tone clipped. "I've got a deadline. I'll leave right after."

He knew she was up to something — he just couldn't see it yet. But unlike his mother, Elisse never had a poker face. Whatever she felt — anger, resentment, joy, or ill intent — always showed up like a symptom she couldn't hide.

"Okay, love." She smiled, wide and polished, but her face gave her away. The smile was a mask, stretched over something more sinister.

• • •

Later, Nolen pulled up in an Uber, thanking the driver before stepping out in front of the sign: Soulful Bites. He walked inside, spotted her at a corner table, and sat across from her, his eyes shifting between the menu and the clock on the wall.

Elisse leaned in, smiling as she delivered a compliment — the kind that only sounded sweet if you ignored the sting underneath.

She'd ordered his favorites ahead of time, laid out across the table like an offering—or a bribe.

Over plates of fried chicken, collard greens, and cornbread, she made small talk. Asked about his job. Told him how business at Soulful Bites had picked up so much she'd had to hire four new people. All of it filler. He nodded politely, but he didn't care. He knew she was fattening him up for the real conversation.

Finally, she leaned in, her voice warm.

"You've always been a good father, Nolen. Nobody can take that from you. But a husband? Well… let's just say you could've tried harder. You left my daughter drowning."

• • •

He said nothing. Didn't agree. Didn't argue. He just wanted the lunch over with. Every second across from her felt like a ticking bomb.

"I just need you to know I'm not happy with how this is turning out with you and my daughter. But you are still my son-in-love and always will be. As long as you show up for those boys, that's what matters. Being there for them, and for Teanir. Whether you like it or not, how you treat their mama is how much they're going to respect you."

The food. The location change. The waste of his damn time was all starting to piss him off. She could've said this back at the office.

He wiped his mouth, pushed back from the table. "I already called an Uber."

Elisse rose with him, leaned down, and kissed his cheek like an old family friend. Then, with that same wide smile, she slid a sealed manila envelope across the table.

He looked at it, then shoved it right back toward her.

"I'm not taking that," he said. "And if this is more pictures of me and Novi, save it. I've already seen them."

● ● ●

She pulled it back, tapped the envelope, and said softly, "This isn't about you and Novi. This is about your sons."

That hit him in the chest.

He stared at her, trying to read her expression — but it was stone cold. She offered no further explanation, just turned and walked away.

He grabbed the envelope before leaving and climbed into the back of an Uber. The moment the door shut behind him, he tore it open.

His stomach dropped.

Countersuit. For full custody.

Front and center, highlighted in red, was a claim of reckless endangerment tied to his ongoing extramarital conduct.

It accused him of prioritizing a "publicly scandalous affair" over his children's stability and well-being. It alleged he regularly left them unattended, placed them in emotionally volatile environments, and exposed them to chaos in order to pursue a relationship with "a married woman known to the court."

• • •

Attached were video transcripts of his sons. Their voices — his boys' voices — in print describing loud fights between him and Teanir. One even mentioned, "Daddy said he doesn't love Mommy anymore and that she cries when he's not home."

A knot rose in his throat.

Then the photos. Hundreds of them. Not just the truck. Hotel exits. Beach walks. Parking lot kisses. Things he thought were private — sacred — now preserved as evidence, ready to be dragged through the court system and public record.

She'd been watching longer than he realized. Maybe from the start.

Tucked inside was a Post-it, written in Elisse's sharp, unforgiving cursive:

"Call me when you've reviewed everything. We can work this out — if you're willing to play smart."

He leaned back, running a hand over his face. The Uber driver glanced at him through the mirror, concerned, but stayed quiet.

• • •

He'd keep all of this from his mother. From his grandparents. They didn't need to know — not yet. Not unless it became necessary.

But the truth was pressing in on him, harder every day.

It was getting impossible to hide.

His grandfather had already hinted that he knew about the social media post that briefly circulated — the one the family paid a PR firm a small fortune to bury, spinning it as AI-generated slander. So far, the cover-up had worked. Half the people believed the AI story. The other half didn't care enough to dig deeper. Either way, the Jahlil name was safe.

For now.

But the contents of that manila envelope had shaken Nolen more than he wanted to admit. This was far beyond anything he'd anticipated.

He was angry. Nervous. A slow burn of dread coiled around his chest like a noose.

He needed to protect Novi. She hadn't signed up for this. All she did was love him — love him the way he needed, the way he deserved. And he loved her back with everything

● ● ●

in him. Loving her is what started this. Being loved by her is what made it worse.

And his sons — God, his sons. Three boys, dragged into this like pawns. The idea that transcripts and accusations could follow them for years, that school parents might access the public records, that his own children might one day read those words against him — rage ripped through him. All because his mother-in-law couldn't accept the truth: he *didn't* love her daughter.

He grunted loud and sharp as the elevator doors opened into his building, his face hot and red. People waiting in the lobby instinctively stepped aside, sensing the storm radiating off him. Even his secretary, usually quick to greet him with messages, quietly set them aside and stayed at her desk.

Still, he was head of his department. He didn't have the luxury of falling apart — not in public.

As soon as he walked into his office, he shut the door, closed the blinds, and pulled out his phone.

Then he called her.

Elisse answered on the second ring, voice sweet like syrup poured over a trap.

• • •

"Hey, son-in-love," she said, a smile practically audible. She knew he'd opened the envelope. She knew the fire she'd lit.

"What do you want?" he asked through clenched teeth. "Why send all this to me?"

"If you think you're about to separate me from my boys, you're sadly mistaken. You don't know who you're dealing with."

"But I do," she replied calmly. "That's where you're mistaken. You're going to go back to Teanir and make it right. The embarrassment my daughter has endured ends now. If you value your reputation, your family's legacy, and if you ever want to live in the same state as your sons again, you'll do what needs to be done."

His hand gripped the stress ball so tightly it deflated in his palm and never refilled.

"I've already filed for divorce. It's in motion," he said, each word delivered like a blow.

"I know all about that," she snapped. "And you're going to stop it. Because if you don't, here's what's going to happen."

Her voice dropped, dark and full of venom.

• • •

"I will send every single photo to TMZ. Every angle. Every location. Senator Jahlil's son caught in an illicit affair with a married woman — inside a church no less. I'll release the audio tapes. TikTok, YouTube, Instagram — hell, even Reddit will have a field day."

She paused for dramatic effect.

"They'll meme you. Humiliate you. You'll never be able to run for office — any office. Your power-hungry mama's dreams of building a dynasty? Gone. How can she lead the country if she couldn't even raise a decent son?"

He swallowed hard. The lump in his throat wasn't fear — it was fury.

"And don't think I'll stop there," she continued. "Your neighbors will know. Your co-workers. Your donors. Your sons' teachers. Everyone. You'll stain the Jahlil name trying to play house with a hoe. And I *will* do it."

"You are *not* taking my boys away from me," he growled.

She didn't flinch.

"You'll be handing them over with a bow. A judge will look at your reckless behavior, your priorities, the public

• • •

scandal, and hand full custody to Teanir without a second thought. And your sons? They'll grow up knowing their daddy chose her over them. You think they won't resent *you*? You'll be worse than your *own* father."

He leaned back in his chair, chest tight, vision blurry with rage. If she had been in the office, there was no telling what he might have done. He clenched his jaw so tight it felt like it might crack.

Elisse's voice dropped to a whisper, still smug.

"Nolen, either way, I win. If you fight, I scorch the earth. If you surrender, I get my daughter's life back. Either way, you'll be the one to bleed. So, you ask yourself — is she really worth it?"

That was the last straw.

He hung up without another word.

His entire body buzzed with adrenaline. Rage. Hurt. Betrayal. He pressed his palms into his eyes and leaned forward, trying to force himself to breathe.

He couldn't stay here. Not like this. Not after that.

• • •

He left the office without saying a word and drove to the only place where he could think: The Spot near the lake. It was quiet. Empty. Sacred.

He parked, turned off the engine, and sat in silence, staring out at the darkening sky. This place had always been his escape — the quiet hill overlooking the city, wrapped in trees, untouched by the noise of the world.

But this time was different.

This was where everything changed.

Where he had first touched Novi in a way that was more than physical, it was spiritual. Intimate. Consuming. He remembered the moment, and exactly the way her breath had caught when he kissed her thighs, the way her body opened to him like it had been waiting for him all her life. He hadn't just performed for pleasure that night — he had made love to her. Tasted her like she was all he'd ever need. Every kiss, every movement was deliberate, reverent. Not a single part of him hesitated. And when she whispered his name under that starry sky, he felt renewed.

He didn't regret it. Novi made him feel seen. Loved. Chosen.

● ● ●

They dreamed the same way. They thought in the same rhythm. She was the only one who had ever matched him soul for soul. He never had to explain himself to her — she just knew. And when he kissed her, when he touched her, it wasn't just desire — it was home.

To sacrifice her... or risk losing everything: his reputation, his future, his job, his family name, and most of all, his three sons. This wasn't just about love anymore — this was legacy. Custody. Public humiliation. Everything was on the line now.

And that night, the most intimate night of his life — was now a weapon in the hands of someone who hated him.

Now, that memory stood like a flame in the cold night air. Mocking him.

Now, what was once his refuge, felt like the scene of a crime.

His chest ached and it was hard to breathe. His face felt wet — tears? He didn't realize it. He wiped them away quickly.

If he went back to Teanir, the scandal disappeared. The photos? Shelved. The recordings? Buried. His mother's political machine would stay clean and he'd keep his reputation. Keep his career. Keep access to his sons.

● ● ●

But he'd lose *her*.

Novi.

The only woman who had ever seen him. Heard him. Loved him fully. Fiercely. He could live without her… but he'd never feel again.

His eyes welled again with tears, and he looked down, covering his face with both hands. It was habit. Even though no one was out here, it was an instinct — an acknowledgment of weakness.

And in this moment, he *was* weak.

He was angry at everyone. Angry at his mother for pushing him into a marriage he never wanted. Angry at Teanir for never understanding him. Angry at the church for treating him like a pawn. And yes, even angry at Novi — for showing him a love so real that now he couldn't unsee it and couldn't unfeel it.

If he had never loved her, he wouldn't be in this mess. He wouldn't know what he was missing. He could've stayed numb forever.

Now, he was bleeding from the inside out.

● ● ●

He screamed — loud, guttural, raw. So loud that every bird in the surrounding trees scattered in flight.

That pissed him off too.

Even nature was running from him now.

The night sky above felt heavier than usual. The same sky that watched him fall in love was now watching him fall apart.

He kicked the rocks under his feet, then slumped forward again.

This was the cost.

He'd gotten himself into this.

Now he had to find a way out.

Alone.

He looked down at his phone and noticed a missed call from Novi. He hadn't spoken to her in days. Time had gotten away from him — everything was moving too fast. Too much happening at once. He had told her to call him after her forecasting meeting at the church, but now... that was another day. Another storm ago.

• • •

Just hearing her voice had always been enough to calm him. To soothe the sting. Novi had a way of settling him like no one else ever could. But now?

He couldn't bring himself to call her.

He didn't want to be comforted. He needed to sit in this — this mess, this moment and find an answer. He had already sent her a text when he filed for divorce. It had felt like a milestone. A victory. They were both relieved, excited even. She'd filed for divorce from Zayven, too. They were finally on track to start their own family.

His boys already *loved* her — not just from church, but from all the 'accidental' run-ins at Starbucks, or McDonald's. They always ran to her first.

Now what could he tell her?

How could he explain that the walls were caving in?

He also needed to know what happened. No one had said anything to him, so it couldn't have been that bad... right?

He opened their message thread and texted:

NOLEN:
Hey baby, I'm so sorry I've been really busy.
How did the meeting go?

● ● ●

NOVI:
Bad. Really awful

NOLEN:
What happened?

She was grateful it was through text. Every time she tried to speak it out loud, her voice broke with her tears. The grief choked her. This way, she could breathe between every sentence.

NOVI:
Bishop, Venus, Jeff, and Lady Byrd railroaded me.
Venus and Jeff said I'm to be sat down indefinitely.
No Sundays. No Bible study. No engagements.
And even the song I wrote... the one I sang lead on?
They said Bishop approved Janet to sing it moving forward.

Nolen stared at the screen, stunned.

NOLEN:
We can fight that, babe. That's your song.

NOVI:
That's not even the worst part.
I was kicked out of the church!
Bishop and Venus told me to go find another church
while I work on my marriage — and maybe,
if it's restored, then he'll consider talking
about letting me come back to Devotion Heights.

• • •

Nolen sat back in his truck, heart pounding.

None of that was in the meeting Bishop had with him.

They said nothing like this.

NOLEN:
I don't believe that, babe.
Maybe you heard wrong?

Novi sat up in bed, staring at the message in disbelief.

She re-read it, twice. Tears welled in her eyes again, but this time from a deeper wound.

She hadn't expected *him* not to believe her.

NOVI:
I didn't hear wrong!!
I'm not lying.
I was told that it was an opportunity for you
and Teanir to work on your marriage — and
that me being there was too much of a
distraction. That if I stayed, you'd never
reconcile with your family.

Nolen dropped his phone onto the passenger seat next to him. The air left his lungs. He was reminded of the Bishop's warning — that storm he swore was coming.

He hadn't realized *this* was what he meant.

● ● ●

He didn't just mean him.

He meant *her*. He meant to destroy her in front of the very people who once called her family.

He picked up the phone and typed fast.

NOLEN:
I'm on my way over.

Novi:
Okay.

Nolen pulled up to her house. The porch light was dim, but the door cracked open before he even made it out of the car. There she stood — face flushed, eyes bloodshot, lips trembling.

It crushed him.

He walked straight to her, didn't say a word. Just wrapped her up in his arms as she broke all the way down. Her body shuddered against his. He held her tightly, protectively, grounding her as her tears soaked his shirt.

Anger. Rage. Guilt. It all welled inside of him.

This wasn't just unfair.

It was cruel.

• • •

They'd done this without him. To her. And he'd let it happen. They walked upstairs, silent. She climbed into bed, and he followed. He didn't want sex. Didn't want to take anything from her. He just wanted to be with her.

To hold her.

To keep her safe in the only way he knew how right now. He wrapped his arms around her as she cried herself into sleep.

Her hair smelled like sandalwood, bergamot and jasmine argan oil. That scent had become his peace — it calmed him, lulled him. Helped him sleep like a child.

But tonight, sleep didn't come for him.

He stayed still, her breathing steady now against his chest. And in that silence, that stillness, something inside of him settled. It was always this — always being with her — that made the difference. Not the sex, though their chemistry was undeniable, electric. Not the adrenaline, though it was real every time.

It was her presence.

● ● ●

That soul-deep connection where they could share the same space, say nothing, and still know everything there was to know about each other.

And that alone was enough.

And in that presence... he found his answer.

He pulled her in closer, held her like she might slip away in the night.

A single tear rolled down his cheek.

He had made his decision.

CHAPTER 39
The Price of Peace

He gave something up & no one understands what it cost.

Nolen called Elisse the next morning, asking her to meet him at Starbucks in Harbor East. The weight of the world pressed against his chest. He just wanted to get this conversation over with — so he wouldn't have to see her face again anytime soon.

NOLEN:
Meet me at Starbucks. Harbor East.

ELISSE:
Okay, I'll be there in 25 mins.

He waited in his truck, staring blankly out the window. He ran through every version of this conversation in his head — what to say, how to say it, how to keep himself from flipping the table if she got slick. The very thought of her expression made his stomach turn. Still, he was ready. The decision had been made. And it would change everything.

The radio played low. He saw her pull up. Normally, whether at his house, the church, or in public, he'd get out and

• • •

open the door for her. Not today. That courtesy was gone. He knew who she really was now. There would be no more pretenses.

He climbed out of the truck and walked into the Starbucks. His mobile order was already waiting. He picked it up, grabbed a seat by the window, and waited. No greeting. No smile. Just silence.

Elisse came in, clearly taken aback that he hadn't opened the door for her. She was only parked three cars away. Still, she thought — he called this meeting. He made a choice. She just hoped for his sake he wasn't about to make a dumb one.

She approached him. He didn't speak, didn't even look up. Just sipped his coffee.

"Did you order for me?" she asked.

He gave her a sideways look, half a sneer curling at his mouth, but didn't answer. She ordered her drink, came back, and sat across from him.

"Good morning, son."

"Don't call me that," he said, cold and sharp. "I'm not your son. Never could be. So, let's not do that."

• • •

She smirked, trying to keep her composure. "Okay, you right. Let's get to it then. What have you decided to do?"

He leaned forward, voice calm but heavy.

"My sons mean the world to me. I would never let another man raise them. I'd never abandon them the way my father abandoned me. Don't get it twisted — I never lacked anything. My grandfather was a great example. The Sandifords? Pillars in my life. I'm not missing a thing."

"I know you're not — "

"Don't interrupt me."

His voice dropped low, but the weight behind it made her freeze. For the first time, Elisse felt a flicker of fear.

"Even so, I don't ever want my sons searching for their father in other men while I'm still alive. I'm present. I'm active. I'm loving. I give them everything. I love them more than I love the next breath in my body."

She straightened in her seat, sensing the moment was coming. But she wasn't sure which way it would go.

He continued, his tone steady, final.

"I've decided, after reviewing your threats, to do what's in the best interest of my sons. I am what's best for them. So,

• • •

I'm going back. I'll move back into the house with Teanir and the boys."

Elisse smiled with satisfaction. She'd won. All the planning, all the plotting, all the money was worth it. She was ready to celebrate.

"You can wipe that silly-ass grin off your face," he snapped. "Because just because I'm moving back in doesn't mean I'll *ever* love Teanir. You understand that? I'm doing this for my boys — and only my boys. You knew I never loved her."

"As long as you move back in — " she started.

"I said, don't interrupt me again," he said through clenched teeth. His eyes locked on hers, sharp enough to wound.

She leaned back in her chair, instinctively putting more distance between them. His energy had shifted. Something darker was stirring. For a moment, she wondered if she had gone too far. If she'd pushed a man to the edge — and if her own daughter's life might be in danger.

Still, she masked her fear. In Park Heights, fear was a weakness you never let anyone see.

• • •

"I love my sons," he said. "I still love Novi. I'm in love with Novi. That won't ever change. I've made my choice. I'll move back this weekend. I'll stop splitting time with the boys. But let me be crystal clear — if you ever try to hurt Novi again, your daughter will mourn the loss of her mother."

Elisse sat frozen. Did this man just threaten her life? Over a woman she still called a side piece?

He was serious. His tone, his face, everything about him told her he wasn't bluffing.

"So, any little scheme you have to come for the woman I love — you'll pay for it. Believe that better than you believe in Jesus." He sipped his coffee like he hadn't just issued a death threat in a Starbucks.

"And another thing — you are to never, *ever* mention any of this to my mother."

She remained quiet. Frozen.

He stood, towering over her.

"I don't need to hear anything you have to say. I just came to say my piece. Enjoy your coffee."

He walked out without looking back.

● ● ●

It felt like signing his own death certificate. Something inside him was dying. And he still hadn't told Novi.

How could he?

How do you explain to the woman who lost everything for loving you... that you're about to break her heart?

But he had to. For the sake of everyone else. This decision wasn't about his happiness anymore — it hadn't been for a long time.

He wondered if his whole life would be like this — choosing what's best for others, while dying a little more inside each time.

Would he ever get to rest in love again? Would he ever know peace? Or would he leave this earth with nothing but the memory of what it felt like to be loved by her?

The knot in his throat returned.

He climbed back into his truck and drove to another Starbucks drive-thru. He ordered Novi's favorite. He wasn't ready for this conversation. But he had to tell her.

And this time... it would break them both.

● ● ●

CHAPTER 40
When the Leaves Fell

He left, not to escape, but to protect what he couldn't carry.

He pulled into her driveway just after sunrise, the morning air still wrapped in a hush. The city hadn't fully awakened yet. It felt sacred — quiet, still, as if time itself had paused to give him space for the hardest thing he'd ever have to do.

He picked up her coffee from the console and walked to the door. She was already waiting, like she knew. She *always* knew.

"Hey," he said softly. Her natural beauty held him, like it always did. Radiant even in the pale morning light. But beneath it, he caught the sadness in her eyes. He tried to counter with a smile that said, I'm here. Focus on me. Right here.

He'd learned to take advantage of the now with Novi — because looking ahead always carried consequences. And right now, the future felt unbearable.

"Hey," she whispered back, trying to smile, but it didn't reach her eyes. She knew what he was doing — this urging

• • •

toward the present — but something in her spirit tugged at her, heavy and sorrowful.

She lingered in thought, the way she often did, and he could almost hear himself saying what he always said: I'm right here. Can you stay here with me?

She closed her eyes as he stepped closer, pressed the cup — her favorite — into her hands, then gestured toward the truck.

"Come ride with me for a bit?"

He leaned in and kissed her lips. That's when she felt it stronger. The weight. The knowing. Something *wasn't* right.

She fought back the tears and the lump rising in her throat. Nodded. Reached for her denim jacket from the coat rack. She didn't ask where they were going. She didn't need to.

Her spirit had already told her everything her mind refused to believe.

The drive was quiet at first. He took her down roads lined with trees, past rivers and into places untouched by city noise. He didn't want her heartache to attach itself to anything familiar — no intersections, no signs, no neighborhoods they

• • •

laughed in before. He needed this goodbye to exist somewhere unmarked by memory.

But even here, where the world was golden and undisturbed, she could feel the ache in his silence.

Her hand slid across the seat, curling around his fingers. His grip tightened instinctively, like it always did. But today, it felt different. There was no comfort in it — only countdown.

"I feel like this is the end of us, Nolen," she whispered, barely able to breathe through the words. Her voice broken, her eyes fixed on him, pleading. Pleading for him to call her crazy. To tell her she was wrong. To tell her, We're solid. Don't read into this. I love you. We're moving forward.

She had given up everything for him and didn't regret it. But was he regretting? Her thoughts spiraled — his sons, the weight of their presence in his life. She loved those boys, all three of them, and they loved her… didn't they? Or maybe they didn't. Maybe that was why.

She beat herself up with questions. Is it this reason? That reason? Something I said? Something I failed to be? All she really wanted was for him to say the words that would silence the storm in her chest.

• • •

But he said nothing. His jaw clenched tight, his eyes locked on the road ahead.

He could feel her too — her sorrow, her dread — so heavy inside of him it made his chest ache. Their connection ran so soul-deep it betrayed him. He couldn't hide from what she was feeling, just as she couldn't hide from him.

And it broke him — because he knew he was the reason for her pain in this moment.

"Baby... " he finally murmured, voice thick. "Can we just enjoy this view...*Please?*"

She shook her head, tears welling up, her stomach twisting into knots. "How can I enjoy anything when I feel like I'm dying inside?"

He didn't answer. He couldn't. Instead, he held her hand tighter, as if it could somehow delay the inevitable.

They pulled into the gravel path leading into Patapsco Valley State Park, the trees arching over them like a cathedral. Sunlight filtered through branches, painting soft light across her skin. He parked and sat in silence.

She stared out the window.

"I don't want to get out," she whispered.

• • •

He stepped out and walked around to her door. He opened it and reached out his hand, voice breaking.

"Baby, please."

She looked up at him, eyes glistening. Then, wordlessly, she stepped out of the truck. The moment her feet hit the ground, she collapsed into his chest and sobbed. Her whole body trembled in his arms.

"Why?" she choked out. "What happened? Things were finally starting to work. We were building something real."

"I had to make a decision, baby," he said quietly, pressing his lips to her temple.

She pulled back just enough to search his eyes. "We could've made it work. We could've figured it out. Tell me I'm enough or tell me what's missing. I'll do it, please just don't...don't leave me....with my heart broken like this."

Her desperation cut him open. He gripped her shoulders, shaking his head as a lump rose in his throat. Sadness and fury collided inside him — sadness for having to forsake the one woman who truly loved him right, and anger at being forced into this corner at all. Even now, part of him was clawing for an exit plan, a way to keep Novi. But every

• • •

road led to the same dead end: destroy her or destroy his sons. He couldn't do either.

This was the only way.

"This has nothing to do with you not being enough. You're everything. Everything I didn't even know I needed until I met you. You gave me love, peace, and purpose. You made me feel alive again." His breath shook. He looked away. "And that's exactly why I have to let you go."

"I'll wait" she said. "Even if it's not fair. Even if it hurts."

"I know," he murmured. "I won't ask you to wait. You deserve love. I just want you to be happy."

"I'm happy with you," she whispered. "*Please...*"

"Novi," his voice was rough, low. "Any man would be blessed to have a woman like you. Once a man's been with you, he can't be happy with anyone else. You leave a mark... like you left one on me. A mark I'll never forget. You gave me love, and it changed me in every way. Baby, this isn't about you. You give. You pour. You love without conditions."

Her throat ached. "If that's true... then stay. Stay for me. For us. I need you. I don't care about the world or the

* * *

whispers or the church. Just... stay. Please. We can figure it out. We can make it work. I'll do whatever it takes."

His jaw clenched, the words dragging out of him like they weighed a thousand pounds. "I'm doing this for my sons," he said quietly. "They need stability. They need me. And right now... this is the only way I know how to give that to them."

"But what about us?" she asked, voice raw. "What about our love?"

He had no answer. Only silence. His eyes carried every memory — every night, every laugh, every touch — and it ripped him apart.

"If I choose you," he finally said, "I lose them. And if I lose them, I lose the chance to raise good men. I lose the one thing I swore I'd never be — an absent father."

Her chest heaved with grief, the kind that carved itself deep into the soul, leaving scars that never fully heal.

He pulled her close, pressed his forehead to hers, and whispered the truth that would never change.

"I'll never stop loving you."

• • •

"I don't want your love if I can't have you," she sobbed. "You asked me to believe in this. I did! I believed in you, Nolen. I believed in us."

"I know," he said, his voice breaking. "I know, baby. And I'm so sorry."

They stood in the middle of the woods, where the ground was covered in leaves — and regret. She clung to him as if letting go meant losing more than a man. It meant losing the part of herself that had come alive with him.

Eventually, he kissed her forehead and gently pried her arms from around his waist.

"Come on. I'll take you home."

The ride back was silent. Her hand stayed in his, even as the warmth faded. She stared out the window the whole way, blinking back tears that refused to fall.

When they reached her house, he put the truck in park but didn't cut the engine.

"I don't know if I'll ever heal from this," she whispered.

"Me either," he admitted.

She opened the door slowly, then turned to look at him one last time.

● ● ●

"I'll always love you."

He nodded, unable to speak.

She shut the door. He watched her walk back inside — the house filled with dreams they once planned to share. And as the door closed behind her, something inside him closed too.

Forever.

He drove off, tears streaming, the road blurring ahead.

It was the end of them.

But never the end of his love for the one woman that was his match in every way.

CHAPTER 41
Sonshine

She wanted his heart. He left it with someone else in exchange for his sons.

It started to rain just as Nolen pulled into his driveway — a quiet, weary kind of rain that softened the edges of everything. The kind that felt like restriction. Like defeat. He stayed in the driver's seat long after the engine went silent, his hands still gripping the steering wheel like it might hold him together.

The boys' backpacks were on the porch. Jordon's tiny rain boots were tipped over near the mat. Inside, he could hear Teanir's voice — not angry, not kind... just tired.

The way she always sounded now.

He stepped into the house and peeled off his jacket. Teanir appeared in the hallway, holding a dish towel.

"My mother-in-law called," she said flatly.

"My mother," he corrected under his breath.

"She stopped by."

Nolen didn't answer.

• • •

Teanir's face twisted, repulsed as he stepped back into the house like he'd never disappeared, like he hadn't walked away from her... from their family.

"Well, are you back now? Maybe you do have some loyalty to someone other than yourself after all."

That hit. But he didn't defend himself. The words were buried too deep beneath everything else—hurt, heartbreak, anger. Anger at himself for coming back to the cage she still held the key to.

And now here he was again, sitting in the silence of his own making. Alone with thoughts he couldn't name. With nothing but the hollow ache where love used to be.

He exhaled.

"Tea, don't start. My bags are here."

She stepped closer, her voice sharp but breaking. "The boys ask me when you coming back home. I didn't know what to say. Because you're never... here."

"I know," he said quietly.

Her voice cracked, but her eyes flashed. "You come and go as you please. You don't touch me — not anymore. And when you do talk to me, it's only about them. What am I

• • •

supposed to be, Nolen? A babysitter? A roommate? Or am I still your wife?" Nolen's jaw tightened, his voice dropping low, bitter.

"So now you wanna play house again?"

She stared at him — pleading, wounded, humiliated.

"I can spread my legs and scream loud too, Nolen," she said, bitter and shaking. "Will that make you stay? Will that make you love me?"

Silence.

He flinched — not at her words, but at how deeply they mirrored everything he'd tried to bury.

"You never even liked having sex with me like that," he muttered, voice low and tight. "So, what is this now?"

Tears burned in her eyes, but it was fury that ripped through her throat — her voice rising with rage and heartbreak tangled together in every syllable.

"Because I'm trying, Nolen! I know I'll never be her. I hate the fact that bitch came into our lives and destroyed our marriage! She gave you this false, lying-ass hope of what a woman should be for you. That shit ain't real, nigga! I was the woman for you. I'm your wife. The mother of your children.

• • •

She ain't lived with you in real time, through the bills, the fights, the sleepless nights. How the hell am I supposed to compete with that? I can't! But I'm here, trying to save something — anything — for the sake of our sons. Your sons!"

Her words sharp like glass, cutting them both raw.

Nolen snapped. The restraint shattered.

"Novi didn't ruin this — YOU DID! With your manipulation, with your guilt trips, with the way you turned this whole damn house into a war zone! You never wanted peace, Tea. You wanted control. Competing with my own sons for my attention instead of being their mother — how twisted is that? And then you wanna stand here and blame her? No! This? This wreck we're standing in? That's on you!"

His voice ricocheted off the walls, hot and jagged, the words coming like gunfire he couldn't call back.

Her face crumpled, but she fought back with what little she had left.

"How else could I get you to notice me in this fake-ass marriage?"

He scoffed, the sound sharp and bitter. Even she admitted it wasn't real — not what it should've been.

• • •

"You said vows, Nolen."

"You knew I never meant them."

The words stung — even as they left his mouth.

"I can't do this anymore," he said.

Teanir folded the towel in her hands slowly, deliberately, her voice low and shaking with fury. "So, what now? You leave? Be with her out in the open?"

"No."

He pulled a manila envelope from his coat pocket and tossed it onto the counter with a sharp thud.

She blinked at it, then back at him.

"What is this?"

"The agreement you and your mama made up," he said flatly. "I signed it. I'm staying. You happy now?!"

His face twisted with resentment and rage—an expression she'd never seen before.

Teanir froze, breath caught, her eyes wide. For a split second, she saw him like a stranger. But she steadied herself, forcing her voice to hold.

• • •

"Whatever the reason, you finally did the right thing," she said, voice steady but edged. "I know this ain't the picture-perfect life you wanted, but choosing us? That's what you should've done all along — instead of letting your dick make decisions for you." Her eyes sliced into him. "That's called sacrifice Nolen. Forget that hoe, and start putting me and my boys first — for once."

Her breath faltered the instant the words left her mouth. Nolen's head snapped toward her, eyes blazing.

"Sacrifice?"

Rage surged in his chest, unstoppable. And before he could catch it, everything spilled out—

The resentment.

The heartbreak.

The bitterness of being blackmailed into staying.

The grief of losing the only woman he'd ever truly loved.

"I gave up *everything* for you!" he roared. "I gave up the woman I loved — because of you! So don't you stand there acting like I'm a selfish man. I've sacrificed myself since the beginning of knowing you. I buried my own heart to be there

● ● ●

for my boys. That's all I've ever done — sacrifice! Sacrifice! And even that's not enough for you."

His voice rose so sharp her ears rang. He had never yelled at her like this before. He rarely raised his voice at anyone. But now —

"But she's a hoe?" he seethed. "She's more of a woman than you'll ever be."

Teanir shuddered, the words slamming into her chest. A phrase that, if true, she knew she could never live up to.

Nolen's voice broke, raw, but he pressed on.

"I didn't stay for you or the threats from your conniving-ass mama. Not because of this damn house — which I paid for and would have gladly left you in the divorce. I'm staying because I refuse to let my boys grow up without their father. That's why. It is about the Jahlil legacy — my family's legacy. Not love. Never love. Not with you."

He stood there, chest heaving, watching her as she sank into the chair, caught off guard by his honesty with each word grew more brutal.

Then he stepped closer, leaned down near her ear, and said, cold and low:

• • •

"I'll never love you."

Teanir's hands trembled, but she held herself together, eyes locked on him as he turned to leave. Tears welled, silent and heavy.

"You really love her then, Nolen?" she whispered. "Or you just mad at me?"

He paused at the door, one hand resting on the knob.

"I'll always love her," he said. "With everything that still beats inside of me."

Then he walked out—past the kitchen, past the hallway, past all the wreckage.

Somewhere across town, Novi was praying for a miracle.

And Nolen was trying to survive the one he'd already lost.

• • •

Acknowledgements

To my good girlfriends and firstly my best friend **Celine**. Thank you for being there for this entire book and the before (when I was talking about writing it) and the after (when I decided to get it done). I hope I represented you well since I used pieces of who you are as the inspiration for the character Velani. I feel any woman would be blessed to have a ride-or-die friend like you. Love you always!

And to my good girlfriend **Nicole,** you came right on time and were on board for it! Thank you sis! I look forward to celebrating with each of you together soon.

And to my "let's sweat it out and exercise" sister **Ann**. Thank you for taking time out of your days to read, support, and help me finalize this book. Your efforts, insights, and encouragement are the reason we're now at the finish line. Won't He do it! The feedback from you, your time, your energy, and the laughter we shared — whether on the phone or during our intense muscle building climbs were appreciated.

I love each of you ladies for life. I love each of you for your time, your talent, and your beautifully open eyes.

Here's to Novi & Nolen!

• • •

One year later, Devotion Heights isn't the same. The music that once filled its walls has spilled into the world — charting albums, sold-out tours, and a new kingdom built on fame instead of faith. But behind the lights, betrayal simmers. Novi has walked away from the church and from God, her voice now backing the very artists she once prayed for. Nolen still plays the drums, still smiles for the cameras — but every note played is haunted by the love he couldn't keep. And as cracks spread through Bishop Byrd's empire, secrets threaten to topple everything. The fire hasn't burned out. It's only changed its fuel.

Devotion Heights – Book 2 coming soon

Keep up with all things Devotion Heights by visiting the website for all of our "Devotees".
www.devotionheights.org.

• • •